# THE HYDROGEN FRONTIER

# THE HYDROGEN FRONTIER

*Power without Pollution*

A novel

by

Roy Le Blanc

ISBN: 978-0-578-64649-7 (paperback)

Water will one day be employed as fuel, that hydrogen and oxygen which constitute it, used singly or together, will furnish an inexhaustible source of heat and light, of an intensity of which coal is not capable.

—Jules Verne, *The Mysterious Island,* 1847


"Life's but a walking shadow, a poor player who struts and frets his hour upon the stage and then is heard no more,"

—Macbeth

Don't ask me if everything in this story is true. I'm just the author. Truth is something for you to determine. If you are truly interested in the truth, you will have to find it on your own. After all, who could make all this up?

# 1

I am the son of a forgotten man. Everyone knows about those famous New Orleans jazz funerals. But most burials here are not that way at all. The common man never gets a parade. This was the day I had long anticipated but dreaded. My polished black shoes were at the foot of the bed, and my only suit had been set out the night before. I chose a dark-red tie. My alarm was set two hours early. On the breakfast table was a half-full cup of cold coffee and the morning paper opened to the obituaries section. The two-paragraph item was the only time my dad's name ever appeared in print. "Pierre Delacroix, a plant worker, died of natural causes…" It was never going to win a Grimmy Award for the best-written obit. The photo was the one Dad had picked out.

It was a damp, overcast morning. I stood alone; my tears mixed with misty raindrops that washed down my checks. The few friends and family standing around wore their best "going-to-town" outfits. It was obvious they were all uncomfortable in fancy clothes and, like me, were wearing suits purchased years before. The going-to-town outfits were saved for special occasions. These are the same clothes they will be buried in when their time comes. Condolences were exchanged with glances, not words. Our limited time is but a brief candle, as described by Shakespeare's Macbeth, that adds up to very little in the total scheme of things.

Dad was raised Catholic and remained faithful. He attended mass on a regular basis and always took Communion. He asked for a traditional Catholic burial. The priest sprinkled holy water on the casket and broke the deepened silence with a few half-hearted words. A young altar boy dressed in a long white-and-black vestment extended his arm as far as possible and struggled to hold an umbrella over the priest. "We are gathered here today to celebrate the life of Peter Delacroix, who has gone home to the house of God. Ashes to ashes, dust to dust, and to dust you shall return. May the souls of the faithful departed, though the mercy of God, rest in peace. Amen."

I stood in the same out-of-the-way spot under a small overhang. The weather worsened. Gusts of wind howled through the live oaks hammering rain against the tombs. Nearly everyone started running to their cars. I handed the priest an envelope containing fifty dollars to cover his time.

"Sorry for your loss. Your father was a good man," he said in a matter-of-fact way without looking directly at me. The priest fiddled with the buttons on his raincoat. "Give me the damn umbrella." He was aggravated with the altar boy and seemed annoyed that Dad had picked a rainy day to die. It wasn't worth the trouble to tell him Dad's name was Pierre Delacroix, not Peter.

I watched graveyard workers slide Dad's inexpensive casket into the crypt. They smoked unfiltered cigarettes and complained about working in the rain. A stone mason quickly placed the original marble plaque back in place and sealed the edges with mortar and grout. He covered it with a sheet of plastic. The workers all ran off, trying to get someplace dry.

An engraver would show up tomorrow morning to add my father's name below the forgotten names of my other forebears interred in the same tomb.

Anticipating this unhappy event, I had spent a week pulling weeds and vines around the tomb and painting. The vine root systems had dug deep into mortar between the crumbling bricks, clinging tight like leaches to the falling walls their roots had helped weaken. I repaired some of the old plaster and painted everything with a fresh coat of white Tomb Paint. That is a New Orleans thing. The aboveground crypts can only be painted with special paint manufactured locally. Tomb Paint is very expensive. I saved a few dollars doing these things myself, but I still made a payday loan to cover the remaining final expenses. Dad was penniless, and as a part-time freshman college student working restaurant jobs, I did not have $800. "What are you doing? Don't pull those vines down!" The graveyard director interrupted my work. "The sweet smell helps to cover death's stench!" he said.

Clearly, overgrown vines had weakened the old mortar holding the bricks together. The misinformed director was unknowingly encouraging the cemetery's decline, not preserving it.

Cemetery workers were supposed to keep things up, but the poorly paid, overworked crews never seemed to get things done, and the cemetery's perpetual care agreement wasn't worth the paper it was printed on. The contract was seventy years old anyway and probably not enforceable. Other aboveground tombs were also crumbling and open to the elements. They were constructed during the administration of Andrew Jackson and abandoned long ago. Names engraved into their marble plaques had been worn smooth by time and were now invisible. Only the dead remember. The graveyard was crumbling like forgotten ruins, and no one cared enough to bother anyway. In Central America they believe spirits stay around until they are forgotten by the living.

I ran my fingers across the forgotten names. These unfortunate souls had departed long ago. Many names on my family's tomb also sounded strange and foreign, the older ones having not been spoken aloud for generations.

The first name on my family tomb was added in 1843. My dad's name will be the ninth. The only thing my downtrodden ancestors left behind are the names carved into this single thin slab of marble. It is the only proof that they ever existed. It is our Rosetta Stone. New Orleans has many prosperous families. They inherit priceless art, businesses, and historic Saint Charles Avenue mansions passed from one generation to the next. They learn culture, etiquette, and expectations for success. They have the confidence and means to take risks. Bank presidents solicit them.

The city also has families like mine. We have been in New Orleans for nearly three hundred years, and the only real estate we have managed to acquire is this simple six-by-ten crumbling brick-and-plaster tomb. Dad tried hard and worked nonstop, but the generational disadvantage he faced was an inability to pick prosperous ancestors.

"I told your dad to buy a modern in-ground burial plot across the lake like everyone else. This crumbling old place should be bulldozed. No one ever accused your dad of being smart." My uncle Larry was not one to hold his tongue, although nobody took him seriously since he quit school after the tenth grade. He said education was too time consuming.

"Good to see you again, Uncle Larry. Be safe driving home. Weather is awful!" These were the same scraggly working-class people I had known my entire life—with one exception. At the end of the service, an attractive middle-aged woman I did not know arrived and stood still under a black umbrella. In a snug-fitting dress and expensive pearls around her thin neck, she seemed out of place. She acknowledged no one. The woman bowed her head for a moment, clinched her pearls, said a short prayer, and then made the sign of the cross. Touching the tomb gently with her fingertips, she seemed to whisper something, then just as quickly drove away in a green Land Rover.

Rain continued to fall. Alone now, I placed my hand on Dad's tomb and said a short prayer in my own way. "It's been a tough go. Now it's time to get some rest." Walking to the cemetery's main gate on Washington Avenue, I watched uni-formed doormen at Commander's Palace hurrying about with giant umbrellas protecting their important dinner guests. Expensive Bentleys, Cadillacs, Jaguars, and BMWs lined the street. Stylish women in tight-fitting low-cut dresses showed off large diamond rings, pearl necklaces, and sexy, thin legs. Prosperous aristocratic men smoked cigars and handed res-taurant workers twenty-dollar bills. Like a child with his face pressed against a candy store window, I stood rain soaked, across the street, a lost soul looking in.

"Move along, buddy! If you stay around here, I'll have to call the cops! There's a Salvation Army shelter a few blocks away!" the parking attendant yelled at me from across the street. His stance was determined, with his legs slightly apart and his hands on his hips. I pulled my lapels tight across my chest and walked away.

# 2

I am now the age my dad was back then. He was vibrant and full of life. But time is a vicious adversary offering no mercy to vanquished opponents. I wish I had had more years with him, but he fell victim to the ravages of a working man's tough life. The time between hello and goodbye is always too short. "Good morning, Sebastian! Looks like cows sneaked into your bedroom again. We better check that window!" My dad playfully combed his fingers through my hair, teasing about my cowlicks. I rubbed both eyes, yawned, and hugged his leg. He bent down to my level and kissed my forehead. He worked two shifts, and it was always dark when he left for work in the morning and late when he returned home in the evening. At 4:30 a.m., my dad wanted to be very quiet and always tried to suppress his repeated coughing by placing a paper towel tight over his mouth. But in our small two-bedroom home with thin walls, even those muffled noises sounded like alarm clocks. Dr. Hobbs, director of the company's health clinic, insisted everything was fine. He prescribed weekend bedrest.

Our home was built in 1943 as housing for junior naval officers stationed nearby. At the time, it was considered temporary construction designed to last five years. Still, the three of us felt happy and comfortable in its eight hundred square feet. I slept in a twin bed and kept all my stuff in one dresser. Mom and Dad had the front bedroom. There was also a small living room, a bath, and a tiny kitchen with a gas stove and a table with four chairs. The kitchen was so small you could not open the refrigerator door if someone was sitting at the table. We did not have air-conditioning, but comfortable winter heat was provided by a floor furnace between the bedrooms. Our Christmas tree was usually a small, inexpensive Virginia pine purchased from the neighborhood tree lot on Orleans Avenue. We didn't have a clothes dryer, so everything was hung on a backyard line. During the holidays Mom went to a local coin-operated laundromat and collected lint from the electric dryers. Returning home with a bagful, she placed it on the pine tree branches. In the eyes of a four-year-old, it looked beautiful—just like real snow.

Dad bent down low to my level. "Looks like the sandman got you again last night," he said as he wiped the sleepy crud from the corners of my eyes. He kissed my forehead and put his hand on my shoulder. "Listen to your mom today." Dad was worried about waking me up every morning and concerned about my lack of sleep, but I couldn't think of starting my day without seeing him.

My father picked up his black plastic lunch box with the Perfect Circle Piston Rings sticker on one side and an organized labor sticker on the other. He always packed it the night before with an olive loaf sandwich on white bread, chips, and a hot coffee thermos. We had an old wooden chair under the kitchen window. I stood on it and watched until his blue Chevy turned the corner. Just at that time, Dad rolled down the car window and waved. He assumed

I was still watching, and he was right. Dad had purchased the Chevy when it was about two years old, but he always referred to it as his "new" car.

Perhaps that was because my mom's car was a 1954 Ford and so worn out it was nearly in a coma. It was given to us when a neighbor moved to South Florida. The old Ford couldn't make the long drive to the Sunshine State, and shipping it was not worth the cost, so he gave it to us. Dad was always hesitant to sell it because it was unreliable and unrepairable. The junkyard paid twenty-five dollars scrap value when they hauled it away. "The Ford was just about right," Dad said. "If it ran any better, it wouldn't have been given to us for free. If it ran any worse, I would not have taken it."

My father polished his new Chevelle by hand every Saturday until the accident, and then he lost interest. With no insurance and no way to pay for a professional repair job, he purchased a junkyard fender and installed it himself. Things worked fine, except the new fender was a gold color, and the inexpensive blue spray paint he purchased from the hardware store never matched the original GM finish. The paint cans had to be shaken well before use. That was my job. They had a small ball bearing inside that rattled around. Dad said we were doing "a first-class rattle-can repair job."

I loved looking through my father's old scrapbook. The photo of him proudly leaning against the front of his green hot rod 1947 Mercury coupe with the hood up was my favorite. The engine had three carburetors, special Fenton aluminum high-performance heads, and a chrome air cleaner. Internally, the engine was completely redone with high-compression aluminum pistons and a high-performance camshaft. Dad called it the Green Monster and hand painted the name on the glove box door. During his high school graduation ceremony, Dad parked the Mercury nearby and kept the engine running. His name was announced, he walked fast across the stage, shook the principal's hand, received his high school diploma, blew a kiss to his girlfriend (my future mother), and ran out a side door. She grew up nearby on North Miro Street. They had known each other since the third grade.

Dad slammed the transmission shifter into first gear and floored the accelerator. The rear tires screamed and smoked, and the Mercury's back end fishtailed back and forth, leaving black streaks on the parking lot pavement. His fast hot rod gave him a huge advantage over all the other boys in slower cars. The city streets were clear, and most lights were green. It seemed even the New Orleans police were coconspirators in this annual ritual. The Mercury was nearly airborne as it cleared the Judge Seeber bridge at ninety miles an hour. Pedestrians covered their ears as Dad rocketed by.

Chalmette Aluminum was seven miles south of Nichols high school. Everyone in New Orleans just called it CA. The smelter was opened in the early 1950s and was the world's largest. The plant had nine potlines and a capacity of 275,000 tons. It promised good benefits and a defined retirement plan, job security, and high pay. All jobs at the plant were organized, and union labor rules applied to new hires. The first hired would always enjoy seniority, even if the time difference was only a few minutes. Dad skidded the Mercury to a stop, jumped out, and ran into the employment office. He was number three in line. Within a few minutes, there were seventy-five eager teenage boys waiting behind him.

HR personnel checked to make sure all the job applicants had a valid high school diploma and then directed them into a larger room with small wooden desks lined in rows. "Please take a seat." They were given twelve minutes to complete a short Wonderlic aptitude test.

One frustrated boy set his pencil down and walked out after five minutes. "The hell with this. I thought I was finished with tests. I can go work for the post office!"

Half the applicants failed the test and were told to leave. Dad's score was one of the highest. He was given a quick physical.

"You will learn to feed the cells. Alumina is added intermittently in short intervals with a breaker feeder system. It also helps with cleaning of captured cell gasses used as feed for the reduction process. You will earn seventy-five cents above minimum wage to start. Sign here," the HR person said in a disinterested tone. The minimum wage was one dollar in the 1950s. The extra seventy-five cents per hour was hard to resist.

Dad wondered why the salary was so high.

"You get extra pay because you will be working sixty hours a week in a foundry full of smoke and soot around molten aluminum at 2,192 degrees Fahrenheit. But you get time and a half for everything worked over forty hours and free health care at the company clinic as an added perk."

"Free health care! That's a real deal," Dad said.

My father started working at CA as a proud apprentice potroom trainee the Monday after his high school graduation and was offered overtime on his first day. Dad believed he was on track to becoming a millionaire. He asked my mother to marry him the next Tuesday. They enjoyed the Mercury's back seat many times but always managed to stop. Now with a high school diploma, a good job, and a pending marriage, there was no reason to wait any longer. A loud wedding reception was held in a meeting room behind Linda's All You Can Eat Family Crab and Catfish Restaurant. The happy couple rode from Saint Dominic Church to the reception in the back of a neighbor's Studebaker sedan. Music was provided by an RCA hi-fi radio with a scratchy speaker. The bride and groom danced to "Tenderly" by Rosemary Clooney before leaving for a three-day honeymoon at the Fountain Blue Hotel in a cheap room with a parking lot view. The entire event cost less than seventy-five dollars.

Mom never finished high school, but she did attend cosmetology college for six months and landed a job at Silhouette's Beauty Shop on Canal Street. She worked part time as a shampoo girl earning tips. Usually, she made ten dollars on a good day. Mom took a short leave of absence when I was born but never went back to work or finished a GED. She was very proud to say that she invented a new beauty shop chair and expected to get rich. But her "invention" just added common features to an existing chair design. Her patent application was rejected without comment. "I think the patent office is trying to steal my invention." She claimed to be looking for a high-powered corporate lawyer to make things right.

In the eyes of a youthful eighteen-year-old from a blue-collar family, the CA job was a remarkable opportunity. Dad could buy a house with a white picket fence and a car, marry, and raise children. He believed long three-day weekends spent relaxing on Biloxi's beach was within reach. At retirement in forty-two years, he would have a comfortable pension and union benefits. Life was good!

Dad could never bring himself to sell that beloved first hot rod. The old Mercury sat in our backyard under a magnolia tree with four flat tires for decades. He always dreamed of restoring it. On hot summer afternoons I climbed in, sat upright on the old soft leather seats, held the steering wheel tight, shifted the gears, and imagined I was racing to set a land speed record on the Bonneville Salt Flats.

Ironically, Chalmette Aluminum closed for good in 1983, barely thirty years after groundbreaking.

# 3

Although I was always curious about his childhood, Dad never talked much about growing up in a run-down old shotgun home on Piety Street in the ninth ward. It had no gardens or flowers. The house was in a constant state of neglect. It was run down and worn out. The dilapidated little structure with its sunless brown yard and flowerless garden conveyed a strong sense of defeatism. It had capitulated long ago.

Most of the things I learned about his upbringing during those years were pieced together from family conversations, old photos, neighbors, or the occasional comments Dad made himself. Obviously, everyone has an angle or ax to grind; I know that. These family members and neighborhood acquaintances were in and out of jail, bankruptcy court, divorce court, jobs, and marriages. Some of them never finished the tenth grade. The best man in dad's wedding spent seven months as an Orleans Parish Prison inmate after he masterminded a daring but poorly planned midday caper involving the theft of a Chrysler Imperial hood. Lawyers would consider them all unreliable.

"I'm not worried about those people," Dad said when I asked why I saw Mamaw and Papaw Delacroix only a few times a year. Looking back, I think he was trying to protect me.

I do remember certain things about them. They had two dogs, Champ and Powderpuff. Powderpuff was a pug and lived inside. He was supposed to be house trained, but not really. They said he pooped inside only when he was nervous. But there was always dog crap on the linoleum floors hidden in the corners. They each acted like they did not see it, so it stayed for weeks. Champ was a sweet old German shepherd that had lost most of his hair long ago. He always came to the fence with gifts each time visitors arrived. I remember Champ gave us a short stick he found under the house and a cardboard milk carton. He was happy to greet everyone.

"I can't keep that damn dog out of the trash." Papaw kicked him hard. Champ cried, put his tail between his legs and ran off back under the house.

My grandparents had a small black-and-white television set with tin foil wrapped around the rabbit-ear antenna like an anaconda snake. It sat in a corner of the living room on a flimsy TV tray. Mamaw loved Lawrence Welk and never missed his show, but the TV's vertical control was out, so the picture constantly jumped around. A strategic slap on its side usually stabilized the picture for a few minutes. "Slap it again, Flathead," she said over and over during the one-hour show. Back in the day, Papaw made his living rebuilding the old-style flathead motors, so Mamaw called him Flathead. No one else ever dared call him that, at least to his face. Eventually Papaw moved his chair closer to the worn-out TV so he wouldn't need to get back up again. It was cheaper to slap it than to replace the worn-out vacuum tubes. Papaw Delacroix slapped that TV for years. "Slapping the TV was a good thing. It was much better than Flathead beating anyone. It was a harmless way for him to blow off steam," Mamaw said.

At Christmas, Mamaw gave everyone rose milk and Geritol as gifts, products recommended by Mr. Welk. She loved *The Lawrence Welk Show* more than she loved a two-for-one sale at the S&H Green Stamp Store.

We all had to be very careful at their house. Mamaw spent a week in the hospital after a case of empty Dixie Beer longnecks fell on her head. Papaw Delacroix liked to drink a lot of Dixie but tried to hide the evidence. He hid the empty bottles and full cases around the house. Mamaw was injured when she opened a hallway closet door. The case of longnecks fell from the top shelf and landed on her head. A neighbor discovered her lying on the floor a few hours later and called the hospital. She had lingering side effects for years.

Mamaw and Papaw Delacroix hung an inexpensive wooden picture frame holding some old military medals next to a shadow box in the dining room above the table. The shadow box contained a kitchen scene with tiny furniture and a stove carved from wood. A shiny old silver dollar rested against the back behind the glass. "Always keep a silver dollar tucked away somewhere. If you do, you'll never be completely broke," Mamaw said. She was very superstitious about things like that. On New Year's Eve, she always swept a dollar bill wrapped in a cabbage leaf in the front door and out the back, and after that she ate a large bowl of black-eyed peas.

None of her superstitions were very effective, since they were always short of money anyhow. "I'm in kind of a bind now. How about helping me out? Can you spot me fifty dollars until payday?" Dad had only been married for a few months when Papaw asked to borrow the cash. "You have a great job at CA and plenty of money! I only need the fifty dollars until I get paid!" Some people have good fortune or are born into

17

wealth. They are the lucky few living easy lives separated from the rest of us, who work every day just to pay the rent and keep food on the table. "No one in this family has ever had anything. All I will ever inherit is more work," Dad said after he reluctantly wrote the fifty-dollar check knowing that the money would never be repaid.

Perhaps Dad was such a good father to me because he wanted to be the opposite of Papaw Delacroix, who constantly put his son down, berated him, ignored him, and beat him. Dad was humiliated in public and called worthless. Papaw gave him the nickname Shitass and called him that for years. He was told fifteen times how to properly close a car hood. "Close it again, Shitass! Again! Again! Pay attention to the small stuff! We'll be here all day until you get it right!" Papaw never took his son to the movies, played ball with him, or took him fishing. When my father was about four years old, he tried to kiss his dad on the cheek. He was pushed to the floor. "Men don't do that stuff," Papaw Delacroix said.

He believed the same thing about books and learning. "That's for sissies. Real men work with their hands. You must be tough. To survive you need to be the meanest bastard on the block." That was a difficult lesson for a four-year-old.

Papaw came home late one evening complaining of terrible itching. He said he must have caught a case of crabs from the dirty shower at the Reliable Reconditioning machine shop. "It itches like crazy. We got to do something." Everyone knew he had a habit of spending time with French Quarter prostitutes. He went into the bathroom and asked Mamaw to shave him. Trying to avoid trouble, she did as asked. Why would anyone humiliate another person like that? She should have sliced his penis off.

I learned that Papaw joined the marines in 1942. He saw action on Tarawa atoll, Iwo Jima, and Guadalcanal. When a nearby marine was shot on Iwo Jima, Papaw picked up the dead marine's flamethrower and spent the next two weeks torching Japanese soldiers hiding in caves. They say he killed dozens. He threw up after he torched the first few, but eventually he got used to it. Then Papaw started to like it. That old military medal hanging in their dining room was not just some random award. It was the Navy Cross, awarded to Papaw for extraordinary heroism!

They say he was a sweet boy before the war, but after, he was never the same. Papaw used to save food from his dinner plate to feed hungry strays in his poor neighborhood. Now he enjoyed kicking them. This was years before PTSD treatments, and any indication of mental fatigue was considered a sign of weakness. Everyone said he was shell shocked. Papaw never talked about his World War II experience.

His local mechanics union was affiliated with the Teamsters. Every Fourth of July, the union held a giant patriotic picnic in City Park at shelter number four. The shelter was decorated with flags and red, white, and blue banners. Dozens of families with kids everywhere showed up. They grilled hamburgers and hotdogs, a band played patriotic music, and kids played kickball and kick the can. Tug-of-war, sack races, and Hula-Hoop ring toss competitions were organized, with the first-place children awarded five dollar US government savings bonds.

The adults sat in lawn chairs drank beer and discussed politics. Then the talks started. This was Dad's favorite part of the day. He sat cross-legged in front of the stage and listened carefully to every individual story about grisly European land battles, dive-bombing on Japanese ships, or flying Hellcats and P-38s. He hung on every word. World War II veterans stood up and one by one talked about their experiences. Dad admired them all. The D-Day and Anzio invasion stories were interesting, but Dad loved hearing the tales of exotic adventures in the South Pacific most.

One guy had been a PT boat crewman. He walked slowly to the stage but was proud and told thrilling stories of adventure. "As chief engineman, I sat on a small seat inches above three giant V-12 Packard marine engines. Each one was supercharged and produced one thousand six hundred and fifty horsepower. The engine room on a PT boat was noisy, hot, and cramped, with no portholes, but those beautiful Packard motors could push that boat at fifty knots. Who needs windows when you're looking at such beautiful engines? We chased the Imperial Jap navy all over the South Pacific, attacking everything from subs to heavy cruisers. Usually we attacked at night, fast and unseen, let go of the torpedoes, then turned and ran. My skipper came on the intercom. 'Time to go hunting! Give me all you got! Full power!' Aye, sir! So I jammed the throttles forward and held on! Those Packard ladies made a sound sweeter than Glen Miller. At full power, the roar was like a big band symphony to me. The Packard motors were loyal, reliable, and always thrilling. Like a true girlfriend, they never disappointed or complained."

Dad loved the PT stories most and sat mesmerized dreaming of South Sea adventures in fast boats with powerful engines hopping from island to tropical island, sinking enemy ships by moonlight.

Papaw just sat in the back, drinking beer and ignoring the talks, or he left early. "Listening to these knuckleheads talk about war is like talking to the pope about picking up women. They know nothing about it," he said. I don't think anyone realized he was a recipient of the Navy Cross. He liked it that way. He was invited to speak onstage many times but always refused. "I don't have anything interesting to say."

There were over four hundred kids in my dad's high school class. There was one guidance counselor. In four years of high school, Dad received advice regarding his future only once, and that was the first day of his freshman year. "I never knew this school even had a career counselor!" Dad and his buddies used to joke about that. Still, he received more advice from the exhausted counselor than he ever did from his own father.

"The counselor doesn't talk to us because we're poor and dumb. He figures we'll all become GI grunts anyway. Ain't none of us rushing home to check the mail for a Harvard acceptance letter, that's for sure!" Dad and his band of friends were all considered part of the same knucklehead group, like the characters in Kipling's *The Jungle Book.*

"The only acceptance letter I expected was from the draft board!" one of Dad's friends said sarcastically.

The truth about Dad was something altogether different. When going through his things, I discovered a dusty cardboard box tucked away in a dark corner of his garage. It contained many books, including some written by Cordell Hull, James F. Byrnes, Dean Acheson, and John Foster Dulles, among others. I recognized the names. They all had been secretary of state at some point. I know the books were read and studied because they were heavily dogeared with handwritten notes and highlights on nearly every page. It was all written in Dad's hand! He also read *Understanding Machines, The Mechanical Engineer's*

*Pocket Handbook*, and a few issues of *Popular Mechanics*. His interest in mechanical engineering helps explain his love for building hot rods with high-performance engines. Dad even had a book published by Evariste Galois, a French mathematician who died in a duel. As I thumbed through the musty pages, I could picture him reading his secret books late at night with a flashlight under the covers, trying to avoid the ridicule certainly to come from Papaw if the books were ever discovered. "Book learning is for sissies." Papaw Delacroix would have thrown all of them into the trash—after beating Dad first.

At the bottom of the box was an incomplete Tulane University admissions application form. The university asked about favorite music. Dad answered Pachelbel's canon in D major. "It moves me to tears every time I hear it. No one should go through life without experiencing its compelling beauty," Dad wrote in pencil. I had no idea he loved classical music. At some point Dad took a part-time weekend job as a Tulane maintenance worker. I don't believe he needed the money at that time; however, I do think it was the best he could do to keep his college dream alive somewhat, even if it was on life support. He wasn't a student, but at least he was on the beautiful campus. That was worth something.

Things at the university didn't go well, and he was soon fired. His supervisor claimed Dad was hiding to avoid work. "He wasn't lazy. At lunch your dad enjoyed spending time in the library, around books. He found a quiet spot and got lost in a Hemmingway novel. Before he knew it, it was three o'clock, and he was fired," according to a former coworker. I think Dad just took the path of least resistance and eventually abandoned his college dreams as unrealistic. I did check with the university to verify this story, but no one there remembered him.

"Come to think of it, we did see the guidance counselor one other time when he came to our shop class," according to an old high school friend. The Huey P. Long bridge over the Mississippi River had to be sanded and painted constantly. It was a never-ending task. Painters hung on ropes swinging hundreds of feet above the Mississippi River with little or no safety precautions.

"Painting the bridge is a great job opportunity with good pay," the counselor suggested.

Eager vo-tech boys pushed and shoved to get their hands on the job applications like hungry lion cubs fighting over a recent kill. I suspect Dad applied trying to make Papaw proud. Painting that bridge was the kind of job a real man would do. Many older boys quit high school and sat for the GED. Then they worked twelve hours a day scraping and painting.

High school boys studying vo-tech had just a few options. The Cold War was raging, and the military accepted everyone with a high school diploma or GED. There was a draft in place, but Dad had not been called because he was not yet eighteen. The federal government offered career opportunities with the post office or other agencies. State jobs usually involved road repair or prison guard work. The city was always hiring firemen and policemen. These civil service jobs offered security and good pay, but you usually had to "know somebody" to get a foot in the door. With no political connections or influential friends, Dad's options were limited. The bridge painting job looked like good work with good pay for a high school kid with no other prospects, but his job application was denied. "You need to be eighteen. Come back in a few years."

Until he was old enough for a real job, Dad took on various entry-level part-time gigs. He cut grass, washed dishes, and tuned up old cars for elderly neighbors. With time on his hands, he went out for the football team and tried for the toughest position on the field. Being a linebacker would please Papaw Flathead. The season's first game was against Chalmette High. His team sweated in a run-down school bus, and they had old equipment and useless leather helmets. He went home every day with terrible headaches caused by powerful head-on collisions. Their worn-out uniforms were old and tattered.

The Chalmette players had the best of everything. The grass field was manicured like LSU's, the locker rooms were remodeled and smelled clean, the stadium was freshly painted, and even the Chalmette cheerleaders had the best of everything. "How do they get so much funding?" The coach pointed to the giant brick smokestack belching out black, blue, and gray smoke, towering over Chalmette High the way Mount Vesuvius watched over Pompeii. "Evidently Chalmette Aluminum has deep pockets."

It was a clear evening, but after the game, the bus driver turned on his windshield wipers. Even with that it was difficult to clear the oily soot off the windshield enough to drive safely. The Chalmette neighborhoods had no clotheslines. Every other New Orleans area had them. It was the way wash was done. The filthy air was too polluted to hang clothes outside to dry. Cigarette smoke smelled better and was probably healthier.

# 4

*It's true. They give the working class just enough to buy a home with a thirty-year mortgage and finance a new car. Workers feel confident, marry, have children, and raise families. But like marionettes, they are manipulated by someone controlling all the strings. Given little opportunity, working-class children fill future labor pools, and the rigged cycle continues. Kids from the political class and wealthy families attend Yale and Harvard; they party on yachts off Nantucket. Working-class kids are lucky to get an associate degree from a community college and land a job managing a retail outlet. The chance of a working-class kid growing up to control significant capital is nearly impossible. Their odds of winning the lottery are better.*

The world's largest aluminum plant was originally planned for construction in the Northwest. Other aluminum industry activity was already in the area, attracted by the abundant and inexpensive electric power provided by the Bonneville hydroelectric dam. However, after meeting Louisiana's governor, the secretary of the interior, Oscar Clemens, canceled those Oregon plans and suggested Louisiana as a new ideal location. He said, "Local representatives in the Northwest wanted efficient industry that could also preserve the environment. That was something Louisiana's governor never brought up."

The interior secretary also suggested that the plentiful supply of cheap Gulf Coast natural gas made more sense than using hydro power. "Even in a drought, America still needs aluminum," he told a Washington state news reporter. That was not exactly the complete truth. Secretary Clemens didn't mention his night on Bourbon Street with Louisiana's notorious governor, Earl Long, or the fact that he was being blackmailed by the half-crazy southern governor. Clemens was a powerful man who always expected to get his way. Never did he imagine he could be played like a Stradivarius by a hillbilly southern governor.

The federal government had significant leverage in the new aluminum plant location selection process. The Interior Department and the Defense Mobilization Department offered a five-year amortization of plant expenses and loans and guaranteed the purchase of all excess production that was not utilized by private enterprise. Essentially, the government was promising to buy all the aluminum the new plant could produce for the defense industry at high market prices, guaranteeing a profitable investment for decades. The new plant would be built in a location agreeable to the government, or these offers would be off the table.

But even without the blackmail, there was reason to question the character of the interior secretary. He was sued over timberland rights in Oregon and California. "Working with the secretary is like sharing a swimming pool with someone who insists on having the top half," said a plaintiff in the case. It was alleged that Secretary Clemens took kickbacks on multiple occasions from established timber interests, placing their bids ahead of small independent mills. According to court documents, the timber bid system was "a charade fostering cozy agreements with the secretary's friends."

He was also involved with an aluminum company that sold substandard artillery shells to the US Navy during World War II. The shells were dangerously out of specification and had been responsible for many deaths in the Pacific campaigns. The owner of the company was a client of Clemens's law firm. Despite his checkered background, Oscar's loyalty to Harry Truman was rewarded with an appointment as deputy interior secretary when Truman took over the presidency after Franklin Roosevelt's death. Then he was promoted to interior secretary after Truman defeated Dewey in 1948.

When Secretary Clemens received an invitation from Louisiana's governor, Earl Long, to spend time in New Orleans, he accepted immediately. Governor Long was famous for entertaining dignitaries with wild French Quarter parties and private get-togethers with Bourbon Street strippers in secret Roosevelt Hotel suites. The invite was viewed as a great opportunity to relax and recover from the stress of a difficult Washington, DC, job. A curious *Times-Picayune* reporter asked Long if it was appropriate to entertain federal officials in such colorful fashion.

"If the people of Louisiana ever elect good government, they won't like it," Long reasoned.

Louisiana's governor had multiple breakdowns and had been confined to a mental hospital from time to time. He once offered an LSU adjunct professor a tenured position in exchange for a week with the man's wife. "They condemned me to the nervous hospital because my wife, Blanche, believed the *Picayune* nonsense about topless strippers and extracurricular activities. *Picayune* editors are crazy, not me!" He hurled profanities at reporters at every opportunity. After he escaped from the state hospital in Mandeville, Earl left Blanche and moved in with Blaze Starr, a young French Quarter stripper who was more famous for affairs with Governor Long than for her stripper routine. He read a *Dixie Roto* magazine article about her and proposed marriage even before seeing her in the flesh. He was still married to Blanche at the time.

The governor's black Cadillac limousine arrived thirty minutes early at the Lakefront airport. He had time to have three gin and tonics at the Crash Landing bar in the main terminal. The secretary's DC 6 arrived on time. "Welcome to the great state of Louisiana!"

Clemens was tall and thin with a serious, narrow face. A papery pinkish complexion gave him the look of someone who spent most days indoors. In another time, he could have found success as some midlevel Prussian secret police functionary. Governor Long suggested a visit to the airport bar before heading to the Roosevelt Hotel and a night on Bourbon Street. "After that flight, a drink would be just the thing. Yes sir, just the thing!"

Both men ignored most questions shouted by the waiting news crews and reporters. "Why are you here, Mr. Secretary? Does your visit have anything to do with aluminum? Are you planning to visit Bourbon Street with Governor Long?"

"We're just trying to do our part to fight the commies. We're good Americans working for our country." Earl leaned over and whispered in Clemens's ear, explaining that all *Picayune* reporters were commie bastards anyway. Long knew that Clemens was one of the first government officials accused by the House Committee on Un-American Activities of being a member of a communist organization. This was the governor's way of keeping him off balance.

It was a twenty-minute ride to the hotel from the airport. Traffic was stopped at every intersection. The governor explained how much fun they would have in the French Quarter. "You will really love the My-Oh-My Club. It's my favorite." The secretary had no idea what he was in for, especially considering how friendly Long was with many of the strippers working the Quarter clubs.

A crowd gathered at the Saint Charles entrance to the Roosevelt Hotel hoping to catch a glimpse of the two famous men as they exited the car and entered the extravagant lobby. Earl kept a bucket of water and a cloth in the back of the black Cadillac limo. "Wipe your forehead and neck with this wet cloth. It won't hurt to wet under your arms a little too. It looks just like real sweat." Long pretended to be a man of the common people and did not want anyone to know he was riding around in an air-conditioned car.

The lumbering Cadillac turned off Canal Street to the Roosevelt, the driver rolled the electric windows down and pulled to a stop, and the governor waved to his admirers. Both men walked quickly into the lobby, trying to avoid questions from more annoying reporters and determined photographers.

On the left was the world-famous Blue Room lounge and the Sazerac Restaurant. "Louis Armstrong plays here all the time, whenever he's in New Orleans," Long said as he pointed to the Blue Room. "And they serve Ojen. It's the official drink of Mardi Gras! Locals call it holy water. We'll try that after dinner." A small, discrete, out-of-the-way elevator was hidden on the right side of the ornate lobby. It went directly to a penthouse suite. Huey Long had used it as his official office when he worked days in New Orleans and as his secret love nest at night. Many believe that Huey hid the famous "deduct box" somewhere in the rooms. Huey usually wore pajamas all day and once caused an international incident when he greeted a German naval officer in the early afternoon while in his white pj's.

After Huey's assassination, Earl inherited his brother's secret Roosevelt Hotel suite and used it primarily to entertain Bourbon Street strippers. Huey was a political genius who developed a national "Share Our Wealth" following. Earl was always more interested in getting honey on the stinger than effective governing. Nevertheless, he believed he had an incredible innate understanding of human nature. He confused his narcissism for vision and wisdom.

Earl often said he looked for weakness in his opponents and exploited their vulnerability. Earl was not particularly strong himself; his confident strength was derived from the perceived weakness of others. But to think Earl was some type of real statesman was like confusing a butcher with a surgeon. Earl believed Clemens was hiding a fault that he kept from everyone, especially his family. Earl could smell it. Gambling, drinking, or a taste for unusual kinky sex, Oscar was hiding something. "We'll see how Secretary Clemens puts the sauerkraut on his sausage," Earl said.

"Your room is right this way." Earl led the secretary to the hidden elevator. One of his armed bodyguards always stood watch at the elevator, keeping reporters and jealous spouses at bay. Earl's official photographer was nearby. "His name is Cain Keller. He takes a few photos for me here and there and snaps a few pictures for the state archives. I grew up with him in Winn Parish, and I've known him since the second grade. We're like Huck and Tom—almost kinfolk. Nothing to worry about," Earl explained after Clemens expressed concern about the presence of a photographer. Cain tipped his hat and faded away into the background.

"We have dinner scheduled at the Sazerac in forty-five minutes—in a private dining room, of course. Then we're heading to the Quarter." The governor had planned a long night.

Dinner conversation went as expected, but the extravagant meal took much longer than scheduled. The secretary had four holy waters with his shrimp etouffee and bananas Foster. Earl's two-hour pitch for Louisiana as the ideal location for the new aluminum plant fell upon deaf ears.

"I see a couple of concerns and unsurmountable problems for Louisiana," Clemens responded. "First, aircraft manufacturing is primarily based in the Northwest. Shipping aluminum across the country adds cost. Second, if something happens to the local affordable natural-gas supply, then plant operation will be negatively impacted. In that case, the plant would have to be converted to coal, or natural gas shipped in from elsewhere as LNG. All very expensive impractical scenarios."

"How you like that supper?" Earl asked while totally ignoring Clemens's objections. He did not plan on taking no for an answer regardless. Governor Long had already arranged lucrative natural-gas pipeline contracts from his political cronies. The kickbacks would fund the Long political machine for decades. He always said money is the mother's milk of politics. The fact is, rich people have it, and poor people don't.

*Ironically, the populist governor had no concern for the health of Louisiana workers or the environmental impact of his schemes. He cared only about campaign funds. But workers like the Delacroix family were just scraping by and willing to take nearly any job. Thus, Long was always hugely popular with the voters he screwed.*

The official entourage of two identical government Cadillacs and five state police cars acting as decoys began to make their way to Bourbon Street. All the while, the governor's actual Cadillac slowly rolled around back, with its lights off, to the My-Oh-My kitchen door on Royal Street. Secretary Clemens assumed they were using the back entrance to avoid reporters. The truth was, Earl didn't want him to see the large neon sign hanging over the front door, "My-Oh-My Club, The World's Most Beautiful Female Impersonators."

The club manager was waiting. "Good to see you again, Governor. Hurry this way. Your usual booth is waiting, and your favorite server, Danni, is working tonight."

Earl and the secretary slipped in unseen and sat at his private booth, which was enclosed inside a small room. It provided a perfect stage view but was hidden from the other club patrons. "This is my best hideaway," Earl said.

Danni brought over the first round of cocktails. "I'll make sure these glasses never go empty, sweetheart."

The large group of reporters waiting on Bourbon Street eventually gave up and went home for the night, convinced the notorious governor had given them the slip again. "Go home and get a good night's sleep. Nothing to see here," Earl's PR man advised the suspicious reporters.

Danni was thin young and beautiful, with tiny feet and spectacular shoes. She shaved her legs and plucked her eyebrows daily. She loved tight-fitting sequined dresses.

Earl ordered appetizers.

"I have never seen such beautiful women," Clemens said.

Earl smiled. "The night is young."

The master of ceremonies started the show with throwaway lines intended to loosen up the crowd. "Everyone gets wet when the man on the flying trap pees! Girls who drink beer on the beach get sand in their Schlitz!" He was not a professional comedian but did get a few chuckles.

The lights dimmed, and the real show started. Danni was onstage first and sang "Tenderly," a huge hit for Rosemary Clooney. Danni was not Rosemary, but at the My-Oh-My, all the girls sang and waited tables. There was no lip syncing. The club was a long way from Hollywood, but it was still outrageously glamorous, and it was still show business.

Clemens was mesmerized by Danni's bewitching style and sensual voice. She sang from table to table with elegant ease. The piano player caressed the keys like a familiar lover, his eyes closed as he fell deeper into a contagious melodic rhythm created by his own enchanted playing. Every man covertly wished Danni were singing just to him, but her blue eyes remained focused on Clemens. All the while she worked her way across the smoke-filled room, moving closer and closer to the governor's booth. She leaned over the table, inches from Clemens, holding out her hand, palm down.

The evening breeze caressed the trees—tenderly.
The shore was kissed by the sea and mist—Tenderly.
You took my lips
You took my love
So tenderly.

Danni sat close to Clemens. They talked like reunited friends. Governor Long ordered a bottle of champagne. "Your best champagne for my friends. Good friends and good drink are my favorite things!" After two or three hours and more and more heavy drinking, Clemens began to relax.

"I still can't believe you're a man." Clemens's hand was high on Danni's inner thigh. He had had an experience like this as a young teen and spent the next fifty years trying to resist the impulses. He gazed at the straw in his cocktail, then twisted it around between his fingers.

Governor Long called over to his trusted bodyguard standing in the shadows. "Have the Cadillac brought around back."

Clemens quietly thought about things for a time. He knew he was about to make a big mistake. Danni snuggled close against his neck. Clemens stood up and reached out for Danni's hand, and they headed down the secret hall to the waiting car.

Eventually, Earl made his way back to the Roosevelt Hotel. He sat at the Blue Room bar and had another drink with his bodyguard. "They're still up there?" Governor Long asked, expecting Clemens to be done quickly, but two hours later Long was still waiting.

"Powerful men should learn to be discreet with their indiscretion," Earl pontificated. The governor was a master at figuring out where a man itched and how to scratch him.

The dial above the elevator began to move, indicating someone was coming down. "This is for you, as we agreed." Long reached into his lapel pocket and handed Danni a thick envelope. "Aren't you going to count it?" he asked.

"Of course not!"

Danni kissed Earl on the cheek. "It's always a pleasure doing business with you, sweetheart."

She placed the hefty pack of hundred-dollar bills in her purse. "You know, Ella Fitzgerald, Lena Horne, Carol Channing, and Marlene Dietrich all appeared in this club! It's sacred ground!" Her stilettos clicked against polished marble floors. Without looking back, she raised her left arm and waved goodbye. It was a sophisticated, stylish side-to-side hand motion, like the Queen of Rex on Mardi Gras day toasting her king at Gallier Hall.

Earl called Cain. "You got the photos, right?"

Cain had the photos and many others. He knew where all the Long family skeletons were buried. Al Capone had the bookkeeper. Earl Long had Cain Keller.

In high school, Danni was known as Danny Hunt. She had few friends but loved track and field. In fact, the 5K was her best event. Winning many meets, she lettered as a junior. All school athletes were required to take a business math class that included an introductory investment component intended to teach basic stock selection and risk understanding. Each student was given $500 in imaginary money to build a portfolio of selected stocks.

Danny placed her entire $500 on Studebaker and Packard common stock. She was ridiculed by classmates for investing so foolishly. Both companies were struggling to survive in the postwar market against the huge production capacity of Ford, Chrysler, and GM. "How can the government allow them to fail? Too many workers, too many plants, and too many defense contracts," she argued. Both stocks soared at the start of the Korean War, with Studebaker building army trucks and Packard building airplane engines. Then both companies announced a proposed merger. Danny's imaginary $500 portfolio was worth $4,300 in short order—the most successful portfolio in the class, by a wide margin.

Recognizing her ability to understand complicated economic principles, the teacher suggested she read certain business books. Before long, Danny had read every title available in the school library.

# 5

*Sometimes even the powerful are manipulated by others who are richer or more fearless or more reckless. When the tables are turned, they don't like it much. Still, the regular Joes on the street are the expendable pawns who have their lives turned inside out as they are jerked around by these clashes.*

Thus far, Oscar Clemens's Monday morning was routine. While riding to his office in the Old Executive Office Building adjacent to the White House, he read the front pages of the *Washington Post* and *New York Times*. Oscar always sat in the front seat of his official Packard government car. He felt safe sitting close to his armed driver, particularly after the assassination attempt on President Truman by Puerto Rican militant pronationalists Oscar Collazo and Griselio Torresola while the president was staying at Blair House.

At his office, Clemens lit a cigarette. His secretary brought hot coffee and the mail. He pinched her on the rear and winked. A large brown envelope on top of the pile caught his attention.

"That was delivered by special airmail courier this morning. It's from Louisiana," she said.

Oscar took another sip of his coffee, then set the cup down on his desk and lifted the package with both hands. It was taped heavily around all sides.

It was from Cain Keller, Official Photographer—Office of the Governor, Baton Rouge, Louisiana. Oscar used a letter opener shaped like a small knife and pried it into the envelope across the top. His secretary offered to help, but he refused. "That will be all for now."

"Yes, sir." She left the office as directed.

His stomach began to turn as he realized the package contained eight-by-ten photos. "This can't be good."

Clemens prided himself on never showing emotion. He was always in complete control—until he saw the photos. The first ten or so were regular publicity-type shots always taken on political trips. The other twenty were not routine. Angrily, he hurled the package across his desk, knocking over his coffee and a crystal brandy decanter, which shattered into a million pieces on the hardwood floor. The photos were flung everywhere. He stood up and pounded his fist into the leather writing pad atop his desk. "That hillbilly son of a bitch!" Clemens ignored the hot coffee soaking into the finely polished finish on his custom-made mahogany desk.

Hearing the commotion, his secretary rushed in and saw the raunchy photos spread across the office. "Oh my! Oh my!"

Eventually, Clemens picked up the ringing phone. The office receptionist was on the other end. "It's Governor Long on the phone, sir. He has called three times already this morning. He would like to speak with you about the Louisiana meeting. He doesn't know when he has enjoyed a visit as much as the one with you. He said you made a wonderful impression. What should I tell him?"

"Tell that piney woods SOB to go to hell!"

This was the first time the professional receptionist ever disobeyed her boss. "I am very sorry, Governor Long. The secretary is in meetings all morning. However, he will return your call very soon. Great to speak with you today."

Long was not going to go away. It was not just blackmail; it was a classic case of checkmate. Oscar Clemens knew he was fucked. He had only one card left to play. He thought about using Danni. What would happen to her if this leaked out? Naively, he wondered if Long was willing to throw her under the bus as well. But Danni was a businessperson. If this leaked, within two weeks she would be a millionaire with a long-term Hollywood contract. Oscar had no way of knowing, but Danni was already considering contacting a Los Angeles PR firm. She dreamed of driving a red Cadillac convertible down Sunset Boulevard.

Clemens begged the governor to destroy the negatives. "For heaven's sake, man. Do you have any decency? I have a family!"

"Nothing personal, just business," Long said.

Construction of the giant Chalmette plant began in February 1951. The first aluminum was tapped on December 11, 1951. Groundbreaking to first production took only ten months, a remarkably fast construction schedule by any standards. Near the main parking lot, rows and rows of new bicycles were assembled in lines like uniformed infantrymen at attention. The lot was forty to fifty acres and would soon be completely full of Fords and Chevys owned by workers. The plant was so large that pedaling was the most efficient way for workers to get around.

The dedication ceremony was planned, with Clemens and Long pulling the crucible tilt lever on the first production pot. Wearing asbestos gloves and safety eye shields, they started the first aluminum flow. The vice president of the United States was present and on the podium. Charles Wilson, director of defense mobilization; both Louisiana senators; and the mayor of New Orleans were also present. Clemens's wife was at his side. Captains of industry including the CEO of General Electric and Kaiser Aluminum were there.

Earl was introduced by the Speaker of the Louisiana House of Representatives. Tipping his hat and waving to the large crowd, he looked like a returning general after a great conquest. He stepped to the podium, dramatically pulled out a handkerchief, dabbed the sweat beads on his forehead, and discreetly winked at Danni.

"Here in the great state of Louisiana, we once had terrible, worn-out roads. During the winter they became deep muddy ruts. In the summer they became suffocating clouds of red dust. In fact, the roads were so bad, the weather could not get around. Schools were decrepit, run-down old buildings unfit for farm animals. Kids had no books to read and no paper for writing. Hospitals were only for the rich. There were no jobs and no hope. Everyone in this state waited around for promised prosperity that never came. But now we have strong schools, a great Charity Hospital system, good roads, and a modern state capitol building just like those skyscrapers in New York City. And lo and behold, now Louisiana also has the world's largest aluminum factory, with good, modern jobs. People here have wept for generations, waiting for promises that were never kept. Now they can dry those tears because Governor Long never lets his people down!"

The large group of regular folks standing behind the dignitaries clapped and cheered the governor they loved.

National and international media covered the ceremony. Danni sat in the front row of seats in the reserved section, a special guest of the governor.

"This is the finest group of yes men ever assembled," Earl whispered to Danni.

"Two married congressmen have already invited me for cocktails later this evening. Do you think they would be interested if I were not so drop-dead gorgeous?"

"Would you be interested in them if they were not powerful wealthy congressmen?" "Touché, Governor! Touché!" Danni said.

# 6

White-collar workers were housed in a series of smaller structures situated in neat rows on a wide avenue neighboring the plant's main gate. The street's official name was Henry J. Avenue, but plant workers all called it Paper Clip Alley. Administrative functions were carried out in designated office space in the numerous buildings. The accounting office was the largest and employed thirty people. All accounting was done with a series of manual double-entry postings, providing a system of checks and balances. It required a lot of filing cabinets, hundreds of them. Twenty people worked in the receiving office. Fifteen people worked at the payroll and record-keeping building. Another small building handled vendor contracts. An attractive woman of Dad's age worked alone there, filing contracts and authorizing payments. She had a desk, a coffee maker, and a wall of filing cabinets. The sales office employed forty sales professionals, but they made sales calls around the country and were seldom there. Maintenance and safety were housed in a small building near the end of the street. Beautiful crepe myrtle trees originally lined the street, but pollution from the plant's smokestack quickly killed them. Nothing was replanted.

The last building on the left was the plant's health clinic. The clinic contained a waiting room with green terrazzo floors, three exam rooms, harsh florescent lights, low ceilings, and an x-ray machine set up in a small room with a lead-lined door. Vinyl and chrome chairs were arranged against the waiting room walls. A fake garden of faded plastic flowers near the front door welcomed everyone. An overworked receptionist sat behind a desk checking patients in. "Please sign in and take a number," she said over and over. The clinic employed one doctor and two nurses.

Dr. John Thomas Hobbs III never really wanted to be a doctor at all. He finished near the bottom of his undergrad class and finished at the prestigious Princeton School of Medicine as a mediocre, unremarkable student. John Thomas was never serious about school, but he loved drinking on weekends with his frat brothers. They got completely smashed every Friday and Saturday and did stupid stuff. Then they commiserated together, nursing hangovers on Sunday. On Monday they all bragged about the stupid stuff they had done while drunk. Next week the pattern continued. He was just following the path his family expected. His father and grandfather were both doctors, and the same was expected of him, but his heart was elsewhere. His lifelong passion was not health care. It was sailing. "Sailing may be the primary activity that separates us from animals," he said. John Thomas built his first boat at age thirteen. It was a small rowing dinghy with a single sail. "I learned about planking and lofting. Building it was a great experience."

John Thomas won many races in his homemade sailing dinghy, even beating older boys in more advanced classes. Overall, he won eleven Southern Yacht Club sailing trophies in three years, a yacht club record. But his victories were not without disagreement, including a charge that his sail was too large and another that he fouled a marker and did not do the turn. In the annual championship event, a competitor claimed John Thomas turned his boat early, missing a marker in the middle of the last downward leg. It was a windy day, with strong gusts. The boats were spread apart, and no one could prove anything.

"John Thomas cheated! I saw him! He cheated! He should be disqualified!"

John Thomas denied everything and admitted nothing. He said the other boy was just a poor competitor and jealous. But with no evidence other than the one eyewitness account, the club ethics committee adjourned the hearing with no action taken against John Thomas.

However, they did disqualify the accuser for making unsubstantiated and unproven claims against another yacht club member. It just so happened that the members of the ethics committee were close personal friends of the Hobbs family.

"Different sailors often remember events in a certain situation differently. They may have different understandings of rules, or they have different interpretations. In these unclear situations, it is unsportsmanlike to accuse another skipper of cheating," they ruled.

Dr. Hobbs's true love was a forty-five-foot gaff cutter. The sailboat was built by a legendary designer in 1915 as a racing and live-aboard. She was beautifully built, with a double-planked hull fastened with bronze fittings, teak decks, and polished mahogany woodwork. Her main saloon was forward, and a table with ample seating surrounded the mast. The interior was lit with sunlight provided by an opening skylight. Although the boat was old, John Thomas restored it to its original pristine condition.

He arranged the helm so that he could handle her solo and named her *Aquilla,* after the star used for navigation by Western Hemisphere mariners. When sailing, he loved the feeling of quiet solitude. With full sails and brisk wind, *Aquilla* effortlessly sliced through waves, creating a magical flying sensation. John Thomas planned to voyage up and down the East Coast toward Nantucket, but for now he kept her in a slip at the New Orleans West End marina. The boat was about passion and obsession. It was a true labor of love, as restoration and preservation costs far outstripped her value. He justified the expense by living aboard, but even that was not a problem for a young doctor with a large trust fund. *Aquilla* was a gift from his family once John Thomas managed to finally finish medical school.

He had poor MCAT scores, a low undergrad GPA, and was unlikely to get accepted to any accredited medical school, but his father arranged letters of recommendation from prominent physicians that fixed that. John Thomas's father was chairman of the board at Southern Baptist Hospital, head of oncology at Ochsner, and president of the Princeton School of Medicine Alumni Association. No one ever turned him down.

There was a stark difference between what was written in the bogus medical school recommendation letters and reality. "I cheated my way through middle school, high school, and college. I was accepted to med school, but the problem was that actually I knew nothing. I'm not saying I cheated in med school, but when your dad hires the dean and top professors as your personal tutors, you know the fix is in," he bragged.

After coasting through med school, John Thomas was looking for an easy job with good pay, no need to build a practice, no long hours, no weekends, and no three-year residency requirements. The Chalmette Aluminum health clinic position would be perfect. John Thomas could leave the plant at 5:00 p.m. every afternoon and be at the marina by 5:30 p.m., enjoying many long summer hours sailing *Aquilla* on Lake Pontchartrain. He expected clear sailing, and like a snake charmer who has never been bitten, he went into the CA job with a cavalier attitude and misplaced confidence.

"What do I do if something happens at the plant? Something with serious injuries?" he asked the interviewer.

"Don't try to be a hero. Just call an ambulance from Chalmette General. They'll be here in a few minutes, and the hospital is better equipped with a modern emergency room. Stay out of the way and never do anything that could in any way create the perception of liability for the company. Understood?"

"Well, if I don't treat injuries, what exactly am I expected to do?"

"You are expected to look professional. Always wear the white doctor's coat with the CA emblem, and keep an otoscope in your pocket and a stethoscope around your neck. When workers show up at the clinic, it is your job to get them back to the production floor quickly. Your effectiveness is measured against worker production hours missed. Your annual bonus depends on this. Basically, it's your job to dispense salt tablets and Band-Aids. That's it! Any questions?"

"Nope!" John Thomas said, unable to hide his enthusiasm. "When do I start?"

Chalmette Aluminum workers received a notification included with their weekly paycheck: "The company is pleased to announce the newest member of our health and wellness staff. Dr. John Thomas Hobbs III has joined Chalmette Aluminum as Director of the Health Clinic. He comes to us with strong letters of recommendations and a degree from the outstanding Princeton School of Medicine. We are eager to see his positive contribution to the health and well-being of our workers."

# 7

The legitimacy of the state is maintained through national ideology. We learn to believe that our rulers are wise, that they represent the best interests of our society, that they uphold the traditions of our founders, and that they protect us from terrible and constant dangers. We are taught that our blessings and prosperity flow from the state's wisdom. It's all based on a contradiction: the existence of an organization powerful enough to guarantee these things is also powerful enough trample upon rights.

*In 1946, Churchill gave a speech at Westminster College in Missouri. He said that communist fifth columns were operating throughout Western and Southern Europe. Churchill explained that there was "nothing Soviets admire so much as strength and there is nothing for which they have less respect for than military weakness." Truman attended the speech and listened intently. "From Stettin in the Baltic to Trieste in the Adriatic, an iron curtain has descended across the continent." With Churchill's speech, on this day the Cold War started. It would last for forty years.*

*President Truman soon announced the Truman Doctrine, hoping to contain the growing communist menace. Things were quickly spiraling out of control. Greece and Turkey were in danger of falling into the Soviet sphere, Western Europe was still war-ravaged and starving, the Communist Party took control in Romania and Czechoslovakia, Stalin ordered the Berlin Blockade, and the American consul in China was held hostage by communist forces. The Soviets said Berlin was the testicles of the West. "Every time we want to make the West scream, we squeeze Berlin." On September 9, 1948, the Soviet Union declared the communist Democratic People's Republic of Korea to be the legitimate government of the entire Korean peninsula. NATO was formed. The Korean War started. America and her allies needed aluminum.*

*At noon, three days a week, towns and cities across America sounded civil defense sirens. Schoolchildren practiced hiding under desks and covering their heads with textbooks. Duck-and-cover practice became a part of the daily routine, as Soviet atomic bombs were expected to rain down.*

*In 1952, the US tested the first hydrogen bomb. On August 8, the Russians exploded a hydrogen bomb of their own. H-bombs employed the fusion of hydrogen and made World War II atomic bombs look like Ping-Pong balls. Before the thermonuclear explosions, the only thing most Americans knew about hydrogen was that it was used in the Hindenburg. Clearly, hydrogen was not just an industrial gas. It is ironic, but the aboveground thermonuclear tests at Bikini Atoll in the Pacific became a catalyst at the foundation of the modern ecology movements. The total and complete devastation at the test sites and the fallout exposure of the Japanese fishing boat* Lucky Dragon 5, *poisoning all twenty-three crew members, focused attention on environmental responsibility.*

*The crew was fishing near Midway Atoll but moved closer to the Marshall Islands, following fish. They were eighty miles west of Bikini when the sky lit up. A fine white radioactive dust fell on the* Lucky Dragon *and her crew for hours. President Eisenhower said, "*Lucky Dragon 5 *was actually a spy outfit commanded by a Soviet agent who intentionally exposed the ship's crew to embarrass the US and gain intelligence on the thermonuclear test."*

*All members of the crew suffered severe radiation sickness, and one died. "I pray that I am the last victim of atomic or hydrogen bombs," the dying man said.*

*Afraid of a thermal nuclear apocalypse, two young New Orleans bank tellers complained that they would most likely die virgins. The branch manager was in the lunchroom sitting at a nearby table. He overheard the conversation and, feeling sympathetic, invited the two young ladies to his apartment that evening. The escapade made the* Times-Picayune *after a father read his daughter's diary. He showed up at the bank and was charged with assault. "I was just doing my patriotic duty," the manager said.*

In my old New Orleans neighborhood, on Harrison Avenue, the air raid siren was twelve feet tall and powered by a Chrysler V8 engine. It was mounted on a telephone pole in front of the neighborhood fire station and next to the K&B Drugstore. It could be heard for miles around and was powerful enough to turn fog into rain. Edward Hynes Elementary school was two blocks away. We never got used to its frightening ear-piercing sound.

The government produced nuclear educational movies such as *Duck and Cover*, explaining what to do in the event of nuclear war. Hynes School had its own copy of the film, and we watched it in the auditorium on every rainy-day schedule. It depicted giant radioactive mushroom clouds rising above American cities and children diving under school desks as sirens blared. Nationwide, thousands of backyard fallout shelters were built as the government tested more powerful hydrogen bombs in the South Pacific and the Nevada desert. The short-lived peace achieved after World War II did not last long.

Backyard fallout shelters were uncommon in New Orleans because the high water table made them impossible to keep from flooding. It was the same reason people here are buried above ground. However, a few shelters were constructed on high ground near the river and lakefront. Pat was one of my rich elementary school friends who lived in a beautiful lakefront home on Egret Street. He had a professional-grade drum set in his bedroom and a pool table in the den. Pat's family had the first microwave oven and the first VHS machine I ever saw. His father was a successful OBGYN, but he also believed the world would soon come to a violent end in a nuclear holocaust. He was a survivalist with an assortment of military-style weapons and a backyard bomb shelter. Looking for summer adventure, Pat and I discovered a way to sneak into the shelter's entrance hidden near a rose garden. It was a thick cement tube with room to stand, cots, shelves, storage space, and a single electric light bulb. Constructed nine feet below ground, the shelter had a small access door hidden behind the rosebushes.

"These new hydrogen bombs make atomic weapons look like child's play. The Russians have enough hydrogen bombs to launch a first strike. It is only a matter of time," Pat's dad said.

His backyard bomb shelter was stocked with enough canned goods to feed Pat's family for three months, until the nuclear fallout cleared, or they had to use the bathroom. There was no accommodation made for that necessity or for fresh air. A vent to the surface provided air, but it was unfiltered. Fallout-contaminated air would have quickly breached the shelter. We enjoyed pork and beans, corn, green beans, and canned meat all summer. We opened the cans from the bottom and carefully placed them back on the shelves exactly as they were. Pat's dad kept a careful inventory of his survival stockpile but never realized most all his canned items were empty.

At the end of West End Boulevard and Robert E. Lee, the civil defense and state government built the largest fallout shelter in the metro area. It was a short distance from Hynes Elementary School. Portions of the shelter were below ground, but much of it was concealed under a huge man-made mountain of dirt, steel, and cement. It was the highest point in New Orleans, even higher than Monkey Hill in Audubon Park. A circular drive led to massive blastproof steel doors. Gray painted International pickup trucks with the "CD" Civil Defense decals were always parked nearby.

"That is for important people like the mayor and governor," my mom said when I asked about the strange building.

"Will the mayor duck under his desk too?" I asked.

"No, Sebastian. He will be safe in there. Our government leaders need to be protected." "When the Russians attack, where do we hide?" She had no answer.

# 8

"How are you, sweetheart? It's been way too long!"

"Nice to hear from you, Danni. How are you?" It was impossible not to recognize Danni's distinctive voice.

"I'm still driving the boys crazy! We should catch up. How about a quiet get-together and a few drinks?" she asked.

Cain was never very close to Danni and was surprised to receive a call from her, out of the blue like this.

"How does tomorrow evening sound?"

"I guess so. Tomorrow should be OK," he said with a slight nervous stutter.

Cain was introverted and very uncomfortable in social situations. He always tried to blend into the background, quietly taking his photos and disappearing unseen. That was his job—to stay invisible, hiding in the shadows like the kid picked last for kickball. Cain lived alone in a small Central City apartment. It was impossible to have a social life when he was always at the governor's beck and call. He had had a steady girlfriend in high school but never married. Cain's life was dedicated to the governor. He accepted Danni's offer because he assumed it had something to do with Earl, and he was not inclined to turn down an offer of free drinks.

"Don't be nervous, big fella. I don't bite. Promise!"

With the election of the Eighty-Third Congress and President Eisenhower, the Republicans swept into power. Washington had grown suspicious about the curious Chalmette selection decision. Congressional committees scheduled multiple hearings, including a Senate committee, two special committees, and one joint committee. They were preparing investigations with oral testimony and public witnesses. The US Justice Department issued orders demanding the preservation of all related documents, and the local US Attorney was issuing subpoenas left and right. President Eisenhower even suggested that the hearings be open and televised. With this political firestorm brewing in Washington, Danni knew it was only a matter of time before she was swept up into the controversy.

"Mr. Clemens cannot be compelled to testify against himself. If full immunity is not conferred upon my client, he will exercise his constitutional right to take the Fifth." Clemens had hired the law firm of Wardwell & Strong, a powerful political firm. His legal team was already calling news conferences and building a defense strategy.

*Danni was worried about possible personal legal jeopardy as the work of government investigations closed in. It was also true that hundreds of reporters with microphones and cameras would pack the committee rooms begging for exclusive interviews. It was becoming a public spectacle. Danni did not see much difference between the crowds of reporters in Washington and the flashbulbs and paparazzi lining the red carpets during the Oscars in Hollywood.*

The Napoleon House was smoke filled, dark, and quiet. The only light was provided by a single candle on each table. All the booths had high backs, providing private seating for lovers, corrupt deal making politicians, and New Orleans businessmen wearing seersucker suits and loose neckties and smoking expensive cigars. The servers were discreet. Danni's favorite booth was the last one in the very back. She ordered a bottle of Hennessy. Cain eventually found her in the dark. She poured two glasses as they exchanged pleasantries.

"How about a tall drink?"

Cain finished it quickly, then shook his head and gently placed the heavy glass down on the table. "That is so good! It's great to see you again, Danni."

They continued drinking and talking like casual friends until Danni turned the conversation to business. "I guess you're wondering what's going on," she said.

"I appreciate the drinks and good company, but yes, you could say I'm curious. Although I do keep up with the news."

"I need something very important. Something I think you have." Danni slid a thick envelope across the table and asked about the Clemens negatives. She said they might keep her out of jail. She called them insurance.

Cain picked up the envelope, thumbed through the thick stack of hundred-dollar bills, and finished another drink. He kept his left hand on the money. Danni lived in a small French Quarter tenement-type apartment. At the My-Oh-My she worked for tips. This was a lot of money to give away. The irony here is that it was the same cash in the same envelope Earl had handed Danni after her night with Clemens.

"The photos could keep you out of jail or make you famous. Right?" Cain said, "Clemens's lawyers have already contacted me multiple times. It seems everyone wants them. But Earl asked me to destroy those photos and negatives a few weeks ago. Sorry, I can't help you."

Danni smiled. "You didn't do that, sweetheart. I know you still have them!" "What makes you so sure?"

"I know because you opened the envelope! Didn't you? Cain, you're bad at being a good liar."

He kept his eyes on the envelope. "It's not about the money."

Danni said she admired his loyalty and understood why the governor trusted him so much. She said friendship is very important.

"You don't get it! Do you? Our Tom-and-Huck friendship is not what you think," Cain said. "I have loved only one woman in my life. We were in high school and dated for two years. We were both virgins, so waiting was not a big problem. We were determined to save ourselves for marriage. One day Earl picked her up from school and talked her into having a few drinks. He parked in a cotton field and had sex with my girlfriend. He told me not to be mad and said he did me a favor by breaking her in! He said I should thank him! Not a day goes by that I don't think about Earl screwing the love of my life in the back of his car, then joking and bragging about it! The pain still cuts deep."

"I'm so sorry." Danni placed her hands over Cain's. "I'm so sorry! Earl's idea of loyalty is a one-way street. He thinks all the toys under the tree belong to him."

"Me and Earl grew up together in a small town in north-central Louisiana called Winnfield. He likes to say we were like Tom and Huck. I read all of Mr. Twain's books. I'm pretty sure Huck never tried to fuck Becky Thatcher. When we were kids, a lot of old mules still worked the cotton fields of Winn Parish. They could work for you loyally for thirty years, just waiting for the one opportunity to kick the crap out of you once."

Danni poured more Hennessy. Finishing the bottle, she ordered another.

"I have followed Earl around like a lost puppy my entire life, taking his pictures and doing whatever he needed done. He tells me to destroy negatives, and I say OK. But I'm not as stupid as he thinks. I have kept every photo I've ever taken. Every single one!"

"Does that include the Clemens photos?" Danni asked.

"Yes."

Although tempted to take the cash, Cain said it was not just about that. "You can't put a price on revenge. Watching Earl's downfall would be enjoyable. Even an old mule can kick like a bastard!"

"Take the money and buy that fishing camp at Toledo Bend. You deserve it, and don't stay too long at the ball. That didn't go well for Cinderella, and it won't for you either," Danni said with a friendly smile.

# 9

Chalmette Aluminum consumed massive amounts of natural gas in the production process, but like some Central American drug cartel leader, Earl was not satisfied with his obscene profits. The plant also used extensive internal electricity for machinery, equipment, cranes, and hoists. In fact, aluminum is never found in nature like gold or silver is. Aluminum molecules bond with oxygen, creating claylike aluminum oxide. It takes a tremendous amount of electricity to break the oxygen bond. That is why they say aluminum is electricity in metal form. Earl's legislative floor leaders in Baton Rouge, eager to generate more natural-gas cash, cooked up a greedy plan to extort more from the plant. They introduced legislation requiring CA to operate at 25 Hz rather than the standard 60 Hz. The bill passed easily with a large majority vote in both houses. "This law protects citizens against the danger of high-voltage lines crossing their neighborhoods, their schools, and their churches," Earl said, but he had alternative motives involving more natural gas and more kickbacks for his greedy political cronies and elected lackeys. The skullduggery and greed had no limits.

The New Orleans Public Service Utility Company could only provide electricity at the standard hertz. Earl's new law forced Chalmette Aluminum to construct their own power grid with additional power stations, substations, and converters. This demand for electricity generation was satisfied with natural-gas-fueled power stations built on the plant grounds. Additional gas pipelines were constructed across Louisiana's swamps, including the Atchafalaya Basin. A new 163-mile pipeline connected the plant with major natural-gas fields at Lake Charles and Saint James parish. This encouraged saltwater intrusion, killing wetlands and marsh grasses that held the deltaic land together and helped protect the state from hurricane floods.

Canals were dredged through the swamps and marshes as they explored for more gas. Hundreds of miles of additional pipelines were built, reaching anywhere a producing well was established. The drilling companies were required to fill in these canals, but that law was universally ignored and not enforced. The canals encouraged saltwater intrusion, leading to additional environmental problems. They were also required to clean up the mess left at drilling sites, but that never happened. The Louisiana marshes became a fossil fuel infrastructure junkyard. When they finished using something, it was just pushed aside and forgotten. Nothing was ever removed because that incurred additional expense. When asked about the wetlands' destruction, Earl said it was "a useful sacrifice."

More environmental devastation followed. Modern electric equipment operated on 60 Hz. A giant, ugly machine manufactured by Westinghouse called the "freak" converted on-site power from the 25 Hz required by Earl's new law back to 60 Hz so that it could be compatible with the plant's new equipment. The freak was a rotating electrical machine that required constant cooling and an unlimited supply of water.

Mississippi River water was pumped through the machine and returned to the river. The superheated water caused additional environmental damage, this time to the Mississippi and its fragile aquatic life balance. Aluminum production during the early years of the Cold War was so important to the defense production that just taking pictures of the freak could lead to espionage charges.

Dad always worked mandatory twelve-hour shifts and tried to pick up overtime at every opportunity, including Saturdays and Sundays. That schedule would drain anyone. Working seven days a week left nothing to look forward to. Exhaustion became a way of life. Dad wore steel-toed asbestos shoes, long-sleeve shirts, and heavy jeans under the heat-resistant and fire-retardant asbestos safety clothes. Deadly hazards were everywhere, and a single moment of carelessness could cost a life. Something as simple as slipping and tripping could be life threatening. The massive overhead electric cranes operating in the blast furnace area were called skull crackers because head injuries involving the massive equipment were common. An apprentice electrician was killed while performing maintenance on the crane. He was struck by a moving beam and fell twenty feet onto an electrical bus panel used for high-current power distribution. Death was instant. Like the unavoidable scent of strong perfume on an airplane, the putrid smell of burning human flesh hung in the air.

Dad saw a millwright slip just as a huge slab of aluminum weighing sixty-five thousand pounds made its way off the production line to the plate mill. The man was inspecting the equipment after recent repairs. He lost his footing underneath the conveyer, wedging his arm in the rapidly moving belt. The slab continued moving.

"Pierre, the conveyer is running over my arm! My God! It's on my arm!"

Hitting the emergency button, Dad stopped the belt. Other workers tried unsuccessfully to free the man. The arm was ripped from its socket. He passed out from pain. Chalmette General Hospital was called. The worker remained trapped until plant electricians managed to reverse the conveyer. An ambulance arrived twenty-five minutes later. Dr. John Thomas Hobbs was not available at the time.

"That was something I never want to see again. I can't forget the pain in that man's eyes," Dad said.

Accidents and injury were common, but many of the most dangerous conditions were invisible to the poorly educated workers. Asbestos was everywhere, especially in the plant areas where Dad worked. Asbestos was not banned in the US until the late 1970s, much too late for my father's generation. Illness also resulted from heat stress. They worked in 130-degree heat and then on winter days stepped outside to thirty-degree temperatures. Pneumonia was common. The heat also caused dehydration, prickly heat, and pyrexia. In certain areas heat was so intense that one could work only five minutes at a time. Core body temperatures over 103F were not uncommon.

Dad's specific job involved drilling a tap hole with a large handheld drill into the top layer of cooler hardened metal in the furnace. Then he placed a splasher plate in front of the tap to prevent splashing of the molten aluminum. A lance was thrust through the hole and into the mix, injecting raw materials necessary to create specific grades of aluminum. After he removed the lance, the tap hole allowed molten aluminum to flow from the furnace into the ladle and then the casting forms.

An inexperienced shop foreman claimed that Dad was working too slow. He ordered another worker to take over and tap the furnace. Workers called the foreman Mussolini, after the inept but dangerous Italian leader. The foreman bragged about being "Eye-talian," and he was dismissive of Dad and refused to listen when Dad told him he was making a mistake. "The process can't go any faster. It's going to screw up!" Dad said. No one bothered to tell the hated foreman that the ladle was not in place. Molten aluminum poured onto the work floor, spread around, and created a white-hot puddle over a wide area. The "breakout" of molten aluminum was a mess that could not be cleaned up until the metal cooled. Then it could be broken apart and carted off to the scrapyard for recycling.

It took a very long time for a furnace to completely cool down. It was also very expensive to fire it back up, but the cool-down process could not be rushed. Workers at another mill had tried to cool a hot furnace with a firehose. Extreme temperatures turned the water into hydrogen gas. When the water molecule is torn apart, hydrogen breaks free with massive energy release potential. The resulting explosion sent twenty men to the hospital with critical injuries. Mussolini was worried about keeping production schedules on time and ordered the area cleaned up before the furnace completely cooled. He wanted it back in production quickly. Wagging his finger and grinding his teeth, he came at Dad like a raging bull. Most shift workers believed the foreman had a drinking problem. He was always a mean bastard.

"Get in there and clean up your mistake, or I'll find someone else to do your job! Dozens of negroes will take this job tomorrow!"

"Yes, sir."

The refractory bricks lining the area were still very hot when Dad was ordered to enter. He wore thick layers of asbestos cloth strapped to the bottom of his heat-resistant shoes. It was so hot even his special shoes would melt under the extreme heat. Refractory brick lined the furnace walls to insulate the vessels of molten metal. The extreme temperature turned some brick into glass. The heat emanating from them was incredible. Like those poor unfortunate Russian enlisted men forced to clean debris from the damaged Chernobyl nuclear reactor, Dad could stay inside the furnace for only a few minutes at a time before being overcome by heat.

His legs began to feel weak and heavy; it became difficult for Dad to take steps. He thought it was the early warning signs of heatstroke. But with each new step, his heat-resistant shoes stuck firm to the partially melted floor. Dad thought his embedded tracks looked like footprints on a beach. "Actually, it looked more like fossilized prints from some extinct dinosaur." He cursed with each step as he trudged on.

After a company review of the incident, Mussolini was awarded a promotion. Dad was given a reprimand and a demotion with a pay cut. Bastards.

Many aluminum workers developed allergic skin disease from repeated contact with metal dust. But respiratory problems were the most common. Upper respiratory infections, chronic bronchitis, bronchial asthma, and pulmonary tuberculosis were 62 percent more likely than in the general population, especially for workers exposed to the plant for more than ten years. Much of the plant had poor ventilation and no extraction fans, and individual respirators for workers were uncommon. Thick clouds of gray smoke clung to the ceilings. At times it was so thick workers could hardly see.

A coworker and close friend of Dad was diagnosed with pulmonary tuberculosis and spent four months in the hospital before his death. "Sometimes we used breathing masks, but usually they were not available," he said. While hospitalized the man received no wages or other compensation from CA. Neighbors and family helped out to feed his family. He went to Chalmette Aluminum as a young man and ended up with nothing to show for his life except destroyed health and premature death. While he lay dying on a hospital bed, he recommended his son to replace him.

Early one morning, Dad was exposed to methyl mercaptan. Breathing the chemical in large amounts can damage lungs, heart, kidneys, and the nervous system, ultimately resulting in death. It is commonly used in conjunction with natural gas. Dad reported the strong odor of the deadly gas to unconcerned management and was told to keep working. They said it was his imagination and insisted that nothing was wrong. "Keep working. You have a break in thirty minutes anyway." A short time later, Dad became very sick, and the ambulance was called. He was unresponsive after gasping for breath.

"Wake up, Sebastian! We need to go to the hospital."

My mother was calm and drove to Chalmette with me still in my Rin-Tin-Tin pajamas and faux coonskin slippers. She did not speed or run red lights or ignore stop signs. I saw no concern in her face. She seemed annoyed and blamed Dad for screwing up her day. "What did he do wrong this time?"

When we finally arrived, Dad was in the emergency room waiting for his release paperwork. He was treated with oxygen and assigned bedrest. I hugged his neck and noticed a cold, clammy feeling. His color was gray and ashen.

Mom changed her demeanor. "I'm so happy you're okay. I was so worried!" She used a handkerchief from her purse to dry fake tears. It was an Academy Award–winning performance designed to preserve her meal ticket.

"I have just a slight headache. It should clear in about twenty-four hours. I can report back to work Monday morning. I'm fine," he insisted. "I like the pajamas, little fella. That's a good look!" He rubbed his hands in my hair, messing it up even more.

"Let's get out of here," he said, smiling.

"It's just a formality, but we need you to wait a few more minutes. Chalmette Aluminum security will be here soon." A doctor holding a clipboard said this was routine procedure. "They will want a statement for the company safety coordinator. Nothing to worry about. They always do this."

"Perhaps you should call the union rep?" Mother smelled a rat, but Dad refused to involve the USW.

"If I do that, management will label me a troublemaker. You know I can't afford to lose this job." I think Dad lived in constant fear of the unemployment line.

The truth was that workers always bore the economic brunt of workplace accidents. The company believed accidents were due to workers' carelessness, and they assumed absolutely no share of resulting expenses or income loss that followed. In most cases Chalmette Aluminum paid nothing.

The company safety coordinator arrived at the hospital and insisted that Dad go back to the mill with him. "Ensuring the continued safety of CA workers is our first priority. Our Safety Leadership Program illustrates this commitment. We constantly complete audits after every incident, learning from past accidents to prevent future problems. The company doctor needs to evaluate you, and we need you to complete and sign a statement," he said.

Dad was driven back and forced to wait over five hours for Dr. Hobbs to arrive.

"If you don't let us out of here, I'm calling the police! You have no right to kidnap us." Mom just wanted to get to her beauty shop appointment on time. It was only after she threatened to involve the NOPD that Dr. Hobbs finally showed up. He was dressed in short pants with a white pullover shirt and topsider boat shoes. He seemed annoyed, and his breath smelled of alcohol poorly masked behind a breath mint disguise.

Dr. Hobbs moved a light back and forth in front of Dad's eyes, listened to his heart, and asked Dad to cough. He dropped the light on the floor, breaking it into many pieces.

"We didn't really need that anyway. The light thing is just a formality," he said. The examination took five minutes. "Don't operate heavy machinery for twenty-four hours, drink plenty of water, and get some rest. You are clear to return to work Monday morning. Please sign this release. If you have any questions, call the clinic nurse." Dr. John Thomas Hobbs III left without answering any additional questions. The release placed all blame on Dad and indemnified Chalmette Aluminum against any responsibility. They said he turned the wrong valve on the wrong hose at a bad time. Dad signed the three-page document without reading it.

I woke up early the next morning and went to the kitchen for a glass of milk. I found Dad unresponsive on the kitchen floor, lying in a pool of his own vomit. "Mom, Dad's sick!"

This time an ambulance took him to Baptist Hospital in uptown New Orleans, where he was hospitalized in a chemical decontamination unit for eight days. Dad was lucky. Two workers at another plant up the road in Norco, Louisiana, died when poisoned by the same deadly gas. Afraid of losing his job, Dad never contacted his union representative or filed a complaint against the company.

Obvious things happen right in front of children, but because they lack a frame of reference, they don't notice what is really going on. While Dad was still recovering in his hospital room, a nicely dressed and polite door-to-door salesman happened to stop by. I was sitting on the sofa with a *Popular Mechanics* magazine, reading an article about the competition to set new land speed records at the Bonneville Salt Flats. I was old enough to be suspicious but young enough to still be naive. He demonstrated a vacuum cleaner on the living room rug. Then he went into my parents' bedroom to clean that rug. Mom followed him in and latched the door. About forty-five minutes later, they both emerged from the bedroom with a disheveled look.

"I'll stop by again next time I'm in the area." "Promise?" Mom asked in a flirtatious coy voice. "You can count on it."

I know Mom had many casual encounters like this. Either Dad did not know, or, most likely, he ignored the obvious, sacrificing his happiness for my benefit. His childhood had been a mess. Dad wanted something better for me. Sometimes Mom would ask him to call before he headed home in the evening. "I may need you to pick up something from the store." This was just a ploy so she would know he was on his way home.

Often Dad would ask just enough probing questions about suspicious things to make her squirm. "Tell me about that guy from the Bell Telephone convention. He was staying at the Monteleone, right? You mentioned he bought you a cup of coffee. The Monteleone has wonderful coffee—best in town, right? That was the evening you got home late, wasn't it?" Dad always backed off before delivering the knockout question. I think his intentions were just to let her know he wasn't quite that stupid. The obvious unasked question was what she was doing at the Monteleone Hotel anyway. Everybody knows the best coffee was the café au lait at the Café Du Monde. Even Mom should have answered that correctly.

The vacuum salesman winked at Mom and handed me a piece of Bazooka bubble gum as he left. Once it became clear what Dad went through just to put food on our table, you would think my mother would meet him on the porch every evening with a cold beer and short tight dress. I don't remember her doing anything like that.

# 10

The old State Highway 84 runs east to west across Louisiana from Texas to Mississippi. It passes directly through Winn Parish and the town of Winnfield, home to the Long political dynasty. Cotton drove Winnfield's economy, but the town also had a single sawmill and a slaughterhouse for hogs that employed fifteen workers. Heading east, the road hits the Mississippi River at Ferriday on the Louisiana side and Natchez on the other. In this slower age before interstate highways, traveling forty-five miles per hour in a Packard, Cadillac, or Lincoln was perfectly acceptable. It was an age of unhurried dignity. Earl made the slow-paced trip across the state many times wearing suspenders and a straw hat. The governor never wore a jacket or tie when he was meeting ordinary folk. He usually loaded up the Cadillac's back seat with produce from Winn Parish and handed out vegetable baskets as gifts while driving along, instructing his driver to stop anytime he saw a group of people, even children. If he left Winnfield in the early morning, Earl could reach Natchez in about four hours. That was without stops. Sometimes his trip across the state took much longer.

"Stop the car!"

The driver turned off Highway 84 and pulled up to a quiet farm area with a run-down home, chicken coop, small barn, and broken-down rusty tractor. Earl walked to the coop, re-moved his straw hat and set it on a post, unhooked the wire latch, and stepped inside. The twenty or so chickens looked well cared for. He got down on his knees, level with the roost, then lay on his back under the row of nesting boxes. Earl had never actually seen a chicken lay an egg and figured now was as good a time as any. A young sharecropper boy showed up asking questions.

Earl used the straw hat to dust off his pants. "Give this eggplant to your mother. Tell her it's a gift from Earl K. Long, governor of the great state of Louisiana!"

That huge Cadillac limo pulling off the highway was a re-markable sight to a barefoot sharecropper kid.

"Nosir, I don't know. Is you really the governor? Why you fallin' down and rollin' in the coop? Why you coved wit chicken dirt all over?"

"That man driving my Cadillac is a bonified Louisiana state trooper. See that license plate right there? It says LA 1. That proves I'm the governor of Louisiana. Who else is going to be riding in a car like this, on this road, with that license plate, giving out baskets of vegetables?"

The suspicious boy kept his arms folded and stared at the Cadillac. Earl pinned a political campaign button on the boy's shirt. "Elect Uncle Earl. I Ain't Crazy."

"Now run along, son, and tell your maw that Governor Long sends his best regards. Enjoy that eggplant."

Governor Long met with his cronies in Natchez for many reasons. Most importantly, he always wanted to avoid the good government types, especially the annoying women with the Good Government Alliance in New Orleans. They hated his womanizing and drinking. The city was never friendly to the

Longs anyway. New Orleans was the only Louisiana city to support Franklin Roosevelt over Huey Long's Share the Wealth programs. The city's largest political organization was the RDO. The Regular Democratic Organization was always anti-Long. The group supported Mayor deLesseps Morrison in his three unsuccessful attempts to defeat the Longs. Between the Dudley Do-Rights of the RDO and the Good Government women from New Orleans, Earl had no peace. That is also the reason Earl had the Chalmette Aluminum plant built just outside New Orleans and Orleans Parish—economic punishment. He was a spiteful man.

"Those bloodthirsty witches track me like hound dogs. They'll never give up until they turn me into a toad. I think they've spent too much time in home beauty shops sniffing Aqua Net and soaking up cheap drugstore hair dye into their brains. If their husbands did their duty properly, maybe these hags would stay home more and bother me less. Everybody has a cross to bear! I have these hags!" he said.

But in Mississippi, Earl felt removed and somewhat isolated from the political and legal pressure of his own state. He also felt secure enough to bring Bourbon Street strippers to the Jefferson Hotel in historic Natchez. They worked the private gatherings topless. The corrupt hotel manager with an old-style pencil mustache, which he mischievously twirled constantly, looked the other way while putting Earl's cash into his pocket. He never recorded the governor's name in the hotel registry, unless it was the fake name Earl used from time to time, Mr. Cotton Field. A devious hotel manager and a corrupt governor, they got along famously. Once a month Earl gathered with his natural-gas cabal members at the hotel to divide their ill-gotten gains. He called the group his "trade association." There were no direct payoffs or kickbacks offered to the governor, but there was poker.

The smoky, noisy games lasted all night, with Earl winning every hand. "Gee, Governor, you won again! You are a remarkable poker player. Never seen anything like it." If anyone beat the governor, they would never be invited back. Hands with four aces, royal flushes, or straights all folded. Earl always won. "There is nothing dishonest about being a good poker player," he said. Other hotel quests called the manager to complain about the noisy, raucous parties, but he did nothing. "I'll look into it," he said.

The political blank check is a legend in Louisiana. In this case it was fact. Earl's business partners signed blank checks during each election season supporting the governor's political machine. "Write in the necessary amount," they said. The political kickbacks were considered the cost of doing business. Earl called it honest graft.

Earl was a superstitious gambler, and before turning over a new hand, he followed a specific routine. First, he placed the expensive Cuban cigar he was smoking in the ashtray, then he called over one of the Bourbon Street ladies.

"Come over here, sweetie. Give me some luck." Earl held her left bare breast with his right hand and licked her nipple exactly nine times. Not ten and not eight—exactly nine. He won incredible amounts of cash and always headed back home with suitcases full of fifties and hundreds. The poker cash made Huey's deduct box look like chump change. Earl even "won" a house in uptown New Orleans on Audubon Street near Saint Charles. After the late-night poker games concluded, he invited two or three ladies up to his room for a private nightcap. The women followed him up three flights of stairs to his large suite. The bathroom still contained an original copper tub. Earl liked brunettes most. He was generous and gave the ladies hundred-dollar bills as rewards for doing the things he enjoyed. Soaking in the tub while smoking another cigar, he especially liked watching.

The New Orleans "hags" of the Good Government Alliance filed a complaint with the Louisiana attorney general demanding a full investigation of the governor's immoral poker games. The attorney general was named Bolivar Edwards Kemp. Earl's full name was Earl K. Long. His middle initial stood for Kemp. The Louisiana attorney general was Earl's cousin. Behind his back, Kemp's political enemies just called him Lemon Head. He had had that nickname since the second grade. His birth was very difficult, and the doctor used forceps a little too aggressively. Resembling a lemon, his head never recovered its natural shape. Not surprisingly, Bolivar found nothing inappropriate with Earl's Natchez debauchery. The three-paragraph opinion concluded that there was nothing illegal about card games played at Mississippi hotels. "Furthermore, the Louisiana Attorney General's Office has no jurisdiction over the operation of Natchez hotels or the fashion choices of bar maids working in Mississippi."

The real "trade association" business started the next morning in a private meeting room adjacent to Earl's suite. Breakfast included fried eggs, grits, bacon, and biscuits. With a black alligator belt, matching briefcase, seersucker suit, blue bowtie, oxford shoes, and perfect hair, Luke Sparrow was not in Natchez to play. He never touched alcohol, favoring only sweet tea or coffee. His thick gray eyebrows looked like wiry caterpillars. The *Times-Picayune* called Sparrow the best political lawyer in the nation. Successfully defending Huey Long against a close impeachment vote in the Louisiana Senate and fighting a team of blue-blood Ivy League lawyers representing the Standard Oil Corporation cemented his reputation as a ruthless son of a bitch. "No one needs a nice lawyer. This bastard is mean as a snake. Dignified, but mean," Earl said as he introduced Sparrow to the men sitting around the table.

The morning started with idle conversation about nothing in particular until Earl called the meeting to order. Sitting next to Earl, Sparrow repositioned his reading glasses on the tip of his nose and carefully lined up his briefcase with the corner of the table. His reading glasses were always suspended around his neck on a silver chain. He kept another pair of glasses in his lapel pocket for distance. The expensive briefcase meant power and authority, just like the Packard Patrician he had driven from Baton Rouge.

Looking over the top of his glasses, Sparrow stared momentarily at each individual and wrote down their names on a yellow legal pad as Earl introduced them. "We have a quorum. I call this meeting of the governor's natural-gas trade association to order. Do I hear a motion and a second to approve the minutes as presented?"

Everyone came to order. Most of the agenda was routine, except for two items under new business. Earl planned to discuss a proposed change of the natural-gas business ownership percentages and the upcoming Washington, DC, hearings regarding the CA location selection process. Like any good politician, he would not bring these things up unless he already had the necessary votes lined up to prevail.

Earl had the floor. Under an unusual "personal privilege" maneuver, he proposed a motion giving Mr. Sparrow a 1 percent ownership interest in the natural-gas operations and equal membership as a member of the trade association.

"This will assure the quality legal representation we need. Everyone is encouraged to speak freely," he added.

No one dared questioned the governor, and a motion for approval from the group was made and seconded without discussion. The men sitting around the table trusted no one. They only felt at ease with Sparrow after he was made a part owner in their illegal arrangement. As a coconspirator, if investigations started, he could not offer testimony against them without implicating himself in the process. It was ironic, but the more deceitful they all became, the more trust developed among the group. Honor among thieves. Nothing like corruption to discourage dishonor.

"I have a motion and a second. Any further discussion?" Earl waited a few moments.

"Hearing no questions, all in favor? Any opposed? Motion carries. Next item."

Earl and Sparrow's motives were more Machiavellian than simply building trust among thieves. The cabal ownership interest had been an even fifty-fifty split. The other collaborators had no way of knowing that Earl had a signed counter letter in his office safe in which Sparrow committed to vote his 1 percent with the governor. They had stolen control of the natural-gas operations with a single vote. Earl now controlled 51 percent.

"Next item under new business. Congressional hearings on the Chalmette plant begin in five weeks."

Sparrow opened discussion. "Everything needs to be discussed here and now, at this meeting. Because once the DC hearings start, whatever is not protected by taking the Fifth will be protected by attorney-client privilege, so long as it is covered in legal strategy sessions."

Earl offered a motion for the group to officially hire Sparrow as lead council. He explained that since Eisenhower's election, the nation's political climate had changed.

"They will come after everything related to the Truman administration, including Clemens's aluminum decision. It is a real witch hunt. But Sparrow will never back down or run. I promise each of you that!" Earl said. "I have known him since Huey's first Public Service Commission election in 1922. Sparrow is a born fighter. He fought when he played baseball. He fought his brothers and sisters growing up. He fights like that now in politics too. The SOB fights everybody. Sparrow loves fights on the Senate floor. He never ran from a political fight before, and he ain't gonna run now. He is going to skin Eisenhower alive!"

Earl's motion to hire Sparrow passed without opposition.

"The congressional committees will issue notices to appear late next week. Opening that letter is like setting off a bomb—everything in your life will be disrupted from that moment forward. You will be overcome by an absolute sense of panic, fear, suspicion, and paranoia,"

Sparrow said. "First, they will publicly accuse you of criminal activity, destroying your reputation. Then they will politely invite you to appear at the hearings. But they will also issue a subpoena and demand that you testify. Finally, they will express outrage when you take the Fifth."

"I never trust Washington politicians. Just because they put on expensive suits and call one another Honorable, they think they can push everybody around. It ain't gonna happen this time." Earl said he had things under control so long as everyone stayed in line and supported him without question. "I'm the fat kid sitting on the end of the seesaw. If they knock me off, all you fellas are in for one hell of a crash."

Sparrow knew it could be more complicated than that. "Let's discuss the Clemens photos. How many copies exist?"

"Clemens has the prints I sent to his DC office. You know that bastard has already destroyed them. The negatives and only other copies were in the personal protection of my photographer, Cain."

"Are you sure Clemens destroyed them? Why would he do that? The photos represent evidence of blackmail and could keep him out of jail. Now, tell me about this Cain fellow." Sparrow took off his glasses, folded his hands on the table, and looked at Earl with a concerned expression.

"No need for worry. I have known Cain since we were kids. He has followed me around ever since."

"What about the photos?"

"I asked Cain to destroy them. Just like always. I promise you. It's done. Cain would never dare cross me. He has followed me around like a lost puppy his entire adult life. I screwed his high school girlfriend in the back seat of my car parked in a cotton field, took her cherry. That knucklehead really believed she wanted to wait. But I convinced him I had done him a favor by breaking her in. The fool thanked me! Cain is a useful idiot. He goes to church every Sunday, drives a beat-up truck, and flunked out of LSU in his second year. The only reason he has a college degree is because I arranged that. Cain is way too stupid and weak to double-cross me—or anyone else, for that matter. The man has no backbone. He is an invertebrate jelly!"

"I want to talk with him nonetheless," Sparrow insisted.

"I haven't been able to reach him for a week or so. He must be off his medication or something." Earl said he had tried calling Cain a few times with no luck.

Using the cash, Cain had bought a fishing shack in Toledo Bend near the small town of Many, as Danni had suggested. He had no phone or mailbox. Cain planned to spend his time fishing and refinishing an old canoe, all the while hoping to stay out of the limelight. The wooden canoe came with the camp and rested on two old sawhorses under a lean-to. It had not been in the water for years. Cain anticipated the enjoyment of witnessing Earl's downfall, but he didn't want to go toe-to-toe with the governor. He just wanted a quiet life and hoped he would be left alone. He used the name Sawyer Finn to help conceal his identity.

"How the hell should I know where Cain is? Maybe he's out somewhere guessing weight and age for a traveling carnival. I don't know," Earl said.

Cain had moved five boxes stacked with his most secret photos to the old state capitol building. He thought it was funny to hide them a few blocks from the new state capitol building. "Hidden in plain sight," he thought. Cain put them in a basement storage room already holding hundreds of similar boxes. His files were mingled with dusty old revenue and appropriations records. He kept his forty-five favorite photos with him. These were the most salacious he had ever taken. Cain looked at them nearly every night. "Better than porn," he thought.

"The only other person with knowledge of the photos would be Danni," Earl said. "She's a team player. Always has been. Besides, I pay well. Nothing to worry about with Danni."

"How can I reach her?" Sparrow had his pen in hand, ready to write down her number and address.

"Well, it's a little strange, but I've been unable to reach her for a few weeks now too. This happened once before, and she was at a casino in Havana with a salesman from Nash-Kelvinator

Appliances. This time she's probably met some rich New Orleans businessman and is sitting at a bar in Rio drinking White Russians right about now. Danni just wants to have a good time. Washington politics is the last thing on her mind. She'll show up soon. I assure you!"

"If something unusual happens once, it could be just happenstance and nothing to be concerned about. If something unusual happens twice, I suspect enemy action. Cain and Danni—that's two!" Sparrow said.

"Maybe it's just bad luck. Plain and simple."

"I don't believe in luck, good or bad!"

"Well, if we can't reach them, neither can anyone else," Earl said.

"We'll see."

Danni was not in Brazil. She was in Hollywood meeting with her new PR team, PRC Public Relations and Consulting LLC. PRC was one of the largest firms of its type, handling A-list actors, actresses, politicians, and executives. They were working on a complete makeover with an entirely new look for Danni, teaching her to handle difficult questions with poise and how to respond to the press while handling herself professionally in all stressful situations.

Eisenhower wanted to destroy the Democratic Party and with it Truman's legacy. Half of America's households now had TV sets. The president insisted on televising the hearings from beginning to end.

"Thirty million Americans tuned in to watch the televised Kefauver organized crime hearings. This aluminum scandal will be much bigger! Once the nation meets Danni, the entire country will come to a halt! Business will grind to a stop, babies will go hungry, shops will close, and everyone will be glued to their TVs. This national event is going to make Danni a household name, worldwide! Talk of the town!" the agency's publicists said.

The firm hired a ghostwriter to work on Danni's autobiography. The writer promised to produce a captivating story. Danni met with her multiple times and provided an outline of the major turning points in her life. PRC also had a political division that was building the groundwork for Danni's upcoming introduction to the national stage. They selected the most scandalous Clemens photos, grouped them into press packets, and planned to "leak" them to key California senators, congressmen, and friendly members of the press. These politicians routinely worked with the firm. In return they could always count on generous campaign contributions and expensive fundraisers held in the hills above Hollywood on Mulholland Drive. Nothing was left to chance.

The Richard Lee Cadillac showroom was nearby in Pasadena. It was the largest dealership on the West Coast. Danni was there every afternoon, sitting in a beautiful red DeVille convertible on the showroom floor. Her short blue dress with white polka dots was hiked up high. On top, it was held snug by straps that Danni allowed to hang loose, showing some of her right breast with just enough nipple exposed to drive the salesmen crazy. A red bow was tight around her tiny waistline. She became friends with Marty Finn, the dealership's showroom manager.

"I'm going to buy this car someday soon, and you are going to be the first one to ride with me down Sunset Boulevard. Trust me, sweetheart!"

"I've heard that many times. They never come back to buy. But you sure look great behind the wheel! Better than Hedy

Lamarr and Sophia Loren!" Marty said as his hand maneuvered up and down Danni's thigh. She opened her legs just enough to express willingness. The manager had seen many young hopeful starlets dream about owning a Cadillac convertible. It almost never worked out, but Danni promised to surprise him!

"Are you going to give me a good deal, sweetheart?" she asked with a wink.

There was a white convertible on the showroom floor near the red one. Danni liked that one too. "It's a tough decision. Perhaps I'll just have to buy them both!"

"Maybe you'll surprise me and do just that!"

Marty was particularly attracted to Danni's petite but very firm breasts. They reminded him of his first girlfriend. When he was sixteen, a tiny peek was enough to give him an erection. Some things never change. It was impossible for Danni not to notice his eagerness.

"Oh, I will surprise you, sweetheart. You have no idea."

# 11

Maintaining a wooden boat is an expensive, full-time commitment, especially when it involves a forty-five-foot oak-planked sailboat built in 1915 and sitting in the polluted, brackish water of Lake Pontchartrain. Nothing can be deferred. Painting, varnishing, and sanding is a weekly chore. It is a true labor of love. No one else would ever remain committed to the demanding maintenance obligation for long unless they were head over heels in love.

*Aquilla* was beginning to look a little neglected. Wooden boats should be pulled into dry dock for hull repair and refastening annually. *Aquilla* was eight months behind schedule. It seemed even Dr. John Thomas Hobbs III was growing tired of it. Caulking and wicking needed attention. Some brass fastenings had weakened, and a few oak hull planks were loose and leaking. If the overworked bulge pump failed, she would sink. Like a distracted husband in a dying marriage, Dr. Hobbs had gradually stopped caring, and now he could not care less.

It was sad to see the beautiful *Aquilla* sliding into a state of disrepair. Dr. Hobbs was also in a state of hopeless decline. He claimed his drinking was just "social." Drinking heavily with friends can lead to many problems. Heavy drinking alone is far worse. Dr. Hobbs had a few acquaintances at CA, but no one he could call a friend. If anyone asked about his drinking problem, he lied about it anyway. It had started innocently with a preference for Gordon's gin served over ice. Drinking after work on *Aquilla*'s aft deck helped him relax. He was always alone and enjoyed the solitude, at first. One thing led to another, and now he was a lonely drunk. He hid gin bottles everywhere, behind medical books in his office and above ceiling tiles in the clinic exam rooms. He even replaced rubbing alcohol with gin, hiding it in plain sight. A fifth would last just two days, and when Hobbs ran short, he hunted through the trash hoping to find a few last drops in empty bottles. Just like Don Birnam, the main charter in Charles Jackson's 1944 novel *The Lost Weekend*, Dr. Hobbs was losing his battle against the bottle.

At first the drinking made him feel relaxed, with less anxiety, taking the edge off the day. But he became irritable, and his ability to concentrate deteriorated. He paid less and less attention to personal hygiene. He gained twenty-five pounds and seldom got haircuts. He sweated constantly, and his hands trembled. Dr. John Thomas Hobbs III became angry and insulted clinic patients and employees with personal attacks. One nurse quit, and another retired early. Employee turnover became a problem.

Still, he believed he was functioning well until his brother's wedding fiasco. Dr. Hobbs was best man but drank himself into a coma the night before and overslept. "Where the hell are you, man? I'm getting married in fifteen minutes." Dr. Hobbs grunted and said something senseless, rolled over, dropped the phone, and continued sleeping. His future sister-in-law called him a drunken ass. He missed the wedding, and his brother never spoke to him again. The drunken stupor was just an excuse. John Thomas could not stand seeing his brother move on with a happy life.

"Pierre, you come to the clinic every month. There is nothing wrong with you, and working here is perfectly safe." In an ineffective effort at sounding personable, Dr. Hobbs checked the chart to see Dad's name, and then he passed a light back and forth in front of Dad's eyes, just like he did for everyone.

"But I still spit up blood, and my chest hurts."

"That discomfort is just a result of heat exposure. It should clear up quickly if you follow my instructions correctly."

Dr. Hobbs gave Dad the same advice and a handful of salt tablets, and he suggested bed rest and hydration. A simple chest x-ray would have revealed the shadowed mass growing in the lower portion of Dad's left lung.

"X-rays are for broken bones, not coughing," Dr. Hobbs explained. "Do you have any broken ribs?"

"No, I don't think so."

"Then you don't need an x-ray! I'm the doctor, not you. I won't tell you how to melt aluminum, and you don't tell me how to run a medical clinic. Pierre, think of your work here the way you would a lifeboat. Being stuck in the open ocean on a small lifeboat would be a horrible experience. Floating aimlessly with no food or water, baking in the sun with sharks all around waiting for dinner—it would be hellish. Should we get rid of lifeboats because they're uncomfortable? Of course not! Working here is difficult, but you don't have another option, do you? Be thankful for the boat you're in."

"I'm sorry. I'm not questioning anything. It's just that my chest hurts so much, and the salt tablets don't seem to help. I'm worried, Dr. Hobbs!"

The clinic x-ray machine was never used. Dr. Hobbs had not bothered to learn the manual, and he had gin bottles hidden behind the safety partition. A respected professional is always given the benefit of the doubt when they assure you repeatedly that all is well.

# 12

Marty worked long hours every day, but he loved being around beautiful cars and enjoyed the modern advancements offered in the new Cadillacs. "The Fleetwood has nine coats of hand-polished paint. The interior and body panels are all hand assembled. Cadillacs are almost as custom made as Rolls-Royces!" He considered his sixty-five-hour workweeks to be an enjoyable privilege. He never took personal time off or had a serious long-term romantic relationship. Driving a different Cadillac home each evening was one of his favorite management perks. Marty was constantly amazed that he was paid so well to do something he loved so much. Even when sick he still worked; in fact, he had not missed a single day in eight years. Until now.

He loved technological advancements and considered himself to be an early adopter of everything modern. He was the first in his neighborhood to have a dishwasher, a washer and dryer, an electric oven, and a car with an overhead valve V8 and automatic transmission. Marty was probably one of the first to eat his dinners on trays in front of the TV. The Zenith Flashmatic fourteen-inch black-and-white TV set he had recently purchased to watch the aluminum hearings cost three months' salary. Marty loved the handheld flashlight device it used as a remote control to change volume and channels. Changing channels without getting up from the couch was considered remarkable technology. Neighbors showed up at Marty's house just to try it out. But the infant technology did not work as advertised, since any ambient light activated the TV's photocells, causing volume and channels to change at random. Keeping the living room completely dark was the only solution. Marty covered his windows with newspapers and turned off all the living room lights. "There you go. See? It works great."

"I'm taking time off to watch the Washington aluminum hearings live on my new Flashmatic TV! Clemens testifies today!" Marty announced to the surprised dealership employees.

"Can't believe Marty is taking a day off to watch political nonsense!"

"It is not boring nonsense. The tricks and skullduggery involved with these hearings are an amazing thing to watch. High-intensity light bulbs and flashes make it impossible for witnesses to see anything beyond the table in front of them. The hearing room thermostat is set high. Sweat makes hostile witnesses look nervous and guilty. This is all part of the government's technique designed to crack witnesses. It's intended to maintain a thin line between fear and anger without allowing the witness to turn fear into aggression. They constantly keep witnesses off guard, beating them into submission and softening them up, then offering a carrot at the exact right moment. It's the way they ferret out the truth."

Like most Americans, Marty was enthralled with the drama playing out in the nation's capital. It was estimated that over forty million Americans were watching every day. Many were viewing from bars or TVs set up at other local businesses, as predicted. Most were at home with new TVs purchased for the hearings. The technology was changing the country and changing politics. Marty mixed his favorite martini, opened a fresh pack of Lucky Strike cigarettes, turned on his Flashmatic TV, and sat back in his favorite armchair to wait for the drama to unfold.

The first witnesses called were mostly lower-level officials, some of Earl's Louisiana cronies and politicians from the Northwest. Washington State officials complained about the economic development they had lost and claimed the selection process was hijacked by crooked Louisiana politicians and skullduggery. But they neglected to mention that most Washington State politicians had voted against another polluting plant in their neighborhood. In fact, community groups had organized effective opposition.

Next to Sparrow, Earl sat in the back of the hearing room with a confident smirk. "It's like taking candy from a baby," he said. He was cavalier because the aluminum plant had been up and running for years now. It was not going to move north or anywhere else. Earl believed all this was just political theatrics intended to influence the upcoming midterm elections. Sparrow advised Earl that the best answers to stupid questions is give no answers.

Everyone with any real knowledge of events invoked their Fifth Amendment right against self-incrimination and refused to turn over subpoenaed documents, claiming lawyer privilege, or refused to appear.

"With all due respect, Senator, I have to plead the Fifth!" "With all due respect…" It went on and on.

"On advice of counsel, I respectfully decline to answer and invoke my Fifth Amendment right."

Danni was called to the witness table also, but on advice of counsel, she also took the Fifth. Nevertheless, partisan senators shouted questions at her, trying to discredit everything she might know while trying to destroy her credibility.

"Are you some type of Bourbon Street drag queen?"

"Is Governor Long your pimp?"

"Can we subpoena your birth certificate?"

"Are you blackmailing Secretary Clemens with raunchy photos?"

"Are you a prostitute? Are you some kind of freak?"

"You call yourself an entertainer. Are you more like Hedy Lamarr or Lizzie Lape?"

The committee chairman hammered his gavel over and over, demanding order and proper rules. "The rules, customs, and precedents of this committee, promoting orderly and deliberate discussion, will be followed."

Danni sat stoic, trying to take the abuse and harassment with dignity. Small tears ran down her cheeks. Danni wept. Her tears were very effective, just as her PR team expected.

Marty was now next to his fourteen-inch Flashmatic trying to get a better look. He put down the cigarette, looked at his martini, and wondered if he was drinking too much. "That's Danni! Well, I'll be damned! That's Danni!"

Luke Sparrow sat next to Governor Long. He had already indicated in his written responses that the governor would take the Fifth on everything not covered by lawyer-client privilege. Sparrow expected Long to be dismissed without a required appearance. Bored with the political theatrics, Earl left the committee hearing and went to the bathroom. He complained that his bladder seemed to be shrinking as he got older. "It's about the size of a southern pecan now." A small lunch counter located in the building's basement offered sandwiches, pies, and coffee. Earl ordered a ham sandwich and black coffee. He put a dime in the paper machine and sat down to read the morning news. He ordered the sandwich with Swiss cheese, lettuce, tomato, and mustard. "I hate mayonnaise!" After taking one bite, Earl tossed the sandwich in the trash and threatened to have the counter lady fired.

"Please don't do that. I need this job. I have a family!"

"If you expect to keep a job at a lunch counter, you should learn the difference between mustard and mayonnaise!" Earl waved his arm dismissively as if he was annoyed by a fly and went back to the hearing.

Clemens indicated through his legal team that he did not intend to answer questions as well. "The secretary is an honest government servant with nothing to hide and is eager and ready to testify. It is the best path to exposing the truth behind this Republican political stunt. However, it remains in our client's interest to protect himself against self-incrimination in this aggressive political environment. Secretary Oscar Clemens will exert his Fifth Amendment rights."

Clemens's lawyers did not find Cain. They gambled that the photos were all destroyed. "Speculation without evidence is just unproven conspiracy theories promoted by charlatans pontificating on soapboxes," they said, referring to the Republican leadership confidently leaking misstatements and asking off-the record questions about Clemens's personal life.

"What is the Justice Department up to?" Sparrow asked Long without expecting an answer. On the witness list was the manager of the Jefferson Hotel in Natchez.

"Anyone who has a job still requiring them to wear a name tag when they are forty years old has problems. How the hell did they dig him up anyway? Not a problem; I'll stomp him out like a cigarette butt on the sidewalk," Earl said.

"He's not a problem for us. Playing cards in Mississippi hotels is not a federal offense."

Of special interest to Sparrow was the unidentified surprise witness scheduled to speak after Clemens's legal team. Sparrow had a certain feeling of dread. "I think the Republican administration has found Cain and perhaps his photos!"

"What!"

"Not to worry. He was just a hired photographer. Like the mechanic that maintains your car, he keeps it running but doesn't know everywhere you go. Cain was paid to take pictures. He knows nothing else. Besides, all the photos he took over the past twenty years are for the public record and historic state archives, nothing more. Reckless talk of blackmail is unfounded speculation. Nothing more, regardless of what Cain may do or say. If anyone wants to see Cain's legitimate photographs, they should visit the state archives building. If Cain took compromising photos of Clemens, he did it on his own expecting to make a buck," Sparrow said.

"I always suspected Cain had a perverted mind! He thanked me for taking his girlfriend's cherry. For Christ's sake. Who does that? The man spends too much time peeping in bedroom windows," Long said.

It didn't take much time for US Justice Department investigators to locate Cain. Rumors of the existence of incriminating photos had first surfaced in California months ago. If there were photos, then the governor's photographer would be a person of interest worth tracking down. Cain believed he was completely untraceable, living quietly in the remote pine forest of rural Louisiana with no phone or utility bill in his real name.

He paid cash for everything else. However, his love of fishing was well known. The best fishing in Louisiana is at Toledo Bend. Cain entered the Sportsman's Paradise Bass Tournament at Cypress Bend under his assumed name, Mr. Sawyer Finn. The government's investigative work was almost too easy.

Two men in gray suits were waiting on the dock when Cain returned. Their black Ford Fairlane government sedan was parked nearby.

"How did you guys find me?" Cain asked while maneuvering his small bass boat. They reached over and gave him a hand tying up it to the dock. The agent to Cain's left pulled an envelope from his lapel pocket and handed Cain three subpoenas. Included was a demand for any and all photographs related to Governor Long and Chalmette Aluminum.

"We simply looked for you where the fishing is good. Every fisherman in this tournament has a Cajun French name, except for Mr. Sawyer Finn!"

"We would like you to come with us. We have a DC6 waiting at the DeRidder Airfield now."

The Senate Republican majority, working with information and evidence obtained by federal investigators, began to unravel Earl's scheme. They offered Cain absolute immunity for his truthful testimony against the governor.

Clemens sat quietly and constantly used a handkerchief to wipe away sweat from his forehead. His wife was at his side offering support. She could not imagine the public humiliation heading her way. Without any legal representation, Cain sat at the witness table prepared to tell the complete truth.

"Please state your name for the record."

When nervous, red splotches appeared on Cain's face and neck, Earl called it "psychological eczema."

"Cain Keller, former official photographer, Louisiana Office of the Governor.

"I was with Governor Earl Long and Secretary Oscar Clemens the entire evening, from start to finish. The day began at the Lakefront airport when the secretary's airplane landed on time. I took some photos to memorialize the historic handshake. It was about a twenty-minute ride to the Roosevelt Hotel on Saint Charles Avenue, near Canal Street. A short time later, everyone had dinner and drinks at the Sazerac Restaurant. I stayed invisible, tucked away in the background while taking multiple photos."

When Cain requested a water break, Marty ran to the bathroom, made another martini, and was back in his favorite chair without missing anything. But the bathroom light caused the Flashmatic to jump channels. Instead of watching ABC News, he was seeing *Commando Cody: Sky Marshal of the Universe.*

"This damn thing!"

He clicked the flashlight control fast like a machine gun, eventually getting back to ABC. "The two men drank heavily at the Sazerac before and after dinner. They enjoyed Ojens, ate shrimp étoufée, and had bananas Foster for dessert. Discussion about the aluminum plant went on for a few hours. But Governor Long was unable to persuade the secretary to change his location decision. It was then that Governor Long sprang his trap. Two identical Cadillacs pulled up to take the men to the My-Oh-My. One car was used as a decoy to misdirect and confuse the media. The governor and Secretary Clemens were in the other. The entered the club secretly from a seldom-used back door and took their seats in the governor's private booth."

"Mr. Keller, Mr. Keller," a Republican senator said. "I've heard of the debauchery and wickedness that takes place on

Bourbon Street down there in New Orleans. Mr. Keller, what kind of club is this My-Oh-My?"

The committee chairman called the senator out of order but allowed Cain to answer the question.

"It is best described as a Broadway-type club specializing in personal entertainment." "Mr. Keller, what exactly does that mean? Personal entertainment?" "Senator, it's a different type of club."

"To your knowledge, did Governor Long introduce any of these entertainers to Secretary Clemens?"

"Yes, sir. He most certainly did."

"Mr. Keller, did you happen to take pictures of this encounter?"

Two doors in the back of the room opened as if on cue, and six young congressional pages began passing out brown envelopes containing some of the notorious photos.

"Yes sir, I did."

Reporters ran from the room fighting over a bank of pay phones against the back wall, all struggling to reach their editors first. Photographers pushed one another out of the way, trying to get the best shots. Clemens's wife grabbed her purse and stormed out.

Finally, an ABC reporter approached the camera. "Many of the pictures are not fit for family viewing. However, these will give our audience an idea of what went on down there on Bourbon Street." One by one, he held up a series of nine photos.

Sparrow stood on the capitol steps and held an impromptu news conference. Surrounded by seventy-five print reporters and photographers, he defended the governor and effectively discredited Cain.

"Governor Long has taken care of Mr. Cain Keller nearly his entire adult life. Mr. Keller has been in and out of mental institutions, including the Mandeville Mental Asylum in Louisiana. As a loner, Cain has struggled to satisfy deviant sexual urges and has compensated by taking many highly inappropriate pictures. The governor believes Cain took the Clemens photos on his own for private personal sexual use and perhaps financial blackmail. Cain now says Governor Long paid him cash! Well, how convenient. This is all a sad tapestry woven by a sick mind crying out for professional help.

"Governor Long is deeply saddened by the obvious deterioration of his old friend's condition. The unfortunate behavior Mr. Cain has recently displayed indicates a worsening of his syphilitic symptoms. The governor has offered his assistance to the Keller family during this most difficult time."

Under his breath Long said Cain was "crazier than a runover dog."

Claiming respect for the privacy of Cain's family, Sparrow walked away without entertaining questions shouted by the inquisitive pack of reporters.

"Mr. Sparrow!"

"Mr. Sparrow! Please, a few questions!"

"Did Governor Long pay Cain for the photos?"

"Did he pay the My-Oh-My entertainer? Did he set up Secretary Clemens?"

"Mr. Sparrow, please!"

Federal immunity meant nothing to Bolivar Edwards Kemp, Lemon Head. The Louisiana attorney general quickly impounded a grand jury in East Baton Rouge Parish to look into misogyny and voyeurism. Every criminal judge in the state is elected. Most owe their careers to the Long political machine. Cain never had a chance. State troopers found Cain's private collection of salacious photos hidden under a mattress in his fishing cabin. They did not find the file boxes hidden in Baton Rouge. After three days of hearings, the grand jury indicted Cain on thirty-three separate counts. His court-appointed lawyer advised him to plead guilty. "Take the deal. It will mean a few months jail time in Baton Rouge, then it's all over." The lawyer was promised a civil district court judgeship in Shreveport by Long's machine.

"The Cain indictment clearly indicates the innocence of Governor Earl K. Long in this most unfortunate series of events. We hope Secretary Clemens and his family can find some closure," Luke Sparrow's press release reached every major American newspaper. Cain was sentenced to eighteen months in the East Baton Rouge Parish jail. However, the state director of hospitals intervened and committed Cain to the Mandeville Mental Asylum instead. "Cain will receive the proper treatment and care he deserves at Louisiana's finest psychiatric hospital. He has spent time here before. The doctors and staff are eager to help Mr. Keller again." The director of hospitals was also a Long appointee.

With the grand jury indictments and Cain's involuntary hospitalization, the Federal Republican case against Earl Long evaporated like rain from a summer shower in New Orleans. Cain could spend the rest of his life committed to a mental asylum. Earl Long walked away free and clear, able to collect his natural-gas kickbacks for years.

"This is another of Earl's tricks. Can't I just go to the Baton Rouge jail for a few months like I was promised? I can't go back to that asylum again! This is not fair. It's a setup. Don't let them take me." Cain was dragged from the courtroom by two huge men dressed in white medical outfits. He was strapped into a straitjacket, placed in a white ambulance, and driven away.

*The Soviet Union claimed they did not operate political concentration camps. It would have been nuts to challenge the power of communist leadership anyway—only certifiably crazy people would try that. The Politburo did not admit to operating political prisons, but they did have a large system of insane asylums where they committed political opponents. Malcontents were locked away and forgotten about until their reeducation was complete. Similarly, Cain was crazy to think he could challenge Earl Long.*

Excitement at the Los Angeles Richard Lee Cadillac dealership was nothing new, but this was different. The black limousine with professional driver pulled to the curb first, followed by a caravan of hawkers, hangers-on, and groupies. Flashbulbs lit the showroom as if a Fourth of July fireworks display were going off. Danni strutted in like Cleopatra. "Hello, sweetheart. You still have those two Cadillac convertibles?"

"How are you, Danni? I see you've been busy!"

"Half the country hates me. Half the country loves me. But they are all buying my book. How about you, Marty? You still love me?"

Danni sat in the red Cadillac first. Marty leaned in close and placed his hand on her knee. "Can't decide between the red or white. Should I just enjoy both? I told you a surprise was coming. Do you like surprises, sweetheart?" Danni asked while rocking her knee back and forth.

"I always love the thrill of trying new things!"

The Delamater Lodge was hidden on a quiet state highway north of LA. The mom-and-pop operation specialized in discreet visits. Originally, it had been a large family home on ten acres. The twenty secluded cabins were added over the years as a source of income, each constructed with a Pennsylvania Dutch architecture influence and built with stone walls, polished wood floors, and slate roofs. Enclosed attached garages could hide two cars. Eventually, the main house was converted to a lobby, restaurant, and lounge. The restaurant was open twenty-four hours with a chef on property. Catering to wealthy and famous people, lodge management could be counted on to keep secrets. Two brown fiberglass horses were hitched to an authentic buggy and mounted at the front drive, and an adjacent sign said PRIVATE. Cameras, photographers, reporters, gawkers, and snoopers were prohibited.

Marty always borrowed the most inconspicuous cars he could from the dealership's used-car back-row lot. Usually he showed up in an old DeSoto or Nash. He was very careful not to draw attention to himself. Marty and Danni met here once or twice a month, then the rendezvous became nearly every other day. Cabin 6 was always reserved for them. Management had fresh flowers, a bottle of California red, and two crystal stem glasses on the coffee table. They gave Marty and Danni each a key and never asked questions. Cabin 6 became their secret sanctuary, the only place where they could relax, enjoy each other's company, and escape from the pressure of Danni's fame and growing career.

"I just saw Errol Flynn! I think he's in the next cabin! Do you think Ruth Roman is with him? What do you think they talk about when they're alone?" Marty asked Danni.

"Marty! Nobody rents a secret cabin just to have deep, penetrating conversation!" Danni playfully straddled him and began to unbutton his shirt. Marty smiled in an understanding way.

# 13

One nagging question kept Clemens up during many cold and lonely nights. *Why is the Long organization so determined to keep Cain secreted away under lock and key? What does Cain know that has the Long family so scared?*

Clemens wintered in seclusion at the Crater Lake Lodge in southern Oregon. He spent the years fly fishing, sipping cognac in front of a stone fireplace, hiking in the snow, and writing his memoirs. He especially enjoyed quiet early-morning coffee in the wood-paneled café. The *Wall Street Journal, New York Times,* and *Los Angeles Times* were available every morning. Spending three months alone was easy for him since his wife had left, his children no longer spoke to him, and his former political allies all ignored his calls. Even former president Truman canceled a planned meeting at his home in Independence, Missouri, with Oscar.

Clemens was not ostracized because he had lost a political war. He was cast aside because of the sexual nature of his scandal. He was angry, and the isolation and lonely solitude gave him time to plan his revenge uninterrupted, something he did well. "Revenge is a dish best served cold," he liked to say, especially when it is unexpected and overdue. He solicited the only people he knew he could still count on, his Washington,

DC, legal team of ruthless mercenaries. "We've been expecting your call."

In theory they were regular lawyers like most others, but in truth they were highly paid fixers working for powerful clients. They handled disagreeable mistresses, disgruntled business partners, troublesome political candidates, and scandal. Hiding behind the cloak of lawyer-client privilege, they worked outside the political mainstream. Retribution was a specialty of these legal mercenaries.

Oscar was nearly bankrupt after fighting multiple political battles and his recent divorce. The lawyers were expensive. They say politics makes strange bedfellows, and this was especially so with the skullduggery and backstabbing common in Louisiana. There was one other person he hoped would take his call. The enemy of my enemy is my friend.

"Hello, sweetheart. How are you?" Danni was happy to speak with him. She eagerly agreed to funnel significant funds to Clemens's legal mercenaries through one of her multiple corporations. "I want to see that SOB hanging from a light post with his eyeballs plucked out, like Mussolini. Earl leaves a trail of destroyed lives everywhere he goes. He's a two-bit demagogue, a political barbarian, a sadistic adventurer!"

"Danni, I have one more question. Will we ever have the opportunity to be alone again?" "You are a good man. But I'm sorry."

Danni was able to charge everything off as a legitimate business expense. "Legal services," she called it! "I can help destroy Earl Long, and the IRS will reimburse me. That's perfect! Poetic justice—it's better than a novel about the ultimate revenge. You can't make things like this up!"

# 14

Earl Long charged onward in classic Tennysonian grandeur, riding into the valley of death. "Danni. How are you?"

"Earl, I'm doing great. I was just thinking about you!"

"I'm in a bit of a pickle down here. It seems my opposition is much better organized these days. We're circling the wagons, but political enemies are everywhere. They're like New Orleans roaches in the summertime—I can't get rid of them. Enemies are everywhere, and my friends are like ancient Greek mariners. They hear the siren call of the FBI, and they all abandon ship! They got my arm in the woodchopper! Danni, you're on the cover of *Life* magazine. Your fame could be quite helpful to an old friend like me. Governor Earl needs to know that he can count on your support." Like, many arrogant politicians, Earl often talked about himself in the third person.

"Well, Earl, wish I could be more helpful. But I have so much going on these days. I have three screen tests coming up. I'm working on an album with Tony Bennett, and I'm cooking business deals out here in California. Things are hectic! My managers and PR professionals are working to build my brand. They all advise me to avoid politics. I'll be appearing at the Blue Room in a few months. How about I send you a couple of tickets. Great seats. Besides, you always said it's not the people voting that matter, it's the people counting the votes. Wish I could do more sweetheart. I'm sorry."

"Danni, you know its impolite to show ingratitude. I helped you. Now you help me. It's a square deal. That's how it works. Anyway, where would you be without Governor Earl K. Long?"

"I wonder if Cain is thinking that. Good luck, Governor." Danni hung up the phone.

Louisiana law did not allow governors to succeed themselves. Earl cooked up multiple crazy schemes to get around that inconvenient legal reality. He was wrong about one thing. The people of Louisiana wanted good government, and they had finally had enough of Earl's foolishness. He planned to resign, turning the governorship over to his lieutenant governor. Then he could run for governor as an outsider, not the incumbent. Earl also introduced a scheme where he would run for lieutenant governor. After the election, the governor elect would resign, thereby giving the governorship back to Earl.

Unfortunately, getting to Cain while he was committed to a high-security mental hospital would require a certain amount of clever creativity. The hospital was a complex maze of buildings with enclosed courtyards and covered walkways. During the day, patients spent hours walking in circles, the attendants keeping a close eye on everyone. An undercover investigator with Clemens's Washington, DC, law firm managed to land a custodial job at the Mandeville asylum. He cleaned bathrooms, floors, and personal spills for weeks, waiting for the opportunity to speak privately with Cain.

Late one Saturday night, he finally got his chance. "Custodian needed on ward five." Pushing a mop bucket, he reached the high-security ward, entered his code, opened the secured door, presented his ID to the guard on duty, and entered the ward.

"Glad I don't have your job. You're going to need more than that mop to clean up this disgusting mess." The guard pressed a buzzer that allowed him to enter. "Good luck," he said. The guard went back to reading a trashy novel.

A nurses' station protected behind stainless-steel wire mesh was at the center of the cavernous ward. It was where patients passed their time staring at walls. It was empty now. Paint was peeling, and the ceiling tiles were yellowed from cigarette smoke. A sickening odor of disinfectant, cigarette smoke, and urine hung in the air. Two LPNs in starched white uniforms were sitting in a break room drinking coffee and talking about boyfriends. A TV was on in the sitting room, but no one was watching. An empty row of dilapidated chairs was lined up against a wall, likely where patients waited to see medical staff. It had been lights out for two hours. One of the LPNs gave him directions. "Go down that hall. It's in the second room on the right." A long-term patient had had an episode after he refused to enter his room for night check. "I made a mess in here," he said. The patient had defecated in his hand and spread it from floor to ceiling. He was dragged away for further observation.

"You think cleaning crap is difficult. Try living in this loony bin. They call me Nero. You can call me Nero too." The undercover investigator had been scrubbing walls for twenty minutes when a nervous patient slipped into the room. He spoke quickly, with his words running together in a mumbled tone.

"Why do they call you Nero?"

"They call me Nero because I set my cheating wife on fire and laughed while the bitch burned. Nero laughed while Rome burned. I laughed too. Bitch had it coming. In my previous life, I taught college as an adjunct professor. Classical Greek and Roman history was my concentration. That's why they call me Nero. A lot of funny fuckers around here."

"Nero, do you happen to know someone named Cain? I believe he's somewhere on this ward."

"Sure, I know him. He's that political fella. He's not nuts. But he will be soon enough. This place makes everybody crazy. Even you. What sane person is going to scrub shit off the walls for two dollars an hour? See what I mean? In physics there is something called the uncertainty principle. Crazy people are convinced there is certainty. I'll see if Cain will talk to you. He probably won't. He's afraid of Dr. Atlas. Also, Cain may be hard to wake up. They give everybody sleeping pills. I don't take that shit."

"Who's Dr. Atlas?"

"He's the psych tech who maintains order around here. We call him Atlas because he's a big old strong fella. Holds you down while they strap you to the bed just before they hook you up to the jumper cables. Everybody is afraid of Dr. Atlas."

Nero put his finger over his mouth. "Quiet!"

One of the LPNs was making her rounds, with her footsteps echoing down the corridor. She walked fast past the shit room, holding her nose. Not stopping, she disappeared around a corner and down the next hall.

"OK, let's go."

They walked quickly to Cain's room. It was at the end of the hall. Nero went in first. "You woke me up in the middle of the night to talk to an orderly?" Cain asked as he rapidly rubbed his eyes. "What time is it? My head hurts."

"This fella is not a janitor. You should talk to him." Nero left the room.

The investigator held out his hand. "I work for a Washington, DC, law firm. I've been cleaning bathrooms here for a month waiting for the chance to ask you a few questions." He pulled a small notepad from his back pocket. "Mind if I take a few notes?"

"You're crazier than me. Why should I talk to you?"

"Because if you don't, Earl will win. If Earl wins, you stay here and rot." Cain rubbed sleep from his eyes. He agreed to talk and asked where to start.

"Earl used sex as a political tool. He always went after the wives of powerful politicians. Earl was looking for political advantage wherever he could find it, but he didn't bother with the wives of hard-drinking officials from the southern Catholic parishes. Their husbands couldn't care less what their wives did. No sir. As a matter of fact, those loose wives were a political advantage to their philandering husbands. Earl pursued the faithful wives of Bible-thumping politicians from the pine belt, especially the Baptists, Protestants, and Pentecostals. You know, the ones that teach Sunday school classes. The more off limits something was, the more Earl wanted it. That's why he opened up the state to prostitution and gambling, taking kickbacks from organized crime. Earl's greed fuels his relentless drive for wealth and power."

Cain continued. "Earl is the best drummer I've ever seen!"

"Drummer? What do you mean?"

"Drummer is an old term for door-to-door salesmen. They were always trying to drum up sales, so they were called drummers. Earl was constantly drumming up campaign donations. As I said, he was a great drummer. The governor made a fortune selling state licenses. The kickbacks were usually disguised as campaign contributions. His most successful scheme was the sale of hospital licenses, but anyone expecting to do business in Louisiana had to pay. The natural-gas deal at Chalmette Aluminum was just one example of Earl's out-of-control greed. Millions in state funds were stolen. Huey's deduct box was a joke compared to the financial corruption Earl perfected. He basically got a piece of every dollar passing through the state. Earl loved his money because it was always loyal to him. Without question, money is loyal."

Cain said Earl created a free-for-all in state government. He explained how Earl abolished civil service, fired political opponents, and created more political patronage for his cronies. "The corruption and graft were unprecedented. Earl was a spider sitting in the middle of an intricate web of corruption for which he controlled everything. Whatever met Earl's web was instantly trapped," Cain said.

"What about Chalmette Aluminum?"

"Yep! Yep! Earl sure played Clemens—and me, for that matter. The governor seems buffoonish, but that's just an act. He knew everything about Clemens before that first meeting. Earl studied Clemens's quirks, habits, and idiosyncrasies. Everything was planned from the beginning. Then Earl set it all up to fall in my lap as a convenient scapegoat. Once the Louisiana kangaroo courts said I was crazy, Earl was off the hook, free and clear. Earl has set me up as the fall guy from day one with all his skullduggery antics. He just never had to play the 'screw Cain' card until Chalmette. Mister, I admit, I did have a collection of very inappropriate photos that I enjoyed too much, and I probably like to masturbate too much because I don't get any female attention. But that don't make me crazy. I'm stupid, but I ain't nuts."

"This is all very interesting, but do you have any real evidence?" Cain's stories were so outlandish, they were hard for anyone to believe, even for an experienced political investigator.

Cain sat quietly for a long time. Staring at the floor, he said nothing. He leaned back and forth and placed his hands between his thighs and nervously rubbed them together. Doubtful of Cain's credibility, the investigator put his small notebook back in his pocket and thanked him for his time.

"Just one second. As a matter of fact, I do have evidence. Lots of it. Without a doubt, I can prove everything I just said! Every single word! Earl always treated me like a mangy puppy with fleas. Now it is time to turn the tables. That's a square deal, as Earl likes to say," Cain said.

Cain told the investigator about his boxes of photos hidden in a basement storage complex at the old state capitol building. He said it represented thirty-five years of Long family corruption, evidence of everything. "There are hundreds of random file boxes down there, some dating back to the Louisiana Purchase. But look in the section marked 'Appropriations.' My boxes all have small check marks in the lower left corner. I hope this is helpful, but I'm sorry you had to work in this terrible place just to talk to me."

"Don't be sorry. We're going to peel the bark off Earl Long, and you are going to get out of here."

"I quit." The investigator turned in his ID card and informed his janitorial supervisor that he had had enough.

"Frankly, I'm surprised you lasted this long. We'll mail your last check." Filling out forms, the supervisor did not even bother to look up from his desk.

"Don't bother!"

The investigator drove out of the asylum's main gate and turned right onto highway 190.

He would be in Baton Rouge and at the old state capitol building in two hours.

Clemens's legal team planted the exposé article in the *Baton Rouge Advocate* originally. But it was picked up by every other Louisiana paper the next morning. Even the Long political strongholds of Alexandria, Pineville, Marksville, and Natchitoches carried it. The article was over five thousand words and with photos took up nearly the entire first section of most state papers.

Earl had dozens of meetings at the Jefferson Hotel in Natchez. He enjoyed the isolation from the political pressure of his home state. Long was too smart for his own good. Since he was crossing state lines, his scandals became a matter of federal interest, especially after the articles appeared. The Jefferson Hotel manager was of interest to federal grand juries and became an important witness. The US Justice Department handles things differently than the grandstanding senators did in their showboat hearings. Not as dumb as Earl thought, the hotel manager kept records on everything. The manager had documents related to every visit "Mr. Cotton Field" ever made to the Jefferson, including the other attendees with Earl. He wrote down the serial numbers of every hundred-dollar bill Long ever gave him, and he recorded the license plate numbers of Earl's friends. "I just figured having an insurance policy might be a good idea."

"How can anyone be trusted that still wears a name tag at forty years old and twists a long mustache like it's still 1920? The man displays an inability to make good life decisions. He's a nobody! He runs such a low-rent dump we had to bring our own prostitutes. A five-cent condom from a gas station vending machine is more reliable than he is," Earl said during a campaign debate in Saint Martin Parish.

When Earl's reelection scams failed and the voters and media turned against him, unable to run for governor again, Earl qualified for a seat on the Democratic State Central Committee, just to keep his political hat in the ring. He lost! Desperate, he ran for congress from Louisiana's Eighth District. Earl had to run for something. That was his best legal defense. So long as he was a candidate for office, Earl could claim the investigations were politically motivated "witch hunts." This was the traditional central Louisiana Long political home base. The Eighth included Winnfield and Winn Parish. Earl beat a weak incumbent and won the congressional seat by a slim margin. Ironically, he had a heart attack on election night and was rushed to the hospital, where he died nine days later.

Bolivar Edwards "Lemon Head" Kemp dropped out of his reelection campaign two weeks before the primary. He was named as a person of interest in multiple federal investigations. Bolivar was expected to coast to an easy victory, with polls showing him up by twenty points. Instead, his political career sank along with the rest of the Long political ship. The entire organization went down faster than the French navy at Trafalgar.

Jimmy Davis was Louisiana's new governor. His first official action was to sign an order releasing Cain. Retreating to his secluded fishing camp, introverted Cain disappeared from public life. Shortly thereafter, a delivery truck appeared pulling a brand-new trailered Skeeter Bass boat with a 7.5 Evinrude outboard. "Is your name Cain?" the driver asked. "This boat is for you. Paperwork says all paid in full. Signed by someone named Danni."

# 15

Things were very different back then. Some people harbored suspicions about Danni's sexuality and called her a drag queen. Everyone knew she had worked as an entertainer at the My-Oh-My, but she was so gorgeous most men wanted to sleep with her, and many women were jealous of her. The controversy generated incredible nationwide publicity. A California radio station said it was impossible for Danni to be anything other than the 100 percent pure, all-American, girl-next-door prom queen.

Although most did not believe the hateful whispers, Danni was still afraid to marry Marty. Marriage involved a state license that would require birth certificates. Churches were out of the question. They could live together openly in Denmark, but that would require forfeiting their US citizenship. Marty and Danni shared an apartment often, appeared together in public, became successful business partners, built a committed relationship, and were written about in glamour and fashion magazines, but they could never risk marriage.

"I'm so sorry I can't offer you a traditional white-picket-fence lifestyle," Danni said.

"Sorry? Nothing to be sorry about. I've never done things the traditional way. Besides, our happiness will really upset mean people. They have it coming. Anyway, those picket fences need paint. I don't want to paint a fence. Do you want to paint a fence? I would rather kiss and have fun!" They both laughed.

It was a poorly kept secret that the Richard Lee Cadillac dealership would soon be listed for sale. Marty loved his job, and he loved selling Cadillacs. "But my most successful sales achievement was convincing Danni to love me," he said.

Danni wanted Marty to be happy. "Everything can be bought, and everything can be negotiated. Except love," Danni said. She never set foot in a business school class, but she had a natural talent for negotiations and recognized Marty's powerful sales personality. Constantly reading business books gave her a business understanding, and she was always underestimated by gullible competitors.

"Businesspeople always seek advantage. But in this competitive marketplace, we can't make money unless we please our customers better than the competition. Elasticity of demand forces us to keep prices competitive, unless we have exclusive products in exclusive markets!" Danni explained.

The Los Angeles Packard dealership building had been vacant since the company's 1958 bankruptcy. It was a grand old building with marble stairs and columns and was located less than two blocks from Richard Lee Cadillac. Danni took out a six-month option to purchase the Packard building and commissioned a well-known design firm to plan its rebirth as a modern Lincoln dealership with an exclusive contract to offer Mercedes-Benz. "I once made a small fortune on Packard stock in high school. I've always had a love for Packard. This may all seem chaotic, but there is a method to all this," she said.

Marty developed an interest in the new Mercedes automobiles he had been reading about. He invited Danni to drive with him to Las Vegas, where some of the new models were on display at the famous Sands Hotel. The German firm had recovered from the war and was entering the US market with expensive, well-engineered luxury cars. "They are some of the world's best-built and designed automobiles," Marty said. Word soon spread around Los Angeles that a well-financed group of Hollywood insiders was behind the new Lincoln-German partnership. The Packard building made sense for another reason as well. The Packard Automobile Company held the Mercedes American distribution rights and planned to sell the German cars through their existing dealer network. The bankruptcy ended those plans. "If Mercedes was good enough for Packard, its good enough for us," Marty reasoned.

When Richard Lee Cadillac was listed for sale, only one qualified investor group entered a legitimate bid. It was a low-ball offer based on the uncertainty created by the pending new Lincoln-Mercedes competition entering the market. The offer was quickly accepted. The successful Cadillac purchase offer was handled by lawyers representing an anonymous group of investment partners called D&M Motors Limited of Los Angeles. The group was secretly led by Danni. "Marty will be general manager and president. This is not negotiable," she said. The partners agreed to her demands. Danni sat at a board table and helped draft the purchase letter of intent. "We are buying tangible assets only! Not a penny for goodwill," she said, insisting that the sellers adjust their expectations recognizing the pending Lincoln-Mercedes competition. Danni inspected the noncompete agreement, letter of indemnity, and the accounts receivable. Satisfied, she instructed the lawyers to "close the deal."

Once the Cadillac purchase was settled, Danni continued with the Packard building purchase option but backed away from Lincoln. She expanded the Mercedes agreement to include all Southern California with exclusive territory guarantees and ten-year automatic renewals. "Mercedes is our long-term future in the beautiful Packard building. Cadillac is our money-making opportunity now." Danni saved her team of investors hundreds of thousands of dollars and secured a remarkable ground-floor opportunity with Mercedes. Marty and Danni celebrated by driving the Coastal Highway in a Coupe DeVille convertible with the top down at sunset. A was a perfect evening.

"Oh my, sweetheart! I've never driven around town with a good-looking president of a motor car company before!" Danni playfully raised her red sunglasses, winked, and placed her hand on Marty's knee.

"Beats the hell out of painting white picket fences! I ain't Tom Sawyer!" Marty said.

They headed to cabin 6 for the evening.

# 16

New Orleans was the perfect place for thirteen-year-old adolescent boys with little supervision to find meaningful mischief during the long summer months. My band of misfit neighborhood friends went everywhere on bicycles, even across Broad Street to Tulane Avenue on the edge of Central City. The old Dixie Brewery building had a dark, cavern-like passageway to Tulane Avenue. It was used as a drive-through for thirsty patrons waiting in line to pick up refilled longneck cases. It resembled an old train tunnel made of red brick and gray flagstones for pavement with ruts made decades ago by heavy steel wagon wheels. The oldest New Orleans buildings always had flagstones. There is no natural stone anywhere near south Louisiana, but flagstones are common. They were used as ballast in the keels of old sailing ships and repurposed as building material during the eighteenth and nineteenth centuries. Decades of neglect took a heavy toll on the brewery. The run-down Dixie Building seemed to have more in common with the ruins of Palmyra than with a modern business. I loved exploring it.

Every Friday a line of cars extended though the passageway and down Tulane Avenue toward Jefferson Davis Boulevard. The brewery provided an unattended free tap so customers could have a beer or two while waiting to exchange their empties. We showed up with aluminum cups we had sneaked from someone's kitchen.

"You boys better get the hell out of here!"

Pedaling fast, we disappeared into the adjacent neighborhood, circled around, and came back. The slow-moving and overweight brewery men attempted to chase us off the property, but they had no chance of ever getting close to us. They ran a few yards and then bent over, placing their hands on their knees trying to slow their heavy breathing. We were harder to catch than bass in city park lagoons. Eventually everyone arrived at an agreeable compromise: the men went about their business ignoring us altogether while we took advantage of the free summertime beer. We might have enjoyed it too much, but it was certainly better than the lemonade offered by neighborhood moms.

The July Fourth weekend was the biggest of the year for New Orleans beer sales. It was comparable to Black Friday for modern retailers. Local breweries made their profits for the year. Somehow iodine ended up in a large Dixie Beer batch. It was undrinkable and ruined the holiday for many thirsty New Orleans beer lovers. The brewery never recovered, most of the men lost their jobs, the free tap was turned off, and the building fell into further decay. It all became a sad metaphor for life in New Orleans.

When we were not tormenting brewery workers, we were trying to sneak past doormen at twenty-four-hour Bourbon Street strip clubs. We pedaled straight down Esplanade Avenue to the French Quarter, where we tried unsuccessfully to sneak into the clubs. Huge doormen in black tuxedos never allowed us to enter, but they did not discourage us from getting a peek. They opened the door wide, revealing forbidden and alluring temptations. "Old enough to want. Too young to get!" And they slammed the door shut. "Now move along, boys." The disappointing message was always delivered in a Louis Armstrong–style cadence that tourists loved.

"Sebastian, you're thirteen now and ride that bike all over town. It's time you do something productive to help support this family. Everybody got to work around here." Dad signed me up to deliver the *States-Item* afternoon newspaper. He built a basket from aluminum strips he recovered from a CA scrap pile. Bending and shaping each piece with pliers and a metal file, he worked like an artist creating a masterpiece. Then he used sheet metal screws to hold it all together. He finished it off with an aluminum lightning bolt on each side. They were painted bright red. "The bolts represent power and speed," he said. The bike was an old Schwinn designed to deliver newspapers or groceries. It was called a Newsboy Special, and it had a heavy steel frame, a motorcycle-size rear tire, and a small front tire configured to accommodate a large basket. Dad had paid ten dollars for it at a neighborhood garage sale.

"You can pay me back next month."

I struggled to handle the heavy bike with the loaded-down basket full of evening newspapers. The bike weighed thirty-five pounds, and the papers weighed about fifty pounds. I tipped the scale at eighty-five pounds. When I turned sharp corners, I did not have enough strength in my broomstick-skinny arms to turn the handlebars back. The bike would go in short, lazy, helpless circles and eventually fall over. Unable to lift it, I removed all the papers, leaned the bike against a tree, and then replaced the papers. I held on to the handlebars, got a running start, jumped onto the seat, and started pedaling again.

I thought Dad had built the homemade basket with lightning bolts because he wanted my bike to look cool. I had no idea he was too broke to afford a real metal one. It was OK, because I loved my custom basket.

Soon I realized it was easier to fill the basket halfway, deliver those papers, and then return to the station to pick up the rest. This took much more time, but at least I could handle the bike. The manager did not want to hang around waiting for me, so he began leaving my remaining papers on a nearby street corner. "I can't be late for supper," he said. The manager thought he was being helpful, until a bundle of fifty papers was stolen. I had to pay for replacements. In addition to paying for the papers, paperboys were also charged for supplies, including rubber bands and plastic rain bags. During rainy months I worked for free after paying additional wet-weather expenses and sometimes actually finished the month in a financial hole. It rains a lot in New Orleans.

At the end of each month's billing cycle, I received an invoice covering all expenses due. It was usually over $100, a lot of money for a thirteen-year-old kid! It was my responsibility to go to each customer's home on the route and personally collect the money they owed, about $2.10. I made nothing until I had collected enough to pay the *States-Item*. I earned the net balance. Once I reached my net positive day and had collected enough to pay the bills, I celebrated by treating myself to lunch at Landry's Lakeview Restaurant. "Our paperboy is here. Hamburger with ketchup and butter only!" The waitress treated me like their most important customer and knew my order by heart. My burger always tasted wonderful because I was paying for it with my own hard-earned money.

"Come back when my husband returns. He's on a business trip." One newspaper customer put me off for two months. "He's been delayed again. Next week he'll be back home, and we will pay. I assure you," she said. Foolishly, I continued to deliver their paper. This went on until I returned one day to discover they had moved out.

"How will I get the money they owe me?" I asked Dad.

"You won't. But you won't ever fall for that again. Will you?"

On a mild spring day, I folded my papers as usual, loaded the basket, and got a drink of water from a hose before pedaling off to start my route. The manager had recently purchased a new blue Dodge cargo van and arrived at the paper station just as I was about to leave. As he pulled into the alley, older boys thought it would be funny to throw rocks at the rear of the van. Intending to avoid any trouble, I rode off, finished my route, and looked forward to supper. After doing my homework, I would have time to watch *The Brady Bunch*. This was the episode where Mr. Brady put a pay phone in the kitchen. I planned to review my word list for an upcoming spelling test one more time before getting to bed.

"Well, Sebastian! I hope you're happy! This little episode will cost a hundred and thirty dollars! What the hell is wrong with you? That is a brand-new van." Dad was standing in the backyard waiting for me. Grabbing my arm, he pulled me into the house.

"What did I do?"

When his rear window shattered, the manager had slammed his brakes and demanded to know who was responsible. All the older boys pointed in my direction. "Sebastian did it. We all saw him." I was already a block away and unable to deny anything.

"If you didn't break the window, why would all those other boys blame you? Are they all lying?" I had never seen my father so angry.

Dad deposited ten dollars a week into a Christmas savings account at the bank. He withdrew that money to replace the cargo van's window. "I expect you to pay back twenty-five dollars a month until it is all paid back in full. If you don't, the family won't have Christmas this year. You caused problems at the brewery and deliberately damaged someone's property! You were not raised this way," he said, expressing deep disappointment.

I made thirty dollars on a good month but was more upset that I was not believed than about working every day for nothing. Dad made me apologize to the manager, who said he hoped I learned a valuable lesson from all this.

I rode my Newsboy Special to school every day. It was easy to toss my schoolbooks, football, and a jacket in the basket. On Tuesday and Thursday, I stopped at McKenzie's neighborhood doughnut shop and always ordered the exact same thing, a chocolate éclair and a small milk. The milk cost about fifteen cents and the éclair about twenty. I enjoyed my morning treat more because I was paying with money I earned. "Our paperboy is here." The counter ladies expected me and always had my éclair order ready. I arrived at school early enough to sit on the steps behind the old school gym and enjoy my breakfast.

Leaning the bike against McKenzie's front brick wall as always, I left my things in the basket and went inside. The McKenzie ladies had my éclair and milk ready. Within five minutes I was back outside. Never to see my bike again—the thief had made off with the bike, my jacket, and my football. He had dumped my schoolbooks on the sidewalk.

"Didn't I tell you to always lock your bike? For crying out loud!" Dad was angry, as expected.

"I was inside McKenzie's for only a minute."

"How do you plan to get another bike and finish paying for the van window?"

It was easy to find entry-type jobs around the city. The employment ad for a drugstore delivery boy sounded perfect. The pharmacy was located on the corner of Ponce De Leon and Esplanade Avenue, one of the city's oldest neighborhoods. The store provided bicycles that were used to deliver small orders and prescriptions to nearby neighborhoods. I was used to pedaling heavy bikes, so my job interview went very easy.

"Can you ride a bike for five hours at a time? Can you collect cash and make change?" the pharmacist asked.

"Sure, no problem." I explained my short career with the *States-Item*.

"Sounds good. You can start tomorrow afternoon."

I was looking forward to an hourly pay rate without having to collect and pay a big monthly bill first, and I could still ride a bicycle every afternoon, which I loved. This was my dream job! The pharmacy closed at 9:00 p.m., but the front doors were locked at 8:30 when we began counting the register and balancing the day's receipts. After that we only allowed recognized customers to enter.

One night Paul, the front-counter salesperson, walked up front to lock the doors. Two men with stockings over their heads burst in waving large chrome pistols and yelling. They ran in my direction!

"Get on the floor, motherfucker! What the fuck you looking at?"

The narcotics and other street-value drugs were kept in a timed safe that was locked at 8:30. It was nearly impossible to open it until 9:00 a.m. the next day. "Get on the floor, motherfucker!"

Paul and I followed their instructions and lay face down with our hands behind our heads on the tile floor behind the front counter. The thugs ignored the cash register, jumped over the counter, and headed for the druggist and the narcotics.

"Open the safe!"

"Open the safe now, motherfucker!"

The pharmacist was too nervous to get the complicated combination sequence correct.

"Open the safe, motherfucker!"

"I'm trying! I'm trying!"

The thugs yelled louder and louder. Then shots rang out. Maybe five, I lost count. The sound of large-caliber weapons fired in an enclosed area is very unsettling. I could smell the gunpowder. My ears rang. I could not see what was happening with the safe, but I knew if the pharmacist was dead, Paul and I would be next. The junkies would not want any living witnesses able to identify them. Maybe I could survive getting shot until the police arrived, but who would call them?

It's interesting what you think about when you're in a life-threatening situation like this. I didn't want to be shot in the head and live in a vegetative state as a burden on others. I worried about who would have to clean up the mess. I worried about my unpaid balance on the broken van window, and I worried about Dad's Christmas Club savings account.

The thugs fled as quickly as they had come. They had shot the safe seven times, damaging the mechanism. It didn't open, and they left with nothing. The pharmacist was curled up against a corner in the fetal position. He was shaking uncontrollably, incoherent, and he had defecated on himself. The NOPD showed up to collect fingerprints. I had survived and felt that I had somehow cheated death. I felt invigorated once the whole episode was said and done.

Many of New Orleans's best seafood restaurants were located at the West End area near the Seventeenth Street canal and the Jefferson Parish line. They were always busy and always hiring young busboys and dishwashers for weekend work. "If you get a restaurant job, you won't need to worry about junkies with guns or people beating you out of your money," Dad advised. I walked into the Bounty Restaurant, spoke with the manager, and started working as a busboy the next weekend. The youthful manager drove a blue Trans Am and had long hair and a gorgeous girlfriend. Dewayne said he had started out as busboy, and now he was a manager making fifteen thousand dollars a year. "Restaurant work is steady and reliable. Everybody needs to eat," he said.

I was paid minimum wage, about $2.10 back then, and all employees were offered a free dinner before starting their shifts. I could order anything off the menu I chose. Of course, I always ordered the same thing, hamburger with ketchup and butter only. The dinner was free, but if you ate anything from the kitchen later, it was considered theft, and you were fired on the spot. I received 10 percent of the gross tips earned by the waiters in my section. I kept track of the tips I saw on the tables and expected to get at least ten dollars at the end of the night when the waiters settled up. Usually I got less than two! Waiters cheated the busboys and laughed about it. Dewayne said it was easy to replace busboys but hard to find good waiters. "Sebastian, if you don't like the way I run things, you can always leave."

The Bounty was built out over the water on wooden piers. Spinnaker's Disco was located next door. On Saturday afternoons the disco's back deck was packed with drinking and pot-smoking happy people enjoying the afternoon. Speedboats were tied up along the deck. The boats had names like *Colombian Gold* and *Fatty*. My section of tables was lined up against the Bounty's glass wall facing Spinnaker's. A woman in a tight black dress leaned over the railing watching the boats. A man walked up, put his arm around her, reached around, and began fondling her right breast. She smiled. I was mesmerized, as I had never seen anything like that.

"If you don't get back to work, you're going to get fired. If you're fired, you'll be unemployed. Sebastian, you don't get laid when you are unemployed!" Dewayne said I needed to stop daydreaming and focus on doing my job.

My job was hard. I was on my feet constantly for ten hours at a time. I worked Friday and Saturday nights and did not get home until after midnight, when Dad picked me up. Starting at 6:00 on Sunday mornings, I worked as a janitor, getting the restaurant ready to open for lunch. I cleaned the filthy bathrooms and dining room and mopped the kitchen floors.

Captain Bligh's bar was across the hall from the restaurant. The restaurant closed at 10:00 p.m., but the bar was open nearly all night. It attracted a totally different crowd. The restaurant and bar shared the same bathrooms. They were always vile and disgusting. I cleaned puke- and feces-covered floors. I cleaned blood off walls and disposed of a bloody tampon someone had tied to the doorknob. When a hand-soap dispenser ran empty in the men's room, someone came in it. Disgusting!

Turning over a five-gallon bucket, I stood on it when I turned on the kitchen lights. Rats as large as raccoons scuttled around. They ran along the pilings and the pier support structure under the building and were impossible to get rid of. I was afraid of rabies.

Another busboy, Bret Stall, asked if I could switch schedules, as he had a family event to attend. I worked his hours as promised.

"Where were you on Friday afternoon?" Dewayne asked. "I switched schedules with Bret. I worked his shift earlier." "Well, he didn't show up, and I was shorthanded. You're fired!" "But Bret didn't show. I did what I agreed to do."

"Bret doesn't matter. You were on my schedule, and I expected you here. You didn't show up. You're fired. Get your stuff and leave."

I didn't want to face Dad with the disappointing news that I was unemployed, so I walked next door to Larry's Seafood Hut and Sand Bar. Some of my earnings went toward the household budget, and Dad counted on that money. I was still dressed in my white shirt, black bow tie, black pants, and black faux leather shoes, the standard busboy uniform. I truthfully explained what had happened at the Bounty and asked for fifty cents more an hour. "Don't worry about it. Dewayne fires everybody. He's on a power trip. But twenty years from now, he'll still be driving that same stupid Pontiac. When can you start?"

"Now."

I didn't want to have to sit and listen to one of Dad's "I'm disappointed in you" lectures about holding on to a good union job, building seniority, vacation days, pension guarantees, health care, and holding the same job for fifteen or twenty years to become a shop foreman or union reprehensive. "Either you get a good job with a forty-hour week at a strong union company, or you work for the post office. You need security in life, and to get security, you do your job regardless. Look at me. I've been at CA since the day I finished high school," Dad always said. He would also explain to me that when you're employed, the people paying your salary have expectations. "You can't sleep late or screw up, and you can't get fired."

I filled out some simple paperwork and started working an eight-hour shift at Larry's. After closing, Dad was in his Chevy on the parking lot's far side. Afraid to tell him about the firing, I walked around toward the Bounty as if I had just left there.

That trick was ineffective. "What were you doing coming out of Larry's Seafood?" Crying, I explained what had happened. Dad wanted to wait next to Dewayne's blue Trans Am and settle things but decided that was not a good idea. "You got fired! Then walked next door and landed another job on the same night with better pay! You the man!" Dad messed up my hair the way he used to do when I was a child. "Let's go home and get a beer to celebrate this remarkable day!"

# 17

I know the lyrics to Frank Sinatra's "It Was a Very Good Year." Every time Mom was out late, Dad fell asleep listening to that song. Our small home offered no soundproofing, and Mom was out often, so I heard Sinatra a lot in those years. One evening Dad received an anonymous phone call.

"You can call me Debbie. That's not my real name, but Debbie works for now." "What is this all about?" Dad asked.

"Your wife has been having an affair for years. I thought you should know." "What are you talking about? Who are you? Why should I believe you?" "Because I can prove everything. Where was your wife last Thursday?"

Dad said she was at a friend's house first, then they went to see a movie. "Typical girl's night out," he said.

"Actually, she was at a Veterans Highway hotel with my husband. Just ask her if room 314 at the Sugar Bowl Inn rings any bells. Ask her if she was there last Thursday. Ask her if she's been going there for the last few years. My husband is a salesman. I never know for sure where he is. So I hired a private detective."

Dad refused to believe and never asked Mom anything about the Sugar Bowl Inn. He never heard from the anonymous caller again.

I can remember Dad ever telling only one joke. A man is in a bar, and he tells a fella that he has been with the same woman for twenty years. "That's great. Sounds like true love," the fella responded. "Yeah, but don't tell my wife. She'll kill me" was the punchline.

Once Dad started drinking, he began hiding his vodka bottles around the house. Some were above ceiling tiles in his bedroom, one was under a sofa seat, and another was in the trunk of the old Mercury. Although Mom seemed more and more distracted, she still believed it would be helpful to get the alcohol out of our home. Eventually she found six bottles, poured the vodka down the kitchen drain, refilled them with water from the faucet, and placed them back in their original hiding places. It took only a few seconds for Dad to figure out something was wrong. He went from bottle to bottle, tasting the contents. The ensuing fight was the worst I ever remember. It was the only time Dad ever hit her. Mom used eye makeup to hide the bruise. It was ineffective and made her look more like a battered wife. "Sorry I lost my temper. I will never do that again," Dad said.

"Gradually and then suddenly" is how Ernest Hemmingway's characters describe the process of going bankrupt. It is also an appropriate description of the final ruin of my parent's crippled marriage.

"The Top Fuel US Nationals Drag Race Finals will be held here next month! Top Fuel!" Dad ran into the kitchen waving his newspaper. "It's the same month as my birthday! What a surprise! We'll see slingshot dragsters, funny cars, 409 Chevys, and 427 Fords. Buddy Garner, Art Ainsworth, and Don Garlits will be there." Dad had been a huge drag racing fan since his high school days building the '47 Merc hot rod. He was more excited than a child on Christmas morning.

"Drag racing? Really? How loud and annoying is that going to be?" Mom rolled her eyes with obvious smart-ass exasperation.

"Can you try to give it a chance at least? For Christ's sake, is that too much to ask? I want this to be something we can all do together, as a family." His excitement drained away, Dad set the paper down on our small table and left the room.

"Just think about it! Please," he said.

The LaPlace Drag strip was shut down sometime in the nineties and redeveloped as a fast-food restaurant, gas station, and strip shopping mall with seven different retail stores. There was no evidence of the property's past except for a small brass marker that everyone ignored.

Twenty thousand fans showed up on race day. I walked along Dad's side. He offered his hand to Mom as we navigated through the crowd, searching for our cheap seats. The smell of fuel and exhaust hung in the air.

"Thank you for coming." He smiled at Mom.

"Whatever."

Dad pulled us past a large, drunk, happy-go-lucky man in a grease-stained T-shirt with a MOPAR logo. His buddies wore T-shirts commemorating GM's engine plant: "Built by Tonawanda-America's #1 Engine Factory." The MOPAR man held a beer in each hand. Mom squeezed by with her back toward him. The man held his beers high and moved his hips jokingly in a clumsy sexual manner.

She turned to him with an ice-cold stare. "That's never going to happen, asshole!" Not expecting the sharp rebuttal, he looked to the side and hung his head down. His friends laughed.

"Gee, lady. I'm sorry."

"Fuck off!"

Dad did his best to keep Mom entertained. He brought drinks, hotdogs, and cotton candy.

He explained details of each race. It made no difference. I can remember her words exactly.

"I've had all I can take!" she said.

"I know this is not your thing. But there are only a few races left. The final eliminations are next. It's for the national title! Just a little longer."

"You are always clueless. I'm not talking about this adolescent racing foolishness. I'm talking about you and this miserable life. You earn nothing. You give me nothing. I have had enough. I want a divorce."

"You want a divorce?"

Saying nothing more, Dad stared into the distance for a long time, lost in the gravity of those four painful words. Mom said something else, but her voice was drowned out by a 409 Chevy and a screaming Chrysler Hemi. Twenty thousand fans stood and cheered as the Chrysler inched ahead.

"It's time to go home," Dad finally said in a weak, beaten-down voice.

The drive home was the longest of my life. Mom looked out the car's side window saying nothing more.

Dad focused on the road ahead. I sat on the back seat, saying nothing. At a red light, Dad wiped away his tears with the palm of his hand.

The vacuum cleaner salesman was sitting on a large Triumph motorcycle parked in front of our house. He enjoyed revving the powerful engine, and he momentarily removed the toothpick he had been chewing. "Hi, baby." He kissed my mom on the mouth and patted her rear. She smiled, rushed inside, and returned a moment later with a small backpack-type duffel bag. Apparently, she had already packed and hidden it away until today, when she planned her escape. They must have been seeing each other for a couple of years.

"Sebastian, don't be angry. I waited a long time to do this. But you're older now and will be going to high school next month. Soon you'll find your own way to figure this out. One day you'll understand." She kissed me on the forehead. "I see a lot of your father in you."

I took that as a compliment, but I think she intended it as a warning. "I hope you see the life you don't want," she said.

"What about the house, your things, and the stuff we have together?" Dad asked.

"I'm taking the one thing I really want—my freedom to start over! You keep everything else."

"Where are you heading?" was all Dad could manage to say.

"West!" Mom hopped on the back of the Triumph.

Dad and I were standing on the sidewalk together. Dad wasn't angry at all, just defeated. "This has been a tough day."

Mom and the carpet guy pulled away and turned left. They did not look back. I was never to see her again.

Dad's old high school Green Monster Mercury was still sitting under the magnolia tree with four flat tires, mice in the glovebox, and rusty floorboards. Out of the blue, he decided to get it back on the road. It was a distraction from his broken heart, and it helped pass the time. My father could rebuild a complete engine and reinstall it in one weekend. Repairing equipment at the CA plant was not all that different. "An engine is an engine, and a wrench is a wrench. It's all the same," he used to say. Working on the 1947 Mercury's simple flathead V8 was easy for such a gifted mechanic. Dad worked with wrenches the way Michelangelo worked with brushes!

"The body is most important. We can repair the trans and engine, but major body or collision damage is too expensive," he said.

There was a method to Dad's madness. Perhaps we could have found an inexpensive antique car already running and bought that, but then I would never learn mechanics, and he loved the Merc like one of the family. "It can't hurt to learn a skill. Even for someone going to college." He always mentioned college, constantly planting that seed. Somehow, he thought I was smart enough. That would be a first for my family. But there was more. The weekends spent with him working on that old car are my most cherished childhood memories. "Maybe this can be your first race car? We will see," he said.

Rather than buy a new expensive generator, he purchased a cheap kit and did the rebuilding job himself on the kitchen table. I watched him clean and paint every individual tiny part. He polished the brass fittings with crocus cloth and carefully reassembled the outer casing. It looked like a Swiss watch when he was finished. Once it was all back together, his great attention to detail was hidden inside, out of sight. "If something is not done 100 percent correct, then it's all completely wrong. Rip it out, start over, and make it right," Dad said.

"You spent all that time, but no one will ever know."

"I will know," he said. "Always do you best even when no one else cares."

He removed the spark plugs and poured Marvel Mystery Oil into each cylinder. With the manual transmission in first gear, Dad would rock the car back and forth. Eventually the engine turned over. Soon it was free enough to turn by hand.

Once the motor turned over, he was able to completely break it down and rebuild it from the oil pan to the intake manifold. Dad rebuilt the carburetor and two water pumps on our kitchen table.

"Sebastian, stand back!" Dad poured gas into the carb and turned the key. It fired up!

Dad was an early environmentalist, although he did not really know it. "The internal combustion engine is a remarkable achievement, but it's very inefficient and dirty," he used to say. "The radiator is hot, the block is hot, the exhaust manifolds are white hot, and the mufflers are hot. That amounts to wasted energy. There has got to be a better way! Just think of how powerful a motor could be! All you need to do is figure out how to use all that wasted energy. If you go to college, you can design and engineer cars, not just work on them. I've had a wrench in my hand for years. It's gotten me nowhere."

He loved turbos because they used otherwise wasted exhaust heat to produce horsepower, and Dad always bored out exhaust valves. "Amateur mechanics think of intake first. They're completely wrong. Doesn't matter what goes into the combustion chamber if you can't get it out." His drawings for a three-valve-per-cylinder head design with two exhaust to each single intake were remarkable. Dad even designed a way to route exhaust gas throughout the intake manifold, heating the fuel mixture for more efficient ignition.

Dad's real interest was in metal composition and new engine-block materials. "Ceramics are the future of efficient combustion design." He believed ceramic motors could run at 1,200 degrees. "The hotter your combustion process, the more efficient and clean the fuel ignition will be. That's true for any engine type. If we figure out a way to control and use heat, everything will change. With ceramic motor blocks, radiators can be eliminated, allowing for the complete redesign of car bodies." He even suggested replacing the unnecessary radiators with catalytic converters heated by the high-temp ceramic engine. "Every car will become a clean-air-filtering system as outside air passes through the converters. Cars could help reverse the pollution problem," he believed.

"Let's get the Merc going and take a weekend road trip. What about Talladega or Daytona? It's just you and me. We can go anywhere, eat anywhere, and stop to pee whenever."

I noticed that his health seemed to improve each time he talked about the car. Dad loved it so much that all his other problems were temporarily forgotten. He seemed energetic and optimistic. His healthy youthfulness seemed to return.

In April, New Orleans received one of those crazy springtime storms. It dumped twelve inches of rain in five hours. Much of the city was underwater. The uninsured Green Monster had water up to the door handles. It was a total loss. A tow truck from Adams American wrecking yard came to haul it away. I climbed inside with a screwdriver and removed the hand-painted Green Monster glove box door. I still have it. The driver paid Dad fifteen dollars scrap value and hauled the Merc away.

"Who am I kidding? It's just an old beat-up car. Not worth nothing to nobody. Marche ou creve," Dad said. He had many French saying like this. I never knew what most meant.

It turned out the flooded hot rod was the least of the problems we faced. Our house was built on pillars with a small crawl space beneath. Still, we had seventeen inches of water inside. The old plaster walls had to be ripped out, the electrical systems were ruined, the old wood flooring was warped and buckled, and the floor furnace was destroyed. With inadequate flood insurance, Dad attempted to rebuild everything himself, working late evenings and weekends. "This is great. Now we can replace the old plaster walls with modern paneling, and we wanted new green carpet anyway. Finally, we can modernize the old place." Dad tried to stay positive.

The mortgage was held by the Crescent City Savings and Loan Bank. Dad made his monthly $114.56 payments on time for years. He drove to the bank's office on the corner of Canal and Carrollton with his payment book, and he checked off each principle payment from his remaining balance. The savings and loan sent an inspector out to the house four months after the flood. "Are you doing everything yourself?"

"Yes. I think it all looks great, and I'm saving money!" Dad said proudly.

"Well! You should have had it done by certified professionals, especially the plumbing and electrical. If money is a problem, you could have applied for a construction loan or equity line."

"Too much credit leads to begging. I'm not a beggar."

"Have you obtained the necessary permits? Have city inspectors been out?" the inspector asked Dad.

His answer was "No."

A certified letter arrived a short time later. It was signed by the bank's president. They called the loan and demanded immediate payment in full. "Evidence of substandard restoration work and materials has impaired the bank's collateral."

Dad tried to make his case about not having the money to do anything else. Still, we lost the house. *Hiraeth* is a Welsh word meaning homesickness for a home to which you can never return. It also refers to a home that never was and exists only in imagined memories. The English language has no such word. It should. After losing our home, Dad and I moved from small apartment to small apartment, and his drinking continued. The truth is, this went on for years. I even lived with Maw-maw and Paw-paw Flathead for about six months. I sat in the same small living room, ate frozen TV dinners in aluminum trays, and watched Lawrence Welk reruns on the same television Flathead had been slapping for years. "You're almost sixteen now. You can get your GED and work at the machine shop. It's a good living. Look around. I've done pretty good for myself," Flathead said proudly.

"At least Flathead managed to keep a roof over his head. That's more than I've been able to provide. Still, you should desire more from life than watching Lawrence Welk on a crappy TV. You're smart enough to go to college," Dad said.

# 18

Even under unfortunate circumstances, Dad managed to remain focused on my education and insisted on the completion of a four-year high school diploma, not a GED. Somehow, he managed to get me into a respected and expensive Catholic school. Though I attended a good school, my working-class roots still ran deep.

"You can make extra money easy by tuning up neighborhood cars in the evenings. Nothing heavy, just simple tune-ups. Points, plugs, condensers, and rotors, just like I taught you. The extra income will be helpful, and it won't interfere with your restaurant job," Dad said.

We made simple paper signs with black markers and posted them on telephone poles around the lakefront. Dad said rich people don't work on cars. "Inexpensive tune-ups. Done fast and right."

I also received financial aid in the form of a scholarship. Actually, calling it a "scholarship" was just a clever welfare disguise. I knew it was just financial aid offered to all poor Catholic families. The deception provided good cover, considering many of my new friends at school were from wealthy families paying full tuition.

I kept my scholarship situation private, knowing that some

people would think it was undeserved and an act of charity. They would say I was given someone's else's spot. The scholarship program allowed me to attend many school activities that otherwise I could never afford. But I still had to have tickets. On game day the stadium had two lines, one for paying students and the other for scholarship students. The free ticket line was near a side entrance, not the main gate. *I felt ashamed. It was like a welfare line. It was humiliating and embarrassing.*

I noticed there was something else different about wealthy lakefront families. It was something I could not quite put my finger on at first. Kris's family lived on Jewel Street and owned a famous French Quarter restaurant. The family drove a sand-color Chrysler Imperial that was a block long and bigger than a whale. It was also the first time I had ever seen a German car up close. They had an Audi Fox in the garage for weekend driving. Kris's mom always ordered lunch from a nearby neighborhood deli. "No, Sebastian, you are not getting a hamburger with butter and ketchup this time. I am going to order a roast beef po-boy dressed for you. You have to try new things to know what you really like!" she said.

"But I already know I like hamburgers."

"Perhaps you will discover something you enjoy more. Take a risk," she said.

Working-class kids are trained to play it safe, find a good job with benefits, and keep it until retirement with a guaranteed pension. Job security and steady pay are prized accomplishments. They avoid all unnecessary risk. By contrast, at every opportunity, lakefront kids were taught to take chances. Failure, risk, and opportunity were celebrated. Their dinner table discussions were always the same: "What new things did you try today?" Kris went out for our school's dance team and announced that she failed miserably. "I didn't even make the first cut!" she said. That evening her family had a special dinner acknowledging the effort.

A 2.0 GPA was required to maintain my financial aid. I usually did fine in most core academic subjects, but I aced shop and other vo-tech classes, helping to maintain a very respectable GPA. It wasn't that I could not handle history, science, math, and English. I just never had role models other than blue-collar working-class relatives. Dad did his best and encouraged me to read everything I could. He even gave me his books, but fighting against entrenched blue-collar custom and culture was hard.

I was surrounded by blue crabs. When catching blue crabs, you can toss them in a bushel basket till it's full. A lid is never necessary. Individually, they climb desperately over one another, all trying to escape, but as soon as one reaches the top, all the others pull him back down. Blue crabs are the perfect metaphor describing the realities faced by kids in working-class neighborhoods.

Soon, I had my first real girlfriend. We enjoyed many unsupervised get-togethers after school and on weekends. We learned to enjoy each other's company so much that our visits became a consuming, overpowering addiction that I enjoyed. Her mother did not trust us alone in a car, so our weekend dates to the movies were on the public service bus. I still held down the part-time restaurant job at Larry's and repaired neighborhood cars in the afternoons. With so many time-consuming distractions, my grades suffered. The two Ds I expected on the next quarter report card would be unacceptable, and I could not visit my girlfriend if I was grounded! I decided to be proactive and break the unacceptable news to Dad early.

"I expect to get two Fs this quarter. I know how disappointed you are in my grades. But I still have a chance to pull them up with the final exams. They count for fifty percent of my grade. I promise! I will study nonstop. I won't let you down. Even a good student can have a bad quarter," I explained while trying to lower Dad's unfair lofty academic expectations. Somehow, he never realized that perhaps my grades would improve if I were not working thirty hours per week. The "simple tune-up" business progressed into something resembling a full mechanic shop. With Dad's help, I was learning to rebuild transmissions and motors while still working at Larry's on weekends.

"You can't fail two classes! They'll kick you out of school! What about your future, Sebastian? Do you want to end up at the aluminum plant like me?"

The report card arrived with the two Ds I had expected all along.

"Son, I am so proud of you! I never believed you could pull up two failing grades. Nice work. You buckled down and got the job done!" He was so happy to see two Ds, he took me out to dinner at the Port of Call. He even said getting the Ds was a remarkable accomplishment.

As part of a shop vo-tech training program, my school supported a drag racing team. Eventually I was helping to build high-performance engines for the team's Mercury Cyclone drag racer. Although we were limited by budgets, we still managed to run a quarter mile in 11.33 seconds at 115.26 mph. That was good enough for a Sportsman Class first-place finish at the Cajun National competition. We managed to win a national title in a worn-out car with donated junkyard parts and a tiny budget. It was a remarkable achievement for knucklehead high school kids. The trophy was five feet tall and proudly placed on display in the school's tallest trophy case. We donated the $1,000 cash prize back to the school's shop program.

The Cajun National event was held at the LaPlace Drag strip—the same place where Mom ended our family.

Early in the season, an engine failed when it spun a main bearing, resulting in an embarrassing, heartbreaking loss. "Are you telling me all these other guys out here are better mechanics than you? Break the motor down and start over. Find out what went wrong, and fix it." Although not really realizing it, Dad used the racing team experience to drive home more working-class lessons. I wondered, Why not take risks? Maybe there was a better way to build faster motors. Why not experiment?

"You promised a ten-second car. Seems we missed it by 1.33 seconds!" Johnny was our team driver and my best high school friend. He enjoyed giving me a good-natured hard time because I had not delivered the top-speed engine I'd promised. "Don't get cocky just because your motor won a national title!" he said.

"OK, Johnny. I'll give you a ten-second car. Don't worry."

Johnny's family lived in a small apartment above a doughnut shop on North Galvez Street, and like me, he was also attending school on "scholarship." He left high school in his third year after the guidance counselor told him education is not for everyone. "Have you considered going to work?" the counselor asked.

"You know, I've been thinking about giving an open-admissions public college a try." "Johnny, ambition is nice, buts let's be realistic. We all have burdens to carry. Further study is not for you. Even an open-admissions school will find a way to place you on the waiting list," the smart-ass counselor said.

Being a part of the drag racing team gave me a feeling of belonging. I was the kid who could build championship racing motors and be a big man on campus. It motivated me to stay in school. I was part of something important. Johnny's confidence in school was completely crushed. He loved the drag racing, but he wanted out.

Johnny managed to build a Trans Am drag car. A gang member was shot, his body stuffed in the trunk of the Trans Am and then hidden off Bullard Road in New Orleans East. The car and body were discovered by the NOPD three weeks later. Eventually, the police department sold the car at auction. The awful smells didn't bother Johnny, since he planned to rip everything out anyway. He was the only bidder and won the car for seventy-five dollars. He stripped it down to save weight and became a competitive professional drag racer with many victories and titles. He always said our high school success was the sweetest.

# 19

"Listen, sweetheart, pumping more money into Cadillac is like giving an adrenaline shot to a dead horse." Danni said they should close Cadillac and focus exclusively on Mercedes. Times were changing, and Americans were no longer buying Detroit land yachts. German sedans were perceived to offer better quality with more prestige and were priced accordingly. A Mercedes 600 sedan had a cost breakpoint comparable to a Rolls-Royce. Higher prices translated into healthy bottom-line profitability. D&M Motors expanded from the original Mercedes dealership in the restored beautiful old Los Angeles Packard building to six new dealerships scattered across Southern California. Marty reluctantly agreed with the necessary Cadillac decision but was sentimental nevertheless.

"It's a bittersweet feeling. I remember when you first walked into the Richard Lee showroom and sat in the red DeVille convertible. Cadillac has been like family, but business is business," Marty said while holding Danni's hand. Mercedes was constantly developing innovative new technologies. They pioneered antilock braking systems, multilink suspension, transaxles, all-wheel drive...the list goes on and on. Cadillac had offered nothing new since the fabulous 1959 fins mimicked airplane looks.

"Jet-age styling came and went a long time ago. Cadillac had its day," Danni said. At certain times Marty appeared to be emotional, but he was a remarkable general manager. In fact, he often traveled to Stuttgart, Germany, and gave leadership presentations to new Mercedes dealership managers. He developed formal training programs with incentives to retain top talent. Marty offered prospective customers tours of the state-of-the-art service facilities. "Everyone working in this service department is certified by the Mercedes factory as qualified to work on your car." He loved bragging about the technology available and the constant investments made to improve the customer's service department experience. He pioneered the idea of hosting maintenance clinics for new owners.

Marty held weekly sales meetings with his D&M management teams across Southern California, discussing planning, business performance, and dealership profitability. He started each meeting with the very same question. "What new competitive threats are we facing?" Marty offered plans to address them. Most importantly, he expected every dealer operation to exceed sales goals. The best way to build sales was to get more foot traffic into the showrooms. Marty managed to persuade top company management to allow D&M to display Mercedes's most famous race car at the California dealerships. People lined up for blocks waiting for a chance to glimpse the remarkable gull-winged 300SL. It was a huge vote of confidence in Marty because thirty years had passed since Mercedes had last allowed the priceless SL classic racer to leave European soil.

Getting invites to visit the Mercedes home office was nothing unusual for Marty. But this latest invitation to a conference at Ulm University in Eselsberg, Germany, was different.

The university was the location of the Daimler-Benz Research Center, and the invite was signed by Dr. Edzard Weule, chairman of the board of management of the integrated technology group. Something exciting and confidential was underway. Marty was sworn to secrecy.

"We have invited you here today to discuss the company's most important recent advancements in electric car development." The presenter introduced engineering and research teams.

*Great. I've come all this way to get another pie-in-the-sky lecture on electric cars. What about the power grid? It's not robust enough to handle millions of cars charging at once. What about battery charging time? Are we going to discuss rare-earth material used in the batteries, such as lithium, dysprosium, and lanthanum? They all come from challenging places such as China and Zimbabwe. Can you name any company recycling lithium batteries on a large scale? What happens to an electric car that is out of warranty? Who will fix it? Can you offer someone a jump start? What about the sharp depreciation curve?* Marty was not excited about yet another electric car breakthrough promise.

He knew the batteries were too heavy and posed environmental issues—mining the necessary elements devastated poor countries, the nation's electric grid was already overloaded, and batteries had to be replaced often. It went on and on. Marty could give his own lecture on how much effort and resources had been squandered on technological dead ends. He expected the meeting to be about as exciting as a funeral. Sitting back in a comfortable position, Marty daydreamed about driving the new 560 SEC on the Daimler test track later that day. He was always given the opportunity to drive the car of his choice. There were no speed limits at the Mercedes proving ground tracks.

Dr. Edzard Weule walked to the podium and introduced CARONE. Hidden under a cover was an ordinary-looking MB 100 van. Edzard dramatically pulled the curtain away. "Turning around a century of fossil fuel reliance won't be easy, but this electric vehicle proves to all the world the basic suitability of electric propulsion systems. Its energy efficiency is significantly higher than that of all internal combustion systems previously developed. It reflects the highest levels of environmental friendliness, and it uses resources sparingly. No company in Europe or America or Asia has obtained our level of success in the development of this revolutionary technology. This marks a milestone in the development of exhaust-free driving."

Marty looked at his watch and wondered how much longer this ordinary dog-and-pony show would go on.

"We call this CARONE because it is the world's first practical electric vehicle that does not use batteries. Hydrogen is the first element listed on the periodic table, and by mass it has three times the energy content of gasoline. The basic idea is simple. When hydrogen and oxygen are permitted to react with each other under certain conditions, this process generates clean electric energy with only pure water emitted from the tailpipe. I call this chemical reaction cold combustion." Edzard enjoyed watching the puzzled expressions spreading across the room.

To his absolute astonishment, Marty was looking at the first vehicle featuring hydrogen fuel cells capable of operating in everyday driving conditions. It had been a very long time since Marty had spent his evenings watching a fourteen-inch black-and-white Zenith Flashmatic TV, but he was still enthralled by breakthrough technology. He had read many articles about hydrogen fuel cells but never imagined Mercedes was this far along in development of practical applications of this remarkable technology.

CARONE used twelve fuel cell stacks producing 50 kW. The special high-pressure hydrogen tank held 150 liters of compressed gas, or the equivalent of about forty gallons. With a forty-one-horsepower electric motor, ONECAR had a range of eighty miles with a 56 mph top speed. The fuel-cell system, hydrogen tanks, electronic controls, compressor, and cooling system filled the van's entire cargo space. Although Marty thought everything was incredibly complicated, Mercedes did prove that the technology worked. Marty was especially impressed with the short development timetable.

"We are proud to say we produced this proof of concept CARONE in just three years," Dr. Weule said.

"Danni! Think of it! Every nation on earth has potential access to hydrogen. No more drilling for oil, no more pollution, no leaking tankers or corrupt OPEC. With cheap and abundant hydrogen accessible worldwide, who needs wars?" Marty and Danni made it a point to speak with each other every evening.

"That sounds impossible."

"I thought so too. But I just drove a hydrogen-fuel-cell vehicle around the Mercedes test track three times!"

# 20

Dad walked over to the company health clinic at his lunch break, just as he had done on the third Thursday of every month for many years. Surprisingly, Dr. Hobbs was unavailable.

"I'm Dr. Gupta. Very nice to meet you, Mr. Delacroix. May I call you Pierre?" "Where is Dr. Hobbs?"

"Dr. Hobbs has taken a personal leave of absence. I'll run the clinic for now."

Dr. Gupta reviewed Dad's medical file. It consisted of only one single page of illegible handwritten nonsense. "How long have you had that cough?"

"Ever since I was exposed to methyl mercaptan. I spent time in the hospital, but then I was back to work. That was many years ago. Dr. Hobbs has been taking good care of me since. I see him every month. He said everything is fine. When will he be back?"

Dr. Gupta was concerned about the lack of any medical records. "You were exposed to methyl mercaptan! I'm worried about that cough. I would like to take a chest x-ray, Mr. Delacroix."

"Dr. Hobbs says x-rays are for broken bones. My bones are fine," Dad said.

"As your new doctor, I must insist. It's important to complete your medical records accurately and see about that cough."

Dr. Gupta studied Dad's x-rays in the privacy of his office. The plant's shift change whistle called everyone back to work. He asked Dad to wait a few moments.

"It appears there are large shadows on your x-rays. Pierre, I've made an appointment for you with the Oncology Department at Baptist Hospital."

"I feel great and Dr. Hobbs says I'm fine, but if you insist, any afternoon next month should be good. Wednesdays would be best," Dad said, not understanding the implications of what Dr. Gupta was trying to say.

"Wish I had better news, but you may have cancer. It can't wait until next month. The hospital is expecting you today."

Dad was sitting in a hospital exam room when I arrived. The oncologist walked in with a thick folder of forms he needed to complete and a metal clipboard. Sitting on the end of the bed, he introduced himself and delivered the sad news in a cold, professional manner. Although still a relatively young man, this was the first time I realized just how sunken, tired, and hollowed-out Dad looked. That was what a lifetime of work at CA would do. It all seemed so meaningless.

"I have consulted with hospital specialists, including interventional radiologists, additional oncologists, and a surgeon. You have cancer, and it has grown. It has spread and metastasized. Surgery is out of the question. There's nothing we can do. You might have a few more months."

The oncologist asked if Dad had any questions.

"I thought I had more time. I always thought I had time."

"We will not let you suffer."

Dad wanted a traditional Catholic burial with a priest, and he wanted to be laid to rest in the old aboveground family tomb on Washington Avenue. He asked me to clean it up and paint it. "Our family members have been buried there forever. It's time to go home," he said. Dad also asked if I would promise to sign up for college classes. "Just give it a try. That's all I ask. I always dreamed that your life would be easier and happier than mine. But just getting by can be so hard, you need all the advantages you can get. That's why I always pushed you. But if things go bad, don't let the bitterness and regret get the best of you. I regret hitting your mother. I regret being an unfaithful husband. I regret drinking too much. I worked a dead-end job my entire adult life. Somehow, I became just like Flathead. I regret that most of all."

He asked for one more thing. "Can we drive to Biloxi? I would love to spend an afternoon relaxing on the beach."

Early-morning phone calls are never good news. My call from the Baptist Hospital duty nurse came at 2:45 a.m. on October 21.

"I'm afraid I have some difficult news," she said. Death had come quickly. I had thought he had more time. Our Biloxi trip was planned for the following Saturday. Dad was three months shy of his forty-seventh birthday.

He had started working at Chalmette Aluminum the Monday after his high school graduation. In the eyes of a youthful eighteen-year-old from a blue-collar family, the job presented a remarkable opportunity. He could buy a house and a car, marry, and raise children. Dad believed long three-day weekends spent relaxing on Biloxi's beach were within reach. With free health-care benefits and a retirement plan, life was looking good. But he never made it to Biloxi, not once. It rained on his funeral.

I made an $800 payday loan to cover Dad's final expenses. I registered to take a few night classes at Delgado Community College and enjoyed the Introduction to Applied Mechanical Engineering class. I had an A-plus. When Dad talked about college, I knew he meant a four-year BS university program. Delgado was wonderful because it was affordable, and all my credit hours could transfer to the University of New Orleans.

I registered as an incoming freshman at the University of New Orleans as I had promised. I knew nothing about course catalogues, majors and minors, requirements and electives, or what the bursar does. UNO was an open-admissions, affordable commuter college with a reputation of supporting nontraditional college students, like me. I showed up for registration and selected some basic courses with the help of a guidance counselor. "I want to study mechanical engineering," I said with great confidence.

The counselor looked over my high school transcripts. She smiled politely and suggested I take it slow. "Your high school GPA is above three point oh. Very solid work, Sebastian. You did well in shop and did exceptionally well in the applied mechanical engineering vo-tech classes you have taken. These classes pulled up the lower grades for your basic required academic work, resulting in an adequate GPA. Additionally, I see multiple high grades for participation with your high school's drag racing team!

"But there is a significant difference between applied high school vo-tech classes and college-level engineering courses. I also see the credits you earned at Delgado Community College. You show remarkable promise. But let's take university-level work slow to start out. I suggest that perhaps remedial math and English along with other remedial-level introductory courses would be more appropriate." She asked more about the drag racing team.

"Our goal was to build a ten-second car. That means it can cover a quarter of a mile in ten seconds. We hit eleven point thirty-three seconds, pushing a one hundred and fifteen point twenty-six mile-per-hour quarter-mile top speed with our team's Mercury Cyclone. We won the Sportsman Class at the Cajun Nationals. I didn't drive the car, but I did build the engine. My dad taught me how to build very fast motors. I don't build motors thinking only about horsepower and torque. I think about utilizing wasted heat energy—efficiency in the fuel-ignition process reduces wasted heat energy. My goal is to build an engine that is seventy-five percent efficient. Currently, most are about fifteen percent efficient!" I explained.

"You won a national title with essentially a junkyard car? Amazing! I am impressed. I don't believe we've ever had a national drag racing champion and future mechanical engineer at UNO! We're very excited to have you here! You'll be successful, but let's take our time getting your academics up to speed." She laughed at her own joke. "Get it? Up to speed!" she said.

UNO students called the remedial math "James Bond math" because the course number was 007. I presented my Louisiana driver's license and completed the registration process. The university said I would receive a tuition bill later. At the end of the day, I was an official college student studying at a respected four-year university. It was a great feeling.

When I sold my rusty Chevy, I was happy to get $525. Using most of that cash, I paid down the payday loan and used $45 to purchase a bicycle from an Airline Highway pawn shop. The university was only about one mile from home, so I figured saving money on transportation would be easy. Even though

UNO was extremely affordable, it was always a struggle to pay the semester bills on time. I put them off for as long as possible, then the university threatened to withhold my grades and cancel my registration as a student in good standing. Making an appointment at the bursar's office, I hoped to explain my difficult financial situation and work something out.

"My I have your name and student ID number?"

I sat across from a friendly man in a blue shirt and red tie. He worked a computer and listened attentively as I discussed my circumstances. He requested my student ID again.

"Our records indicate that your bills are covered. You're set to go." "My bills are covered? What does that mean?"

"You owe the university nothing. Everything is paid in full." "Paid? For the entire semester?" I asked.

"You're covered not just for this semester. Your entire four-year degree program is paid in full. Every penny. Every year! Paid in full."

"What? Who paid my tuition?"

The computer operator rubbed his chin and looked at the ceiling. He seemed to remember something important.

"Hmm. You know? I do remember this. An attractive middle-aged woman came into this office asking about you. She wore a nice string of pearls and a diamond ring bigger than an M&M. She asked about your tuition bills and paid them all. She also made a rather large donation to the Governor Earl K. Long Memorial Library fund. We're building a new state-of-the-art campus library, named after former Governor Earl Long. He's considered the university's founder. During the war this was a naval air station. It was Earl's idea to build an urban university." The bursar administrator said he watched the mystery lady drive away. "She was driving a green Land Rover. That's about all I know."

# 21

I was never to know what became of my mother, except that she went "west." Many years later I received a plain envelope without a return address and a Montana postmark. It contained an obituary from a local newspaper. "Michel Miro recently passed away after a brief illness. She had worked as an aspiring actress but most recently was employed as a truck-stop waitress…" My mother's maiden name was Michel, and she grew up on North Miro Street. The Michel spelling was very unusual. It was an old French family name, like Le Blanc. I could had done some simple research, but why bother? If she wanted to be found, why use a silly made-up name? Death leads to interesting plot twists, but if you walk in the woods and see a log rotting on the ground, the best thing to do is leave it alone. Snakes, roaches, and spiders hide under it. Why disturb it? At the time, the perspective I had on my parents' difficult relationship reflected the limited experience of a child. But things were more complicated than they appeared.

I treasured my dad's small collection of his favorite books he gave me, especially the Dean Acheson biography and his engineering books. I read them multiple times over the years. Taking it upon myself to display the collection, I carefully removed the books from his old cardboard box, dusted each, and placed them, one by one, on a shelf in no certain order. I thumbed through the mechanical engineering texts again. Two nice marble book ends I found at a secondhand store worked perfectly.

At the bottom of the box was Dad's incomplete Tulane admissions application. Sitting on the kitchen floor, I read it again and placed it in a folder. Tulane was expensive. It was out of the question for me. Those students had more weekly spending money than the cost of UNO's annual tuition. I spent the next few minutes humming a few bars of Pachelbel's cannon in D major, Dad's favorite. The old cardboard box was dry and brittle, easy to tear apart. I placed the pieces in my kitchen trash can and discovered the box had a perfectly cut piece of cardboard fitted to create a false bottom. Carefully hidden underneath, I found letters from the woman Dad befriended at Chalmette Aluminum. I had always assumed Dad remained loyal to his wedding vows. I was wrong about that.

"When we finish each morning, I start anticipating our lunch rendezvous. After our lunch dates, I start looking forward to the next morning. I dread the long weekends without you. Always wanting more, I can never get enough. My husband passed his bar exam, but it won't take an expert cross-examination to see that I have fallen for you. If he becomes suspicious, I'm done for! My loveless marriage may be hanging in the balance. But that's OK. I can tolerate a distracted husband because thoughts of you carry me through!" She wrote in perfect penmanship.

She signed every letter with "I will always love you! Sabrina." Judging from the dates written on the pages, their affair did last a long time, and they seemed devoted to each other. But with so many letters, volume can be a form of concealment.

It makes it much harder to figure out what the writer is hiding. Truth lies somewhere between the written lines. I think Sabrina ended the affair after her husband was hired as a junior associate at a prestigious law firm with an office on the top floor of Saint Charles Place. If she made a practical decision, who could blame her?

At Chalmette Aluminum she handled vendor contracts and worked alone in a small office adjacent to the health clinic. Sabrina's office had a writer's desk, a wall of file cabinets, florescent lighting, and a commercial coffee maker. Evidently, she enjoyed coffee as much as Dad.

# 22

As you may have guessed, Dr. John Thomas Hobbs III was not on a personal leave of absence at all. Actually, he resigned his position after his arrest and the revocation of his medical license. Authorities began an investigation after the suspicious death of a clinic patient. The inquiry determined the patient died from multiple drug intoxication.

Dr. Hobbs prescribed medications including morphine for the man's back pain but failed to ask about other prescribed drugs he was taking. The patient was receiving temazepam from another doctor. Dr. Hobbs did not bother keeping any documentation of medical treatment during the three years he treated the patient, and he waited seven months before reviewing urine test results exposing the patient's drug intoxication levels. The man was found on the floor of his Gentilly home. He was unconscious with his left sleeve rolled up, a rubber tourniquet around his arm, and a used syringe on the floor. He died shortly after being admitted into the hospital.

"The man became a junkie during his army service in Indochina. I did everything I could to help him," Dr. Hobbs explained. He prescribed the medications after business hours not from the clinic but from the *Aquilla*, where the man would come to pick up his prescriptions. Dr. Hobbs claimed he worked from the *Aquilla* to protect privacy and help his addicted patients keep their jobs. Investigators alleged he was nothing more than a pusher. "Obviously, he overprescribed," they said.

The medical investigators interviewed Allison Meyer, a thirty-four-year-old former CA employee previously working in the HR department. Eventually, she spent time in the Orleans Parish Prison for prostitution. Dr. Hobbs began treating her after she showed up at the clinic complaining of fatigue and lower back pain. He prescribed morphine during a two-year period. She lost her CA job, her home, and finally her family as the addiction took over her life. She had no money or any place to live. Saving her from homelessness, Dr. Hobbs invited her to live with him on board the *Aquilla*. The two began having sex the next day. He demanded kinky sex frequently and threatened Allison by withholding her drugs if she did not comply.

Upon questioning by medical board investigators, Allison turned over stacks of Dr. Hobbs's blank prescription pads, three complete pads signed by Dr. Hobbs, and several pill bottles of prescribed opioids. She told the investigators that Dr. Hobbs prescribed the drugs in exchange for deviant sex, and she alleged he raped her often after giving her morphine. "He would disappear on weekends. He spent Friday and Saturday nights roaming the French Quarter paying hookers. He didn't pay for sex. He paid them for their dirty underwear. He paid more for their underwear if they had just left a customer. Hobbs came back with a grocery bag full of panties. He forced me to wear them."

He claimed Allison stole the prescription pads while he was sleeping. "She's a prostitute. How is it possible to rape a hooker? I paid for everything. One way or another, I always paid," Dr. Hobbs said.

A pot line worker was brought into the clinic suffering from severe dehydration. Dr. Hobbs inserted an IV needle for fluids and electrolytes. Within a short time, the worker began to feel better and, after thanking Dr. Hobbs, left the clinic with his daughter. Dr. Hobbs prescribed rest, plenty of fluids, and salt tablets. "You are clear to return to work on Tuesday." Dr. Hobbs handed him a piece of paper authorizing his return to a full work schedule.

The man's health deteriorated almost immediately, and within hours he was running a fever of 104 and had breathing difficulty. He was taken to the hospital the next day. "If you had waited just one more day to bring him here, he would be dead," the emergency room doctor said. Medical staff said he had an infection caused by a dirty needle, eventually leading to bone infection and congestive heart problems. The man was never able to work again. Dad's neglected medical condition was a blessing. If not, Dr. Hobbs would have killed him years earlier with opioids or dirty needles. It's ironic— die from drugs and poor medical care or die from cancerous chemicals and contaminants eating away your lungs. Any way you look at it, CA was a death sentence.

CA's parent company structured everything to shield itself from liability. The legal problems related to the clinic and Dr. Hobbs were limited to Chalmette Aluminum. Aggressive plaintiff attorneys tried unsuccessfully to pierce the complex corporate legal structures. The victims of Dr. Hobbs were not likely to receive anything from the parent company. Dr. Hobbs was arrested on March 12, and his medical license was revoked the very same day. He was released from the Saint

Bernard Parish jail shortly thereafter on an $850 bond. In accordance with company policy, he was offered the opportunity to resign from CA before his termination. Somehow, his employee record at CA remained spotless, in spite of his negligence, corruption, and incompetence. Nevertheless, his legal problems were just starting. "Dr. Hobbs didn't resign from Chalmette Aluminum to spend more time with his family. He resigned to spend more time with his lawyers," according to an investigative reporter covering the story.

Dr. Hobbs posted the $850 bail, drove to the lakefront marina, parked his car in a shady, out-of-the-way spot, and took his time walking down the pier to *Aquilla*. He stopped here and there, watching brown pelicans and schools of mullet swimming lazy circles. For the first time, he realized how neglected *Aquilla* looked. The decline had happened slowly over time, the gradual effects of neglect only apparent now. New beautiful fiberglass cabin cruisers had replaced many of the older wooden boats once so common. He believed these owners would soon learn the weakness of the fiberglass fad. "Fiberglass is industrial. Wood is art!"

Walking past shiny new yachts with hardly a sideways glance, Dr. Hobbs knew it was only a matter of time before double-planked oak hulls with bronze fasteners returned to favor.

# 23

*NASA launched Apollo 8 on December 21, 1968. The spacecraft eventually settled into lunar orbit. Astronaut Bill Anders picked up a camera and snapped a 70mm photograph as the Earth began to rise over the moon's barren horizon. He took the photo as a diversion from the routine monotony of completing the mission. Called "Earthrise," the color photo captured a breathtaking perspective of our tiny planet never seen before. In the endless blackness of space, Earth was there with a remarkable radiant blue hue. The photograph led to a collective shift in our appreciation for this fragile world, leading to ecology movements and ultimately to the modern environmental prospective.*

*Early environmentalists focused on carbon dioxide as a dangerous greenhouse gas, overlooking methane. Natural gas emits less carbon dioxide when burned but more methane. New studies show that methane is eighty to a hundred times as powerful than CO2 in trapping heat in the Earth's atmosphere. Methane is the main component of natural gas.*

In addition to the plant's methane problem, Chalmette Aluminum also illegally dumped a hundred cubic yards of wastewater into the Mississippi River daily. The waste was toxic to fish and everything else. The most voluminous solid waste not dumped into the Mississippi was the SPL, spent pot lining. This is the corroded material removed from the pots after they were used to melt the aluminum. The SPL was stored on property in giant outdoor mounds resembling small mountain chains. They planned to ship it all to a processing plant in Honduras. This material was toxic and explosive under certain conditions. The Honduran government blocked the plan, so the SPL just piled up at CA. Additionally, Chalmette Aluminum was fined for the illegal handling of potassium fluoride and sodium fluoride by the US Department of Commerce.

Furthermore, there was still no practical plan for dealing with the tons of asbestos everywhere.

In 1970 amendments were added to the original Clear Air Act of 1963 expanding the EPA's mandate. It was too late for many plant workers and people living in the area. After a Department of Environmental Quality investigation, plant managers admitted that they had been releasing mercury into Louisiana's air without a permit since the plant first opened. "The mercury release was never detected because it was rising from remote steam vents used with heat exchangers," they said. Regardless, the DEQ never permitted mercury release into the air, under any circumstances. Taken in total, the volume and length of the illegal neurotoxin releases made the plant one of the worst polluters in American history.

The company responded to the negative environmental investigations with PR campaigns and full-page newspaper ads proclaiming "Chalmette Aluminum—Longtime Steward of the Environment." They touted well-paying jobs and the company's community partnerships. They claimed progress in harmony with the environment and community with social investment policies. The company promised to build more ballparks and football fields. They made large donations to an early-education program for preschoolers and funded a GED center for adults. CA made donations to groups representing oystermen and shrimpers. They supported friendly politicians guaranteeing continued political support.

The 1979 oil crisis occurred in the wake of the Iranian Revolution. Oil prices increased to $39.50 per barrel. Long lines appeared at gas stations, resulting in nationwide rationing and even-odd fueling days. In 1980 the Iran-Iraq war shut down nearly all oil production in the region. The sale of the traditional eighteen-foot-long Cadillac, Lincoln, and Chrysler land yachts getting nine miles to the gallon and weighing five thousand pounds fell to the floor quicker than a prom dress. Americans began a love affair with practical Japanese imports and well-built German luxury sedans such as Mercedes.

Natural-gas prices increased from $2.56 per thousand cubic feet to $4.29. Earl's deals, setting natural-gas prices with futures contracts and guaranteeing supply to CA while carelessly devastating the environment, were in place for thirty years. They were unwinding just as Middle Eastern turmoil escalated.

Oscar Clemens was right after all when he said locating the plant in Louisiana made no long-term economic sense. "Louisiana faces a number of unsurmountable concerns. If something happens to the supply of affordable natural gas, then plant operation will be negatively impacted. In that case the plant would have to be converted to coal or have natural gas shipped in as LNG. All very expensive and impractical scenarios," he said. As fuel costs increased and environmental concerns grew, operating the plant profitably became impossible. The world's largest aluminum plant was designed with a

150-year expected life span. Chalmette Aluminum shut down after just thirty years, leaving a legacy of environmental devastation and cleanup problems lasting generations. Chalmette Aluminum was incorporated as a separate legal entity, shielding the parent company from any liability. Cleanup costs fell upon the EPA and the shoulders of Louisiana's taxpayers.

Chalmette Aluminum's pension plan was overfunded until the financial troubles started. Plant management raided the benefit plan multiple times to cover increasing operating shortfalls. By the time bankruptcy paperwork was filed, the pension fund was nearly empty. "We are terminating the pension plan in its entirety. The company's agreement was that the company would make contributions to the retirement fund. The fund was obligated to provide pensions. And so the company did not at any time assume liability beyond that."

After the plan defaulted on its obligations, workers were left with nothing, and those already retired lost most of their benefits. "I have no income, no pension, and no health insurance. I lost vested rights. What am I supposed to do now?" a desperate worker said, pleading for help. It was government backstops that saved many from financial ruin. Still, suicide rates climbed as workers saw their retirement plans disappear into thin, polluted air.

In bankruptcy, CA discharged pension, environmental, and financial obligations. The parent company received $143 million in tax-loss credits. This enabled them to wash their hands of Louisiana and purchase a new mill in the northwest. The parent company stock increased from $7.35 per share to $67.50.

"Too many conglomerates build plants and deliberately close them to gain a tax loss. It should not be profitable to do this," said a Louisiana State Representative. Yeah, no kidding.

# 24

"**S**ebastian, you're not going to believe this. I finally got it!" Johnny was sitting on my front steps waving a small business-card-sized license of some kind. He was wearing his favorite blue cotton coveralls with leather work boots and smoking a Marlboro. "This is it! My NHRA level-two professional drag racing license! I got it today! Can you believe this shit?" Johnny was excited to be a licensed top-level professional drag racer, although he complained about the rules and regulations. "The fucking rule book is three inches thick. It's a bunch crap," he said. "You can't even change a knob on the dash. Why do you need a fully braced roll cage for closed cockpit drag racers? It's ridiculous!" Johnny always hated rules and felt they were designed to give less-competitive drivers a fighting chance. "It's the only way the chumps can beat me," he said.

Johnny never paid attention to risk or rules. At fourteen he was arrested by the Orleans Levee Board police for riding a skateboard across the Seabrook Bridge over the Industrial Canal. On a Saturday afternoon, Johnny hopped on a freight train to go to a Metairie fried chicken restaurant and ended up on the other side of the Huey P. Long Bridge over the Mississippi River. He's the only person I have ever known who rode a Schwinn bicycle at 50 mph. Johnny held on to the bumper of a car and did it on a dare.

Girls were always attracted to Johnny. A girl in our neighborhood had dated the same boy for years, and an engagement was planned. It was no secret she had a thing for Johnny. He borrowed his dad's old Plymouth, and we went to a Saturday-night party. "I have a car. Why don't you come outside with me?" Johnny asked her. They locked the doors and climbed into the back seat. The boyfriend realized what was going on.

"I love you. Don't do this!" He ran around and around the car beating on the hood and trunk, trying to open the locked doors. "Don't do this! Please. I'm begging you!"

Johnny asked her if she wanted to stop. She said, "No."

I had never seen a level-two NHRA license. It was a very big deal. Johnny gave me a lot of credit, but all I did was build the motor. He was the driver. I learned a lot from my UNO introductory mechanical engineering classes and was able to apply some of that to building Johnny's ten-second Trans Am. We used lightweight metal alloys wherever possible to save weight. I persuaded Johnny to go with the new electronic ignition setups, fuel injection systems, ceramic components, and a few other tricks that I had up my sleeve. A blower added nearly 45 psi of boost, to create over nine hundred horsepower. I also modified and adapted an old Chevy two-speed power guide automatic transmission. It held first gear to eighty-five miles per hour. With so much power and compression, the engines had an expected life span of about ten quarter-mile runs. Johnny was a naturally gifted driver. His fearless instincts and quick reflexes were remarkable.

"You're the brains! You earned this also. Let's go celebrate at Pizza Pie," Johnny said. "Pizza and a pitcher of cold beer sounds just about right."

We ordered a large thin crust with peperoni and Italian sausage and a pitcher of Dixie with frosted mugs. "To the best engine builder ever!" Johnny raised his glass.

"To the youngest level-two drag racer ever. A remarkable accomplishment."

"You are a real college boy now! Remarkable accomplishment? That's a lot of damn syllables just to say. Fucking right!" Johnny said we made such a great team because we had different skills. "You promised a ten-second car. You did it."

After we enjoyed the pizza, Johnny pulled a folded-up magazine article from his back pocket. "This dude was building jet-engine-powered cars in his Iowa garage and setting world land speed records at the Bonneville Salt Flats! Five hundred and seventy-six fucking miles per hour! You turned a dead dude's junkyard Pontiac into a ten-second Trans Am. Why can't we beat what this Iowa dude did? He ain't got nothing on us! Nothing! He ain't got nothing!" Johnny enthusiastically slapped the article down on the table. He draws out syllables and said "Bonn-uh-vull" three more times to make his point.

"Johnny, I don't know anything about jet engines. In fact, I have never even been in an airplane before. Just because I finished a handful of undergrad engineering classes does not mean I'm an engineer. The article says he was sponsored by GE, McDonnell-Douglas, and BF Goodrich. We were sponsored by Larry's Seafood Hut. We have an old Ram-Air Pontiac 400 engine. This guy runs a Pratt and Whitney Turbo Jet J57 with afterburner and eleven thousand seven hundred pounds of thrust! At five hundred miles per hour, a jet car covers the quarter mile in less than two seconds! Going that fast is suicidal," I said.

The story of Art Ainsworth was amazing. He was essentially a self-taught mechanic and learned basic mechanical skills by rebuilding farm equipment at a rural Iowa feed mill. Always curious about interesting machines, I continued to glance through the article. I took a deep breath and set the article down on the table. My heart raced. I felt butterflies in the pit of my stomach.

"What? You look pale? Sebastian, are you OK?" Johnny asked.

"Art Ainsworth held two land speed records in jet-powered cars of his design. He built everything from scratch, including the chassis and body design. He named them Green Monster 1 and Green Monster 2!"

"Now that is a fucking coincidence for you. Isn't that the name of your dad's old Mercury? The one you always talk about?" Johnny asked.

That evening I opened the bottom draw of my bedroom dresser. In the back, wrapped in a towel for safekeeping, was Dad's glovebox door from the '47 Mercury. Rubbing my fingers over the top, I could feel the letters he had painted freehand with household paint from a hardware store: "The Green Monster."

As an underclassman I was assigned to UNO's Upward Bound program for bright students needing an adamic boost. The program offered campus jobs to students in financial need in addition to the academic math learning labs and the James Bond classes. The student assigned to answering the office phone had worked at a grocery store for a few years. He always answered the Upward Bound phone with "Schweggmann's Giant Supermarket." Old habits are hard to break. I was fortunate because I still had a job at Larry's, and my UNO tuition was covered, so I did not apply for a campus job.

With long hours of study, I worked hard and completed all the prerequisite courses. Spending most afternoons in the math and engineering learning lab, I finally gained the confidence to excel in undergrad mechanical engineering programs. The lab was operated by math grad students as part of their master's degree requirements. They were smart and eager to help. The learning lab also offered VHS tapes covering algebra and trig. During the late-evening hours, I often watched the tapes over and over until I finally understood the concepts. Making up for lost time quickly, soon I was back on track to graduate in four years. No longer intimidated by academic challenge, I completed the most demanding coursework with an A. By the end of the spring semester, I had completed Calculus 2114 and 2124, Physics 1061 and 1062, Chemistry 1017, Engineering Design, and Graphics 1781. My next year went easily, especially as I reached the more advanced levels such as Modern Physics, Thermo Lab, Thermo Fluid Design, and Heat Transfers.

As the assistant bar manager at Larry's, I earned a decent salary, worked a flexible schedule, and earned over thirty dollars each night in tips from drunk college students. At the center of the restaurant was a huge U-shaped bar, with a dance floor and bandstand in the front. The dining area was divided into five smaller rooms around the perimeter. Each dining room had its own name: Blue Room, Red Room, Green Room, Yellow Room, and White Room. Most customers never realized that the restaurant and bar layout was designed to mimic the infamous Storyville brothels from the last century. Larry was a funny guy.

He also allowed me to handle the bar on my own and seldom interfered with my management decisions. Although Larry made a lot of money from the bar, he never touched alcohol. Years ago, he had a drinking problem that consumed much of his life, ruined his family, and nearly bankrupted him. "I haven't had a drop in fifteen years! I am dryer than a bone in the desert. After a few DUIs, the judge offered me two options. Get treatment or go to jail. I joined AA and still attend every week," he said.

Sara had been standing near the bar with a friend. My eyes were drawn to her. She had the look of classic beauty and was the most attractive girl I had ever seen. I am sometimes shy in situations like this, but I knew I would regret forever not talking to her. With fake confidence, I went over. The bar provided bowls of salted peanuts as finger snacks. Sara rummaged through the peanuts like a child playing with food they don't want to eat. "Sometimes you find a cashew in all these nuts. Usually you don't", she said. Intrigued, I asked her to dance. She excused herself to her friend. "I would love to."

Sara liked slow dances, so I asked the band to play them often. She had long, curly blond hair and natural humor. "You dance like Fred Astaire!" she said after I stepped on her right foot for the third time. There was a natural chemistry between us. When Sara reached over and held my hand, my heart raced like a locomotive. It felt wonderful.

"I've never danced with an engineering major before."

"Well, I've never danced with a writer before." Sara was a fine arts major studying creative writing.

Eventually we talked about career dreams. Sara said she wanted to write for the *Times-Picayune* and become the editor and publisher. I told her I planned to use my mechanical engineering degree to build race cars, and I asked if she knew anything about auto racing.

"My dad was a huge NASCAR fan. We went to Talladega every year. It was a family tradition. I even saved every ticket stub and have them all arranged in a scrapbook. The sound and excitement of the races, especially the start, was always such a thrill."

Her mother taught remedial English at the Orleans Regional Vocational College as an adjunct professor. Sara's dad ran a small monthly publication from a converted garage about Cajun and Creole Louisiana culture called 'The Cajun Rue'. It had a small circulation in the southern Cajun parishes and a few out of state subscribers. Sara worked on the publication since she was a young child, but it all came crashing down after her mother's affair with the college president.

I asked Sara if they repaired the marriage. "Relationships are not zombies in a sci-fi movie, they don't rise from the dead." She said.

Sara changed the subject. "I hear that engineers make poor lovers." "That thesis is very easy to disprove!" I said. "Well, I have all night, Mr. Engineer."

She grabbed my hand playfully while walking backward toward the dance floor, pulling me closer. "I love this song. Let's dance."

Even with so much going on, still I was constantly thinking about the land speed record and speed week at the Salt Flats. Johnny's voice was stuck in my head, Bonn-uh-vull, Bonn-uh-vull, Bonn-uh-vull. I reached the conclusion that no one would ever crack the 576 mph record set by Art Ainsworth and his jet-powered Green Monster with the existing technology available.

As a young engineering student, I understood that advancement comes from failure and challenge. The trick is to use reason and experience to address the problem. An engineer doesn't sit around doing the same thing over and over. Effective engineers use a systematic approach to determine why something has failed and solve the issue. Jet engines are large and extremely heavy. It is difficult to build an aerodynamic land-racing body around a jet. Additionally, the chassis would have to be robust enough to handle the torque and weight. It all adds up to a heavy race car unable to overcome further inherent limitations. With these obvious shortcomings, it seemed impossible to push the jet concept much further.

Jet cars did have a significant advantage over their internal combustion competition. They were pushed by thrust only, with no need for transmissions, driveshafts, and differentials. Internal combustion engines have reached 350 mph on quarter drag strips. Pushing that to 576 for a mile was out of the question. Traditional piston motors have too much mechanical resistance and friction. Electric motors deliver necessary torque, but they are limited by battery size and weight.

Not too discouraged, I spent my free time at the UNO Earl K. Long Memorial Library, in the engineering reference section, trying to find a clever way to address the speed challenge. Not trying to fool physics or win a Nobel Prize, I just wanted to smash Art Ainsworth's land speed record in a new Green Monster.

It was hard to miss the many life-size posters of former Louisiana governor Earl K. Long in the library lobby. "Why so many pictures of a dead governor?" I asked the person sitting at the reference desk. "It looks like a political rally in here!"

"Excuse me!" she said. "Earl K. Long happens to be Louisiana's greatest governor. He created our modern system of higher education. The regional universities at Hammond, Monroe, Lake Charles, Natchitoches, Ruston, Lafayette, and Thibodaux all exist because of Governor Long. In fact, UNO was a surplus naval air station left over from the war. Governor Long used it to create UNO. He also created our modern system of vocational-technical schools. Earl Long ushered Louisiana into the modern age. We all owe him a big debt of gratitude."

"OK! Thanks for all the information." Surprised by the elaborate response to my simple question, I was eager to move on.

I stacked five engineering texts on top of an oak desk in the library's reference room and began to thumb through them looking for innovative direction.

"That's quite an impressive collection of study material you have there. Are you working on a thesis of some type?"

I had never met the school's dean in person, but I had seen him during freshman orientation last year. He gave a talk about great careers in engineering. Friendly and helpful, he pulled up a chair and asked more questions.

"No, sir. I'm just researching information for personal use." I explained my interest in the Salt Flats and land speed records. "I've tried everything—blowers, lightweight alloys, high-octane aviation fuel, nitrous, and alcohol fuels." I told him about my jet-engine research and success with Johnny's Trans Am. "Maybe Mr. Ainsworth's record represents the pinnacle of engineering achievement. Perhaps his record can never be broken."

"Nonsense! The science of engineering is always advancing! Success builds upon success."

I agreed with his view but expressed my dead-end frustration.

"So, you mentioned aviation gas, nitrous, and alcohol. They are all wonderful propellants, but you need more kick! Something that will transform everything. You need something that will disrupt the current consensus." The dean picked up my pen and tapped it on the desk in excited fashion.

"You need hydrogen! It's not just an industrial gas. It's one hell of a powerful fuel! For every unit of liquid hydrogen involved, over five thousand units of propellant power result. The difference between hydrogen and gasoline is remarkable. I'll quote Mark Twain, who once said something about the difference between lightning and lightning bugs. You figure out a way to harness the power of hydrogen, and you will own Bonneville records for generations!"

# 25

I don't think Larry ever got a single new restaurant customer from his sponsorship investment in Johnny's Trans Am. He did not have a clue regarding targeted advertising dollars to profitable markets. Larry didn't do it for any financial reward; he just loved watching Johnny race, and he loved seeing his name on the hood of a winning drag racer. "I'm Larry! That's my name. Right there!" At each event, he always made sure every race fan knew who he was.

I approached him first for a financial sponsorship donation to our new ambitious project. "Larry, we plan to challenge the Art Ainsworth's five hundred and seventy-six mile-per-hour Bonneville land speed record."

"Ha ha ha. You're going to beat a jet car's Salt Flat record in Johnny's Pontiac? I love you guys, but that's just not possible."

"Actually, I've done all the calculations. It works out. Our limitation is not thrust, but tires! No company currently produces a six-hundred-mile-per-hour tire. Johnny's Trans Am is a ten-second dragster. I'll build a missile on wheels able to cover a mile in six seconds! Not just a quarter mile, a whole damn mile in six seconds! That calculates to six hundred miles per hour. We don't plan to use a jet engine or a Pontic motor, but we are going to use a liquid-hydrogen-powered rocket! Art Ainsworth's record is going to fall faster than the French Maginot Line." I used the historic World War II reference because I knew Larry had served as a private first class in Patton's Third Army.

Larry looked skeptical and raised his left eyebrow in a doubting way.

"Let me explain. The hydrogen peroxide we intend to use as propellant is nothing more than ordinary water with extra oxygen atoms. The peroxide available in the drugstore is three percent hydrogen. Our fuel will be ninety percent hydrogen. The overoxygenated water wants to release the extra atoms as quickly as possible and become more stable. We can help this process along by introducing an element like silver to the solution, which causes an exothermic catalytic reaction to occur, resulting in heat and steam. The reactions are instantaneous and incredibly powerful. The idea is to force that steam power through a narrow conical nozzle, propelling our rocket car forward. I promise, we will smash all Bonneville records!"

I drew diagrams with pencil and paper explaining the functionality of the concept. I was busy with my slide rule and calculations.

"That sounds great, Sebastian. But have you ever heard of a little thing called the Hindenburg disaster? What about those hydrogen bombs the army was testing in the Pacific? What about Soviet hydrogen bombs? Are you going to blow up a racetrack?" Larry asked.

"The blimp tragedy actually helps build my hydrogen thesis. There were ninety-seven people on board the Hindenburg. Thirty-six people died. The rest all survived. Hydrogen is lighter than air, and it fades into the atmosphere quickly.

That amount of oil or gasoline would have burned for weeks. If it was an LNG explosion, the entire Manchester Township and Lakehurst Naval Air Station would have been destroyed instantly. Tens of thousands would have died in the blink of an eye. It's counterintuitive, but hydrogen was a safe option for the zeppelin. About hydrogen bombs, consider the case of nuclear power. It can be used to destroy cities or destroy cancer cells. It all depends on the application and ambitions of the engineers involved," I explained.

"OK, count me in. How much do you need?"

"We need eight hundred dollars to build a proof-of-concept functioning rocket motor model. The whole thing will be about the size of a roll of quarters. Small enough to build on a tiny budget, but scalable and huge in terms of what it will prove."

"Can you put my name on the hood of the actual hydrogen race car?" Larry opened his office safe and handed me eight one-hundred-dollar bills. "In my youth I would take risks. I'm old now, but I love the excitement of being a part of this. I love this Buck Rogers stuff," Larry said.

UNO's engineering department offered to have my proof-of-concept components machined at a New Mexico government lab familiar with this type of precision work. My professor said he had connections who could be helpful. The offer was generous, but it would take a long time, and the cost was still significantly more than my small eight-hundred-dollar budget could handle. I thanked the university for their support, but I had a better idea.

This old industrial area of New Orleans still seemed familiar. I looked out the window as I drove down Franklin Avenue heading toward the river. The warehouses, machine shops, and storage buildings were grimy and old. The area thrived when the navy built the Port of Embarkation on Poland Avenue, but that was a very long time ago. The people earning a living here today looked tired in shabby work clothes and seemed preoccupied with life's daily struggles.

Reliable Reconditioning had been housed at the same address since 1938. It was a steel frame building covered in rusty sheets of corrugated tin. Large barn-type drive-through wooden doors on rollers opened wide to the street. Giant fans mounted in the rafters kept the place at a pleasant temperature even during humid New Orleans summers. There was no air-conditioning or wall insulation. The lathes, drill presses, grinders, milling machines, and shapers were all made by the R. K. LeBlond Machine Tool Company out of Cincinnati, Ohio. They were the finest quality available at any price, and although old, they were expertly maintained and in perfect working order. The shop was exactly as I remembered it. I bent over to pet the two friendly hound dogs resting near the shop office.

"I would recognize dat familiar face anywhere. Sebastian, how are you doing? You're da spitting image of your grandfather. We still miss dat loveable old curmudgeon. In fact, those two dogs belonged to him. He had a big heart and rescued every mangy mutt dat showed up on our doorstep. It's been a while. How are ya?"

He shook my hand with a powerful viselike grip. I always loved that unique New Orleans accent. I felt right at home.

"Papaw Flathead loved stray dogs?" I asked.

"He sure did. In fact, dat hard and hateful persona you remember was just a facade. Da truth is, he was kind and generous. Your grandfather had some faults but loved stray dogs.

I also know he loved you and your dad more than anything. But he wanted you both to be strong and tough, like him. He wanted you to stand on your own two feet."

"That doesn't make any sense. He was hateful because he loved us?"

"Yes, dat's right. Your grandfather stood right here and made your dad open and close a truck hood for nearly an hour until your dad had da process exactly right. Your grandfather understood better than anybody dat discipline could save your life, especially in life-or-death situations. Listen, Flathead was leading an advance squad into heavy Iwo Jima fighting. He had a flamethrower. Three Sherman tanks had been destroyed in short order. Your grandfather figured out where da Japanese bunker was hidden. After ordering da men to take cover, he crept along on his belly for fifty yards unseen. Japanese bullets whizzed past, inches over his head. He found a bunker air vent and placed da end of da flamethrower down into it as far as possible. For da next few minutes he listened to da cries of twenty men as they were burned alive. He survived Iwo because he learned how to be da meanest son of a bitch around. He wanted you and your dad to be able to survive when da next wars come along. Life is tough, and he wanted you to be tougher. Dat is how he expressed his love. Did you know your grandfather was da only Pacific Theater veteran who used a flamethrower to save a wounded GI's life?"

"No, I didn't know any of this. Papaw never talked of the war," I said.

"Well, Sebastian, he was always quiet about his valor. But dat's right—he saved da man's life with a flamethrower. *Life* magazine wrote an article about it. The GI's leg was blown off just above da knee by a mortar round. He was in danger of bleeding out. Flathead dragged him to da side of a destroyed Japanese tank. Using dat flamethrower, he got da side of dat tank red-hot then jammed da bleeding stub against it and held it there. Da wounded leg was immediately cauterized, stopping da bleeding. A few years back, dat man, his wife, children, and grandchildren all showed up here to thank your grandfather. We cried like babies, including your grandfather.

"You should know, he begged your father to work here with him. Your dad could have been happy here for years, but he was lured to Chalmette Aluminum with promises of better pay and free health care. Da free health care turned out to be at a run-down company clinic with an alcoholic company doctor. CA wasn't a job. It was a death sentence. Bastards should all be rotting in jail. Anyway, enough of all dat. So, what brings you out to dis part of town?"

I explained my hydrogen rocket car idea and the proof-of-concept plan. I opened a folder with the blueprints and drawings.

"Flathead always bragged about how smart you are. Your grandfather was so proud of you and hoped you would become a master machinist. Seems you did, in a roundabout way. Your grandfather was da best machinist around. He loved his job and was a naturally gifted machinist. There was nothing he couldn't repair, build, design, or fabricate. In fact, his idea of a vacation was going to Detroit for a week to attend drill-press advancement updates. We all learned from him. Your grandfather could shave Ford V8 heads blindfolded with one hand tied behind his back. That's da God's truth."

"This rocket project may require a little more precision than Henry Ford's flathead motor," I said.

"Look, Sebastian, around here, accuracy is our religion. But why hydrogen? We all remember da hydrogen bomb tests in da Pacific and da Hindenburg disaster."

"It's all a learning curve." I said. "Sometimes unexpected breakthroughs from surprising places can change the world. Think of the Rosetta Stone. That single discovery unlocked mysteries that had puzzled researches for centuries. I believe hydrogen can have a powerful world-changing impact as well."

"Don't you worry about anything. You have come to da right place. Da Rolls-Royce Marlin engine powered da Spitfire. It was da same engine in da P51 Mustang. Da only American company capable of building dat motor with da dual-stage supercharger was Packard. We called it da Packard Marlin. After da war, da US Defense Department certified a handful of machine shops around da country to rebuild Marlin components. Reliable Reconditioning was honored to be a part of dat important group. In fact, we even had a small government contract to work on da superchargers used on brown-water river patrol boats during the 1960s. We also did a little gear cutting and crankshaft balancing for coast guard helicopters. Accuracy is our religion. Let me take another look at your hydrogen rocket." He studied the drawings and nodded his head. "Interesting concept! Flathead would be so proud."

"How many weeks do you think it will take to machine these parts?" I asked.

"Weeks! Hell, son. Dis little thing? My tired old penis is bigger than dis. We can build it faster than you can say 'Good morning, Vietnam!' You can pick your rocket up Wednesday afternoon!"

"What about cost?"

"Consider it on da house. Don't you worry about a thing."

Johnny and Sara were both there on test day. I set every-thing up in my shed and attached the rocket to a regular bath-room scale I had purchased at TG&Y to measure thrust.

"I didn't expect the rocket motor to be this small. It looks like my grandmother's pill bottle." Johnny sounded disappointed.

"Is this test going to be safe?" Sara was wondering if she was in danger. Who could blame her?

"Not to worry. The rocket was machined by Reliable Reconditioning. It'll test out perfectly. Besides, I rechecked everything, including structural design and the propulsion system. I promise, it's safe."

"Here we go!"

Johnny began counting backward like they do at NASA. "Ten, nine, eight, seven, six, five, four…"

Instantaneously, a trail of steam shot out, filled the shed, and clouded our view. The piercing screaming sound was louder than a locomotive whistle. Its appetite for fuel was voracious! Dogs howled. For two seconds the garage trembled.

"Unbelievable! That is the coolest damn thing I have ever seen. You're a genius mastermind!" Johnny was jumping up and down with his hands on his head, running in my direc-tion. Sara asked Johnny to stop hugging me so she could have a chance.

The scale registered a high of thirty-eight pounds. I did some quick calculations on a yellow legal pad. "If we scale the motor up one hundred times expecting similar results for gen-erating pounds of thrust, then we're talking seven hundred miles per hour! Seven hundred miles per hour easy! That's significantly better than expected!" I was stunned.

"Bonn-uh-vull! Bonn-uh-vull! Bonn-uh-vull! Here we come, Mr. Ainsworth!" Sara wrote a PR article and sent it to the *Times-Picayune*. "Local UNO Engineering Student Successfully Tests Hydrogen Rocket Motor." The paper carried the news as its lead sports story on Sunday morning. I bought five copies.

# 26

I arrived for class on time Monday morning as usual and was told the university chancellor was expecting me in his office.

"When?"

"Now," my professor said.

"Am I in trouble?"

It was a long walk from the Science and Engineering Building on the west side of campus to the University Center, where the chancellor had his office. I felt like an unruly kid being marched to the principal's office. The sun was out, and my books were heavy. Nervousness made me sweat. The heat and humidity contributed to wet circles forming under my armpits and an itchy feeling. Antiperspirant was useless under these stressful circumstances.

I sat in a large leather chair across from the receptionist. He was polite and smiled often. "It's hot as Hades this morning!" he said. A round rug in the center of the room was woven with the university's name in gray and blue. An original oil painting of Dr. Homer Hitt, the university's first chancellor, hung on the paneled wall. His face was painted in half profile, and he seemed to be staring at something just out of sight. He looked distinguished behind wire-rim spectacles resting on his nose. Perhaps the portrait was intended to illustrate the chancellor's visionary thinking. On the other wall was a large framed photograph of former governor Earl K. Long holding a golden shovel. "That's when they broke ground on the University Center," the receptionist said.

"The chancellor will see you now. Right this way." He opened the door, introduced me to the two men seated at a boardroom-type table, and offered coffee. I thought the table was just stained with different wood tones, but it was made of integrated wood veneers inlaid in precise patterns and finished to a high gloss. I accepted the coffee but was too hot and too nervous to drink it. A copy of Sunday's paper was on the table, open to Sara's article.

"Good to see you, Sebastian. Please have a seat." The chancellor patted me on the back like an old friend. "We were just reading the *Times-Picayune* article. This is quite the accomplishment, young man. We are all proud. It's a feather in your cap and in the university's cap as well. Our engineering programs are experiencing significant enrollment increases, and this great national PR will contribute to that continued growth.

"I would like to introduce you to Mr. Frank Porteous. He is a former state senator and former federal judge. Currently he's a partner with the law firm of Jones and Jones and the lead attorney representing the University of New Orleans."

"Have I done something wrong?"

"No, not at all. We want to help you," Mr. Porteous said.

He explained how important it was to establish an "airtight" legal corporation for my personal protection and the protection of the university. "The corporate umbrella shields us all from any liability. It protects your personal assets, and it protects the university's good name. In fact, the engineering program is expanding in a significant way. The planned growth will put UNO on par with Georgia Tech and MIT." The chancellor said that the old Pontchartrain Beach location was being acquired jointly in conjunction with a US Navy marine engineering program. Pontchartrain Beach was an old amusement park located on the lakefront between Lakeshore Drive and UNO. After generations of successful operation, the park had closed as entertainment tastes changed. The rides and attractions were sold off, and the property sat vacant for years.

"You have a remarkable future ahead, and we want to make sure you can stay focused on building the world's fastest hydrogen rocket cars, not depositions and court hearings. You will also have a federal tax ID number, business cards, letterhead, and professional financial reporting."

"I don't have any personal assets to worry about."

"But you will. Additionally, do you have the names of three other people we can list as board members?" the chancellor asked.

"Wow! What can I say? Thank you." I gave him the only three names I could think of, Johnny, Sara, and Larry.

Mr. Porteous opened his leather briefcase and produced five thick copies of the articles of incorporation. The chancellor called in a typist and had the board member names added. He handed me a pen made in France, called Montblanc. It had a white cap and beautiful gold trim. Mr. Porteous passed the stack of documents around the table so that every copy had three original signatures. It was as if he were dealing cards at a Vegas casino.

"This is a lot of pages. It's bigger than a phone book," I said.

"Well, like Grandma's pajamas—everything is covered. It's a comprehensive document." The receptionist was called back in to sign as a witness. "One original copy for each of us, and another to file at the Civil District Court Building, and another for the IRS. My office will certify your true copy and mail it to you within the week. Keep the Montblanc as a gift." Mr. Porteous placed the pen back in its original box and handed it to me.

"Can you think of a name for your new corporation?" the chancellor asked.

"How about JLS Inc.?"

"Does that mean Jet Land Speed or something like that?" Mr. Porteous asked.

"No. It means Johnny, Larry, and Sara."

"Perfect. You had better get back to class now."

We stood up and shook hands all around, and I left the room. Twenty minutes before this meeting, I had been an average college student. Now I was president and CEO of a real corporation working with the university chancellor and a famous lawyer, and I had a two-hundred-dollar handmade French pen in my pocket.

"Sara, guess what?" I was almost too excited to speak but managed to explain my exciting day.

"Sounds remarkable! You did read everything? Right? Did you request a day or two to think it over?" she asked.

"Not exactly. I didn't want to seem ungrateful."

"I guess you're right about that. Well, hurry over. I've never slept with a CEO before," she said in a very flirtatious manner.

"For my favorite writer!" I gave Sara the Montblanc.

"I've always heard about Montblanc pens but have never actually seen one. If you look at photos of Hemmingway, he always had one in his pocket. I absolutely love it." Sara said she loved the feel of it in her hand. "But there is one other thing I would rather grip!"

"Am I a real corporate board member? That's so cool!" Johnny asked if he could have business cards printed with his new title. "That boneheaded high school counselor said I would never amount to much. Boy, was he ever wrong!"

I started developing a long-term plan to earn the money necessary to build the Salt Flat racer, but it was going to take upfront funding. Johnny had saved over two thousand dollars from his drag racing championships. He had planned to buy a Triumph motorcycle. Sara had five hundred dollars from a third-place finish in a novella writing contest. Larry offered additional funds on an ongoing basis, and he increased my hours at the restaurant.

I presented my plans to the guys at Reliable Reconditioning and asked for their help. "I plan to build a prototype hydrogen rocket motor dragster and campaign it nationwide in the unlimited class. This is where Ainsworth got his start. If we can beat jet cars on the drag strip, then we can beat them on the salt flats. The prototype will provide us with operational experience, expertise, and funding. Johnny will win big with a rocket car blowing the doors off everything, especially the jet cars. A hydrogen dragster will back up our claims and make money. Our rocket car will weigh less than nine hundred pounds.

"Last year's national unlimited class champion walked away with fifty-five thousand dollars in his pocket. I can build the chassis from used components and industrial tube framing. Everything else, from disk brakes to front-end parts and the suspension, can come from the junkyard. We'll win a lot of cash and learn valuable lessons that will be worthwhile as we put together the land speed car."

They talked it over for about twenty minutes in the shop office with the door closed. I passed the time playing with Papaw's old hound dogs.

"Ok. We love your enthusiasm and want to help as much as possible. After hours, da shop is yours. You can build your chassis here using every tool da shop has to offer. We will scale up da rocket motor at no charge for labor. Just pay for da materials. One more thing: we want to continue working on the Salt Flat land speed racer when da time arrives. If successful, that may help us get some government contracts again. By da way, da guys passed around da hat. It's not much, but we hope it will be helpful." They gave me a paper bag with $250 in small bills.

"How did the shop lose all that government business?" I asked.

"We were doing great, with more contract work than you could ever imagine. We were rated one of da Defense Department's best subcontractors many times over. Executives from Lockheed Martin even visited da shop. They promised us a tour of da real Skunk Works, but dat never happened because overnight everything went to jet engines. We were outdated piston guys, forgotten men skilled in obsolete trades. Dat is when your grandpa Flathead started drinking. Your rocket car is going to destroy those jets. This time we want to be on da winning side of da disruption."

I studied chassis design and engineering while researching Formula One, NASCAR, European sports cars, and Indianapolis open-wheel race cars. I soon had a large collection of dog-eared reference books scattered around my tiny apartment. Since our hydrogen rocket car was not wheel driven, it had no need for a transmission, differential, or driveshaft. It could be built lightweight with a small low frontal area for better aerodynamics. It was always best to use simple design with minimal parts. Johnny found a retired rear-engine dragster frame suitable for our plans. It had a modern spaced tube construction that was very light and strong. I altered the design by moving the driver's position farther forward and adding four wheel brakes, six mounts for the rocket motor, and a parachute. I added robust suspension on the four corners and additional welds and rivets to handle the rocket torque. I designed a forward area for the hydrogen fuel tanks. With no air intakes necessary for a rocket motor, the driver could be positioned directly in front. I spent time applying the samarium oxide coating process for the silver catalyst screens, allowing the rocket to be throttled during operation.

On the right side of the dash area, I incorporated a small rectangular space adjacent to the gauges and instruments. The small aluminum frame I designed and built was a perfect fit for mounting Dad's old Green Monster glove box door from his '47 Mercury. I planned to move it to the land speed rocket once we had it built. Dad would love what we were doing, and he would want to be a part of it. "I love the glove box. Your dad was such a cool dude," Johnny said. He developed a superstitious habit and would never start a race until he momentarily placed his right hand flat over the glove box. Johnny said it was good luck. I agreed.

The Reliable Reconditioning shop turned out to be perfect for our design and building needs. I worked late into the night and usually brought a liver cheese sandwich on white bread with mayonnaise and a coffee thermos. The old hound dogs were content to lie nearby and watch everything. It turned out they loved liver cheese too. We had plenty of space, all the necessary machine tools, and men with remarkable skill and experience eager to help. Lockheed Martin had its secret Skunk Works. Reliable Reconditioning had its Nutria Works. The guys thought it would be funny and put a metal sign over the shop's back area where we were building the car.

I would return each evening to discover that they had completed many of the welds I had tacked in place the night before. The guys built a heavy steel cart that supported the motor and made it easy to move around while mating it to the tube chassis and hooking up all the plumbing. It doubled as a perfect assembly stand. Pipes, pumps, and lines had a lot of fittings that all had to be perfect. I used compressed air to check and recheck everything for leaks. The shop had a hand-operated hydraulic crane capable of lifting six thousand pounds. It came in handy with the motor-mounting process. Six bolts attached the motor to the chassis. After the chassis was done, the shop guys all signed the rocket motor and christened it with a Dixie long neck, naming it Mercury II. It was not named after any NASA moon shot project. It was named after Dad's '47 hot rod. We all raised our beer bottles. "To Mercury II!"

The dragster body was made of easy-to-cut-and-bend thin aluminum panels that I could attach to the chassis and roll cage quickly with self-tapping screws. The guys in the shop taught me to use an English wheel to shape the panels perfectly. I didn't have a wind tunnel available, but the completed body looked like a championship contender anyhow. It had to be shaped to cheat the wind, and its aerodynamic form had to recruit the wind's help if we were going to set land speed records. The body was designed to function like an airplane wing in reverse. Rather than creating lift, our wing-shaped body created significant downforce. Downforce is not so important when racing on a quarter drag strip. The flying mile at the Salt Flats approaching 700 mph was a totally different matter.

I was unsure of a paint scheme and asked for suggestions. The guys all glanced at one another. "At the end of da war, da US was producing five thousand airplanes a month. Paint was considered an unnecessary expense. Especially considering how beautiful dem aluminum skins looked without paint. Da aluminum skin on da P-51 Mustang was pure art."

"OK, Let's polish the aluminum. With one small exception," I said. "The hood has to be painted with Larry's logo."

We all stood and admired the world's first hydrogen rocket dragster. The finished body reminded me of a line from *Wind in the Willows* when Toad says, "I have a very elegant figure—for what I am."

Sara's articles reporting on our progress appeared regularly in the *Times-Picayune*. Locals sometimes stopped by Reliable Reconditioning to see for themselves. "We haven't seen dis much activity in years." The shop ran an employment ad to hire skilled machinists. They were even shopping around for new equipment. Sara said her articles had been picked up by the AP. I had no idea what that meant, but she said people around the country were reading about our hydrogen rocket car.

In the early 1970s, a residential community was planned in southern Mississippi near Bay Saint Louis for owners of small private airplanes. It was about forty-five minutes from downtown New Orleans. The residents could land and taxi their small planes from the runway directly to their homes and private hangers scattered about the flight-friendly neighborhood. Unfortunately, the idea failed, and the houses were never built. But the runway was built and remained abandoned but in decent shape, hidden in a Mississippi pine tree forest. A forgotten road lined on each side by encroaching pine trees, rusty chain-link fencing, and deep drainage ditches led to a broken gate. Beer cans littered the area. A water tower was visible in the distance painted with the NASA and Stennis Space Center logos. It was ironic, but NASA tested Saturn rocket engines nearby. This was the perfect place to secretly test our hydrogen rocket race car. With no other way to refine the engineering, I planned to use actual tests to address any design-change questions.

The main purpose of these early test runs was to evaluate flow rates, chamber pressure, and rocket thrust. We loaded enough fuel for only a second or two of full operation, about a hundred pounds. That was exhausted in about nine hundred feet. Johnny climbed in and fastened his safety harness. Watching the pressure gauges, he slowly began turning the dome loader dial. "Throttle up!" Johnny followed the checklist perfectly. At 600 psi the rocket was set to go. "We're all set. Everything here is a go!" Johnny said in a very calm voice as he momentarily rested his right hand on the old '47 Merc glove box door for luck.

As our racer rolled forward, the thrust dynamometer was expected to reach 3,500 pounds. Applying power for only two seconds, Johnny would then coast to the end of the quarter-mile markers. We wanted to evaluate the performance of the systems while allowing enough distance to stop safely. The car sat quietly until the rocket started to hiss. The high-pitched hiss turned into a low rumble. "Giddyap!" Now Johnny was getting excited. He gave the thumbs-up sign. Thrust pinned him back into his seat. The car rocked and rumbled, shooting off the starting line like a bullet. It was over quickly, as the rocket ran out of fuel and quietly slowed to a noneventful, gentle stop near the end of the old runway.

Johnny was already unstrapped from his seat, smoking a cigarette and out admiring the car. "She is one hell of a bitchin' race car! I have never experienced anything like it. The thrust and power hit immediately. There's no lag time, power delay, or burning rubber. It's all immediate speed," he said.

I reminded Johnny that smoking near hydrogen was never a good idea. He dropped the cigarette and put it out with the heel of his boot. He hated rules.

I did some quick calculations. "Johnny, if we extrapolate the rocket's two-second performance and use those figures to estimate expected quarter-mile times, and if my calculations are correct, then you just drove the world's fastest drag racer! Actually, it may be faster than a speeding bullet!"

Sara asked us to smile for a photo to go along with her latest article. "New Hydrogen Rocket Car May Be World's Fastest."

Over the next few weeks, we did multiple test runs at our secret Mississippi location, evaluating suspension operation, braking, rocket performance, and many other important functions. After the third test run, we added air scoops for better flow at the rear of the car and minor body and suspension changes. Growing in confidence, we increased the fuel load. This time Johnny hit the quarter mile at 6.30! The official world record stood at 258.62 mph and 6.79!

Johnny's face was covered in blood from a deep gash on his forehead. The plexiglass windshield had shattered under the high-speed stress. "A little blood ain't nothing. We don't need a windshield. I can wear goggles," Johnny said.

"Johnny! You can't drive a three-hundred-mile-per-hour race car without a windshield!" While admiring Johnny's fearless courage, we still replaced the windshield with a new, stronger one made of laminated Lexan.

"Here come the cops!" Johnny said.

We all saw the blue lights.

"Everyone stand down. Stay right where you are." The officer was from NASA security. He continued to talk over his radio. Soon more cars showed up. They were not police. They were NASA scientists and engineers.

"Is this the hydrogen rocket Mercury II dragster we've been reading about?" "Yes, sir. I guess so."

"Mind if we have a look? The precision here is impressive. How do you increase your fuel pressure?"

"I use helium gas for that."

"Is this a closed-loop cycle?" The engineer looked puzzled.

"Yes, sir. It is. Am I in trouble?"

"This is impossible. This can't be. I don't believe what I'm looking at. How did you learn to design this?"

I explained that my dad had taught me the basics. "He said heat, especially exhaust heat, is wasted energy. It became my job to cut the grass when I was about eight. The muffler on Dad's old rusty Craftsman push mower fell off midway through the job. Not knowing any better, I picked it up and received second-degree burns on my hand. Dad applied burn cream and a bandage. He explained how heat is wasted energy. It was an unforgettable lesson. To develop a more powerful motor, it must be efficient. So I designed a way to reroute my rocket exhaust back through the combustion cycle. Thrust increased thirty percent!" I said.

"Your dad was an engineer? Where did he go to college?"

"He went to Nichols High School and worked at Chalmette Aluminum. Dad built a '47 Mercury hot rod. It was fast." I talked about my UNO undergrad education and the precision work done by Reliable Reconditioning, and then I showed the NASA engineers Dad's Green Monster glove box door. They took notes and photos.

"You learned to build a closed-loop hydrogen rocket engine from working on a '47 Mercury and a rusty lawnmower? The Russians developed the concept first. We have never totally mastered it. But you did it in your garage!"

# 27

South Louisiana was not known for jet race cars. There were a lot of fast Hemi and Ford dragsters built by skilled southern teams and enthusiastic shade-tree mechanics with nominal budgets, but no one was offering our hydrogen rocket any real competition. The jet car phenomenon was a midwestern thing; the south was still old-school piston— until now! The $1,000 offered for an exhibition run at the LaPlace Dragway was easy money and great PR. "We should do this. You can't buy the kind of positive free publicity this will create. Newspapers and TV stations will be there!" Sara said. I had avoided the LaPlace Dragway for years, ever since Mom announced she was running off with the carpet-cleaning dude. I wasn't thrilled about reliving all that.

It was a cool spring Saturday morning with blue skies and low humidity. Expecting only four to five hundred people, we were surprised to find the parking area full. Traffic was overflowing onto the main highway. Police were called in to help direct traffic on Highway 90 and handle the huge traffic jams. The crowds were larger than the Cajun Nationals I attended as a family on that sad carpet-dude day. But today, these people were here for me. It was surreal in that sense. "What else is going on today?" Johnny asked.

"Nothing else. All these people are here to see Johnny Rocket and the remarkable Mercury II hydrogen rocket car!" Sara said.

She had given Johnny that nickname, and it had stuck. The race-day programs featured Johnny Rocket on the cover. Already people were swarming around asking Johnny to sign their programs. He stood in the bed of the track's utility truck and waved to the admiring fans. "It's Sunday Sunday Sunday! Ladies and gentlemen, boys and girls, race fans of all ages, meet the famous Johnnnnnnny Rocket! The world's fastest human!" The truck drove in front of the overflowing stands. Johnny waved and smiled. Kodak Instamatic cameras clicked. Sara and I sat quietly on a bench in the pit area.

She whispered in my ear. "I know you're thinking about your dad. It's OK. He's here with you today. He's proud and happy. So am I."

"Those difficult family memories never leave me. They're like ghosts haunting an old mansion," I said.

"Look at this. All these ladies gave me their phone numbers." Johnny interrupted us with a fist full of at least thirty individual slips of paper.

"Which one are you going to call?" Sara asked.

"Which one? I'm calling all of them!"

"All of them, Johnny? Isn't that a bit excessive?" For a moment I thought Sara sounded jealous. "You're an incorrigible adolescent," she said.

Johnny strutted around like he was cock of the walk.

The guys from Reliable Reconditioning helped push Mercury II up to the line. They used cotton cloths to do last-minute polishing of the beautiful aluminum skin. It gleamed in the bright sunlight. Larry was taking pictures of his logo.

Sara got a perfect picture of Johnny holding his helmet and waving one final time as he prepared to fit himself into the driver's seat. That was the photo that made the cover of *Hot Rod* magazine. Johnny placed his hand on the old Green Monster glovebox door and closed his eyes for a moment. "All set. Everything looks good." He gave me the thumbs-up signal as I finished checking the fuel gauge and pressure.

"Roger that! Everything looks good!"

It was very strange how silent the crowd became as the rocket began to hiss. Hundreds of cameras were ready. The Christmas tree began counting down to green, and the flag person began waving the start flag wildly above her head. Johnny turned the dome loader dial. The high-pitched hiss turned into a powerful rumble as the rocket fired up and kicked in. Barely five seconds later, Johnny was at the other end of the track. Everything had happened so fast that the awestruck crowd had failed to snap their pictures. Those who did manage to get a photo in time had only a blurry image. "Oh my god!" "Did you see that?" Many in attendance simply had their hands on their heads in total amazement, not believing what they had just seen with their own eyes. It was a sensory-overload experience. I had only shown a portion of the car's true capability, limited deliberately by the low fuel capacity. We had held thrust down to about 60 percent.

Johnny waved to the excited crowd while sitting straddled on the rocket's front section like a victorious cavalry officer on a great steed. His unlit cigarette dangled from his lips. We towed Mercury II back to the pit area, passing in front of the viewing stands.

"Ladies and gentlemen, you have just witnessed the world's unofficial fastest quarter run ever recorded. You have been an eyewitness to history!" Even the announcer seemed surprised by the rocket's speed and power.

The crowd went wild and stormed the track. Thousands wanted to shake Johnny's hand, get his autograph, and touch the rocket. Flashbulbs went off. Johnny was mobbed by the crowd, but he loved every minute of it.

"Let us through. Let us through!" Local television crews had to fight the crowd for an interview with Johnny.

"Johnny Rocket, how does it feel to be the world's fastest human?"

"Good. Real good!"

The Reliable Reconditioning guys were wondering if they could ever polish out all the fingerprints spoiling their beautiful aluminum skin.

"People will see this Mercury II once and never forget it. They will never forget the experience!" said a local celebrity sportscaster.

I expected the total salt flat speed record attempt to cost well over $1 million, all in. But word about our hydrogen speed and power was getting around, and it was nearly impossible to find anyone in the unlimited class Top Eliminator willing to race our tiny eight-hundred-pound hydrogen rocket. They all refused, and we couldn't win the championship if we couldn't find any willing competitors. "That's like stepping into the ring with Muhammad Ali. Do I look nuts?" Jet car drivers just did not want to look foolish and be embarrassed by our tiny homemade rocket racer. Who could blame them?

"Johnny, I received a call this morning from a race promotor in Ohio. He wants us to race the Shock Wave next month. We'll be paid ten thousand dollars for showing up and another twenty-five thousand dollars prize money if we win."

"If we win! Of course we'll win. That Shock Wave beast is the ugliest damn dragster I've ever seen. It's too fat, too ugly, and too slow. It looks like a damn eight-thousand-pound cyclops! We can beat it easy."

"Well, there's just one catch. The Shock Wave team wants a one-point-five-second handicap. That's nonnegotiable," I said.

"Are you kidding me? They want a head start! What a bunch of wimps! Just fill our hydrogen tanks completely, and we'll still win. They can shove that handicap. Anyway, that ugly bastard won't have a chance of winning nohow."

"Johnny, listen to me. I want to calculate our hydrogen fuel precisely so that we lose by fractions of a second. Mere thousandths of a second will make the ultimate difference when it comes to our Bonneville plans."

"What? Why would we lose deliberately?"

"The Shock Wave is not the fastest dragster. It's too awkward and heavy. We want to race the Lava Maniac! To be recognized as the best, we must beat the best. The Lava Maniac is currently unbeatable. But our plan is like a pool hall hustle. We have to first lure them in for the kill."

"I think we look like low-budget chumps towing the Mercury II on a rented trailer behind Larry's catering van all the way to Ohio! It smells like shrimp in here," Johnny said.

"That is exactly what we want. Appear weak when you are strong and strong when you are weak."

"That is Sun Tzu. *The Art of War*," Sara said with a smile.

"Sun who? All these rules, handicaps, and head starts are driving me nuts. I just want to win drag races and set a land speed record. That's all. I still think we look like a ragtag outfit," Johnny said.

We did splurge on nice uniforms. Sara designed white cotton coveralls with buttons down the front and Mercury II and a capital *H* for hydrogen embroidered on the front right-side pocket. They were a modern take on those worn by dealership mechanics in the 1950s. The white color was also symbolic—we were not grease monkeys. There were no oily rags in our pit area. Sara liked to wear the coveralls with her first few buttons undone. It was an incredibly sexy look. I told her so at every opportunity.

This Ohio event was bigger than any of us expected. Art Ainsworth had unkempt salt-and-pepper gray hair—think of Elbert Einstein. He was there wearing a gold VIP pit pass and introduced himself while firing off many questions. "I'm semi-retired from racing now, but I would not want to go up against this hydrogen thing. I know you guys are holding back. That's a good move." He spent a long time looking over Mercury II. "I love the Green Monster glove box door. Nice touch." I answered his questions about Dad's '47 Mercury. It's a very strange feeling to suddenly be on an equal footing with one's childhood hero. I asked him to sign the door. Dad would have loved that.

"When you get the chance to race the Lava Machine, my money is on you! By the way, you see that gentleman in the red shirt standing over there near the fuel depot?"

"Yes. I noticed him a while back. He's been there for a long time, watching everything. Is he a race official?" I asked.

"Well, not exactly. He's the arrogant owner of the Lava Maniac. I never liked him. He can go through an entire box of cigars in one day. He never smokes them, just gnaws them to death. That SOB will walk around here and fire people who don't even work for him. But I think he may be taking your bait! Beating the Lava Maniac will be a real coup de grace for this season," Mr. Ainsworth said with a slight grin.

Johnny did exactly as I asked. The crowd was disappointed with his loss, and he felt embarrassed. But our finish was calculated to entice the Lava Maniac into our web. We were not there to win a meaningless race against a weak, overrated competitor. I know the Lava Maniac team now believed they could take us. But they had no idea we were running only 60 percent of potential thrust!

"We lost today. The large handicap was just too difficult to overcome. Real competitors won't expect an unfair advantage going forward. The Mercury II anticipates winning a national title this year at Pomona California against the Lava Maniac." Sara organized a press conference after the race. I spoke to twenty-five eager race reporters rushing to get the facts. The story of our amazing hydrogen rocket car was captivating the nation.

"Jet Dragsters Run Scared of Hydrogen," Sara's next article, focused on the handicaps and unfair advantages demanded by obsolete jet dragsters. It never mentioned the fact that Mercury II had lost the race. The jet teams would have to swallow hard after reading that.

Most NHRA (National Hot Rod Association) events took place April through September. We planned to compete in twelve races, including big events in Gainesville, Florida; Charlotte; Atlanta; Bristol; and Dallas, Texas. The nationals would be held at the historic Auto Club drag strip in Pomona, California. Although it was a hectic schedule, we always had a week between races to rest and regroup, and the race calendar fit nicely with school schedules.

It was at the STP Performance Nationals in Indianapolis

where we were reminded of the risk inherent in this very dangerous sport. A young driver was competing in the first round of eliminations. Midway through his run, he suffered a tire blowout, causing his dragster to go out of control. Pieces of tire and rim acted like shrapnel, destroying much of the dragster's control surfaces. It tumbled end over end and flipped upside down. He was unconscious when rushed to the hospital, where he was pronounced dead.

Our rocket car didn't have to heat up massive rear slick tires, and we didn't do burnouts before each race. It occurred to me that in our case, heavy traditional slicks were a disadvantage and perhaps a safety risk as well. The added unnecessary tire weight created more friction and heat, putting additional strain on mechanical parts, including bearings and slowing our hydrogen rocket down. I went to the tire dealer the next day.

"I want two Firestone slicks just like we always buy." I also asked if he could shave off the unnecessary rubber.

"Why would you do that? Who buys new tires just to shave them down to nothing? People only do that with cheap recaps."

"It's an experiment, but if we did shave them, how thin could we actually go?" I asked the puzzled tire dealer.

"We would hit ply belts at a quarter of an inch thickness. But you would shave off nearly three quarters of an inch of useful thread."

"How much do you think all that shaved-off rubber would weigh?" "I would say at least twenty-five pounds for each tire." "Do it!" I said.

Everything was going exactly as I had hoped, except for the money aspects. We all learned so much. Johnny was becoming a great rocket racer and had more easy victories under his belt than a tomcat hunting rats and mice. Sara was the world's best PR person, and we refined Mercury II to perfection. Midway into the season, we were winning races and set up for a run at the championship in California, but our net gain was only $14,000. Travel costs, fuel, insurance, tires, taxes, testing, and NHRA fees all were significantly more than planned.

We talked about additional exhibition runs at smaller drag strips around the south. "What about showings at county fairs or airshows? That kind of thing," Johnny asked.

"I looked at all that. When we factor in the cost involved, we would be lucky to break even. But great idea."

The Reliable Reconditioning team suggested corporate backing to help cover costs. Larry suggested additional sponsorships.

"What about Johnny Rocket and Mercury II merchandise? Coffee cups and T-shirts. We can sell those things at the exhibitions and races."

We all agreed with Sara's idea.

"Corporate backing and additional sponsorships are another great idea but challenging to nail down. Everyone is afraid of another Hindenburg tragedy. They say hydrogen is unproven and dangerous."

"It might help if we set up some type of nonprofit organization promoting hydrogen fuel research, like a 501C3." Larry said that might make potential supporters more comfortable. I would talk to Mr. Portcous about that.

If we could land just one well-known sponsor, others would be sure to follow. "Sara, can you make professional-looking Union 76 Motor Sports and Northrop Aerospace stickers large enough to put on the rear body panels?"

She said it would be an easy task. Major sponsors were reluctant to affiliate with us because our hydrogen rocket concept was outside the mainstream. They were thinking about the Hindenburg and Bikini thermal nuclear tests, and if something went wrong, they didn't want their corporate names involved.

"These two companies have a lot of money. Why do you want to give them free advertising?" Johnny asked.

"True, Union 76 and Northrop are not giving us a penny. But when other sponsors see those names on the Mercury II, they'll line up and beg us to take their money. The more they beg, the more our price goes up."

# 28

"I have great news! You're not going to believe this!" Sara was excited beyond words. "What?"

"The *Times-Picayune* has offered me a job as a reporter on the sports beat. The position is mine as soon as I complete my degree. I'm the youngest reporter they've ever hired. Can you believe that?"

"Congratulations! I'm so proud of you! That's remarkable!"

"I have a great idea. Why don't we celebrate by spending the weekend in the French Quarter at a very exclusive hotel, browse expensive shops on Royal Street, and dine at Commander's Palace," Sara said.

"Sounds great. Pecan-crusted redfish, the famous bread pudding soufflé, and mimosas at Commander's. But can we afford it?"

"Not to worry! The paper gave me a five-thousand-dollar cash advance. I feel like a famous athlete signing with a professional team or something. Let's splurge on a great weekend."

We planned to check in late Friday afternoon and hang out in the French Quarter for a while, then continue to Tipitina's and listen to Allen Toussaint until the wee small hours of the morning. Mimosas at the Monteleone's famous Carousel Bar before going to our room would top off a wonderful day. We booked the Vieux Carre Suite, one of the Monteleone's best. Saturday was reserved for antique shops, art galleries, and seafood. Sara suggested a riverboat ride in the evening if we had time. We planned to save Commander's until Sunday brunch before heading home.

Tipitina's and Allen Toussaint was our favorite. We rubbed the shiny head of Professor Longhair's bronze bust for luck. Charmaine Neville made a surprise appearance onstage and sang about putting the right key in the wrong keyhole. "Do you think the 'key' she is singing about is a metaphor for something very sexual?" Sara asked with her hands on my shoulders.

"Do you think the keyhole she is singing about is a metaphor too?" "I certainly hope so," Sara said.

Instead of dancing we just rocked back and forth on the dance floor, rubbing hard against each other in a tight embrace. We both loved New Orleans music, and this was some of the best the city had to offer. It was so erotic! If a night at Tipitina's listening to this melodic music did not put you in the mood, then you must be dead. We were very much alive.

At this hour the Carousel Bar was closing. A young couple was finishing drinks and giggling about something known only to them. The bartenders wiped things down and put clean glasses away. They were happy to make the mimosas we both craved. We brought the drinks to our suite.

Sara excused herself for a moment. I enjoyed my drink and stared out of our fourth-story window watching the city's night life wind down. New Orleans was such a rough city, but so beautiful. Sounds from a nearby all-night jazz club drifted on the steamy night breeze. A cargo ship navigated the river's crescent bend and continued south. A few tourists here and there were struggling back to their hotels. A restaurant worker was heading home after a long shift. He waved to the prostitutes standing across the street. Closing up, a shop clerk dressed in jeans packed away inventory and pulled down metal security shutters. A couple of NOPD officers were talking on the corner under a streetlight that constantly flickered on and off. I turned and looked around the beautiful Vieux Carre suite with its marble-topped furniture, silk wallpaper, and thousand-count sheets. It occurred to me that members of my family would never have been in a room like this unless they worked for the hotel.

"I know how much you love this look." Sara emerged from the bathroom in her white Mercury II team coveralls already half undone down the front. She leaned against the suite wall and pulled me toward her. I had never seen anyone more beautiful than she was on this night. Breathing heavily with desire, I fiddled unsuccessfully with the other buttons. "Let me help you out." Sara undid her remaining few buttons and guided my hand below her belly button. She was wearing nothing underneath. The coveralls fell to the floor around her ankles. Against the wall like this was Sara's favorite sexual position. My heart raced.

"Is building a hydrogen rocket car any more exciting than this?" she asked while unbuckling my belt.

"No way. Not even close!"

I hoped no one was trying to sleep in the adjacent suites. We were carefree and very loud.

In the morning I rehung a painting that had somehow fallen off the wall during the night. Our breakfast plans at Café De Monde turned into a lunch of beignets and café au lait, as we were content to sleep the hours away. Another hotel guest in a nearby suite was walking down the hallway in our direction.

"Good morning, lovebirds. That was quite the ruckus going on last night," she said with raised eyebrows and an inquisitive grin.

Sara looked away bashfully. "It's not my fault. Mimosas make me crazy!"

The first Royal Street antique shop we visited was very high end with a remarkable collection of amazing things. A security guard sat at the front door and watched over everything carefully. There was a massive bed with sixteen golden stars on the headboard. "Do you have any idea who owned this bed?" the salesperson asked. "It was Louis the Sixteenth, king of France!" she said. The price was $25,000.

I pushed up and down on the mattress with the palms of my hands. "It would be kinda fun to fool around on King Louie's bed."

"I was just thinking the same thing!" Sara said.

I was pulled to the beauty of the amazing impressionist paintings lining the wall. "Do you see anything you like?" The salesperson was following us around like a hungry puppy. "The price doesn't matter. We can always work something out."

"This one is eighty-five thousand dollars!" Sara said.

"That is a remarkable value, and you can finance at an attractive rate! Besides, we offer a value appreciation guarantee! If at any time you decide to sell your masterpiece, we will buy it back with a seven percent guaranteed annual price appreciation. Or perhaps, over time, your tastes in art may change. You can exchange your painting for another with the same price appreciation guarantee. This is a great deal for anyone interested in building a valuable art collection for investment or just the joy of it."

"What is the actual finance rate you mentioned?" I asked.

"It depends on your good credit. Anywhere from ten to twenty percent annualized."

I was not a business major, but it didn't take an economist to figure out this con. If I paid 15 percent interest and subtract out the 7 percent appreciation guarantee, I would still be 8 percent in the hole. "We're just looking. Thanks anyway."

Sara was interested in the Newcomb pottery collection. "This all started out as part of the art curriculum at Newcomb College in the early twentieth century. Now it is priceless. The greens and blues. I love the colors. It's all so beautiful," she said. Next to the Newcomb pottery were three priceless Picasso pieces. They also had a few ancient Chinese pieces brought back after Nixon opened the door to China. In the next display case was a collection of unique and interesting pieces from a Georgia potter named Karen. "She's hottest new artist we've seen in years. Her work sells very fast. It's a great investment at a reasonable cost. Her values are sure to go up fast." The salesperson said Karen worked at a private studio in LaGrange.

Sara loved the magnolia-leaf bowls with incredible glaze work. "You have great art-investment instincts," the salesperson said. "How do I know these are original Karen works?"

"Well, Karen signs every piece. However, think of Rembrandt. Forgers have been trying to copy his work for centuries. But there will always be only one Rembrandt."

"I'll take this!" Sara picked out a beautiful and expensive blue vase.

A huge mahogany office desk caught my eye. "This thing is incredible. I love it. Who do you think owned a desk like this?"

Sara asked if I saw the price. "It's thirty-eight thousand

dollars," she said in a whisper. "How can an old wooden desk be worth that much money?"

"Have you read the write-up about it?" The salesperson handed me the catalog description.

"My god!" I rubbed my hands across the top and felt powerful just by touching it. I was speechless and nearly overcome with emotion. I felt a shortness of breath. "Was this really Henry Ford's personal desk?" I looked over the photos of him sitting behind it. His son Edsel was in one picture. Franklin Roosevelt and Herbert Hoover in others. William Durant, founder of General Motors, was in another. "Sara, just think! The Model T, the Model A, and the first V8 were discussed right here, over this desk! Henry Ford! He sat here! This was his desk!" There was an area on the right side that showed wear. "He probably liked to rest his hand here!" Overcome with emotion, I was embarrassed by the tears welling up in my eyes. I had always considered Ford to be America's greatest transportation pioneer. "Wish I had thirty-eight thousand dollars!"

I showed Sara a grainy photo of Ford with President Calvin Coolidge. She was much more skeptical than I was. "President Coolidge? True, this desk might have belonged to Henry Ford, but I've seen better photos of Bigfoot!"

"I see how meaningful the desk is to you. Every so often, items here have this kind of effect on people. I love your passion," the salesperson said, ignoring Sara's sarcasm.

In the window of Blanchard's Bric-a-Brac and Curio Shop was a vintage coffee mug from the Daytona Speedway in Florida. "Johnny would love that," Sara said.

I agreed, and we made the purchase.

Saturday night was quiet. We stayed at the hotel, had a few drinks, and then relaxed in the suite before falling asleep.

We both needed rest. The Monteleone provided a free chauffer service for their guests staying in suites. We reserved a Mercedes 600 sedan limo for the ride down Prytania Street to Washington Avenue and Commander's Palace. Sara looked beautiful. I was wearing a sports coat she had picked out. It fit perfectly. We looked prosperous dressed like this, and riding in a Mercedes limo was icing on the cake. Sunlight reflected off the perfectly polished hood. The driver kept a white cotton cloth handy to polish away any imperfections. A streetcar stopped and waited for us to clear the intersection. The riders pointed in our direction and probably wondered if someone famous was passing by.

"Welcome to Commander's." The doorman opened Sara's door and made sure she stepped onto the sidewalk safely. It was the same guy who had threatened to have me arrested when I stood across the street in the rain after dad's funeral.

"Did you give that doorman a twenty-dollar tip?" Sara asked with a puzzled expression. "Yes, I did! Yes, I did!"

"Sebastian, we're a few minutes early. Do you want to visit your dad's grave?" she asked.

I looked across Washington Avenue at the aboveground ancient tombs, many still in disrepair.

"You know. I don't think I do."

"Are you sure?"

"Yes, I'm sure. What I really want to do is enjoy this wonderful restaurant on this beautiful sunny morning. I want to order Mimosas and take a long time discussing the menu. Most of all, I want to share this experience with you."

We turned and walked inside.

# 29

*The United Nations Intergovernmental Panel on Climate Change released its first report. The conclusions formed the basis for the important Framework Convention naming human activity responsible for the greenhouse effect. They said the substantial increases of atmospheric concentrations of greenhouse gasses contribute to additional warming of the earth's surface.*

*Additionally, the UN determined that immediate reductions in emissions of over 60 percent would be necessary to stabilize concentrations at current levels. They said CO2 is responsible for most of the greenhouse effect reported in the data. Based on the newest models, the IPCC warned of dangerous temperature increases greater than that seen over the past ten thousand years.*

According to the Lava Maniac team owner, they were not concerned at all about Johnny's successful winning streak. "Johnny Rocket is a young, undisciplined ruffian with no class. He will soon fold under the pressures of competition and the temptations of his newfound fame."

We took Johnny to Rubinstein Brothers on Charters Street and had tailored suits custom made. Sara picked out silk ties and black leather wingtips. She was good at matching the ties with shirts and suit fabric. She knew the latest styles. She even picked out the perfect matching socks. I stood by and watched her work her magic. Johnny looked great.

Secret lovers always think they're fooling everybody, but when lovebirds get together, a certain something gives them away. Maybe it's a lover's glow or something like that. Maybe it's a casual display of familiarity that is slightly too playful. I'm not sure what it is exactly, but I know it when I see it. When Sara was trying to fit Johnny's perfect jacket, I saw it. It was gone in a flash, but I knew what I had seen. It left me with a terrible feeling in the pit of my stomach.

Johnny kept posing like a champion in a body-building competition. "I'll never find the right jacket if you can't stand still!" Sara said as she briefly tickled Johnny's sides with both hands.

It could have been my imagination, but I don't think so. Poets write about the "other side of the rainbow." No matter how beautiful things may seem, there is always another side. I decided to say nothing. Why ask questions you don't want answered?

Pictures of Johnny showing up for races while dressed in tailored suits appeared in papers around the country. Sara realized that the racing world loved controversy and thanked the Lava Maniac team for all the great PR opportunities. Her latest press release was titled "Johnny Rocket, Best-Dressed Man in Motorsports."

Larry came up with a new concept that involved rebranding his successful seafood restaurant. It seemed like a huge risk, but Larry had it all figured out. He asked Johnny to participate in the new venture. With investors already lined up, Larry planned to open a group of three new company-owned casual restaurants, with more to follow within a few years. The first three were planned for Atlanta, Miami, and Houston. The concept was totally new and intended to capitalize on Johnny Rocket's fame. The family restaurants would be decorated with an optimistic jet-age ambience and a menu themed on rockets and jets and a huge offering of rich desserts. They called it "Johnny's Supersonic Cafe." I think Larry pioneered the modern casual dining concept. Sara organized the PR.

I was worried about the distraction of all this with the national title and the Lava Maniac coming up, but for now Larry needed Johnny only for the Atlanta grand opening and a few photo shoots here and there. It was a three-day commitment. Thousands showed up at the Atlanta event eager to meet Johnny. He loved the attention and proved to be a great draw as he worked the crowd like a politician running for reelection. Children were given free ice cream. Commemorative caps and T-shirts were handed out.

Johnny personally greeted everyone. "Welcome to Johnny's Supersonic Cafe!" "Mr. Rocket! Can we get a photo?"

"Yes, of course." Johnny posed for pictures and signed hundreds of specially printed first-day menus as souvenirs.

Sara enjoyed Atlanta, and I decided my friends needed a break from racing. I looked forward to some quiet time making additional adjustments to Mercury II and figuring out a budget for Bonneville. As more restaurants opened, Larry promised the best five-star hotels, Pan Am travel, and paid expenses. He also promised to increase his financial support of the Bonneville speed record. "In a huge way!" he said.

Sara called me very late that night to share the news. "The opening was a success. It was perfect. We're going down to the hotel bar for a few Mimosas to celebrate."

"I knew it would be successful. Enjoy the evening. I'll see you soon."

When Sara said "we," I think she really meant just she and Johnny were going to the bar for drinks. Sara had no way of knowing that Larry had been fighting alcoholism his entire life and would not be caught dead in a hotel bar on a Saturday night. As a recovering alcoholic, he hadn't touched a drop in fifteen years. I tried not to be the jealous type, but an omission is a lie, just the same. It bothered me a great deal that Sara could not be honest.

The Bonneville budget looked hopeless, even assuming we beat the Lava Maniac and won a national title. I even added in another $150,000 from Johnny's Supersonic Cafes. "You can count on that much at a minimum," Larry said. The costs were unbelievable. Building and racing a land speed record car is like running a Formula 1 team. It is outrageously expensive. To make ends meet, we needed at least another $1.3 million from new sponsorships. That would cover everything, including materials, labor, travel, fuel, insurance, tires, and so on. I believed that to be an insurmountable financial mountain to climb.

"In a few weeks, everyone interested in drag racing will be at Pomona for the nationals. We'll be there anyway; why not set up a conference with prospective new sponsors? We could answer questions and announce our plans for a Bonneville land speed record attempt in a hydrogen rocket car! It'll be the perfect opportunity. Maybe we can generate more sponsor interest," Sara suggested.

She said, "We need to spend money to make money." She scheduled our event at the historic and expensive Chateau Marmont in Hollywood overlooking Sunset Boulevard. According to legend, Humphrey Bogart ate dinner there every week. F. Scott Fitzgerald had a heart attack in the lobby, and Greta Garbo had a favorite room. I noticed the oriental rugs were faded, and the velvet couches were showing wear, but the hotel was beautiful and historic. It was the perfect place for our record-breaking announcement.

The turnout was better than expected. Sara said everyone present was a potential large sponsor with the means and interest to support a Mercury III Bonneville speed record rocket. Our guests enjoyed the open bar and hors d'oeuvres. Johnny worked the crowd, taking care to talk with everyone individually. Most major auto manufacturers were represented, and oil companies and even some NASCAR team representatives were there. NASA and Lockheed Martin sent representatives. "I have read all the articles about this hydrogen rocket car. We are very interested to learn more," a woman from General Dynamics said. Her business card said she was a Senior Vice President for Design and Development. Johnny spent a lot of time with her.

"Thank you all for coming. I hope you enjoy this beautiful setting. Please help yourself to the bar." I was nervous but settled down and enjoyed giving my presentation. "Our immediate goal is to beat the Lava Maniac and win nationals. But the Mercury II is just a proof of concept. We plan to apply the lessons learned, scale up the rocket engine, and smash the current six hundred and thirty point forty-seven miles-per-hour record. We will claim the land speed title with a larger Mercury III. This new rocket will develop twenty-two thousand five hundred pounds of thrust! Jet cars have reached their limits. A new hydrogen age is about to begin."

I saw the engineers in the audience doing quick calculations. "That's right!" I said. "Fifty-eight thousand horsepower in a race car weighing less than a Chevy sedan."

Sara asked them to think about the worldwide press coverage of this remarkable record-setting event. "The exposure for sponsors will be priceless," she said.

I answered questions for the next forty-five minutes. A prosperous, well-dressed gentleman from the back asked for a few minutes of my time in private. We stepped into an adjacent room.

"I love new and innovative technology. I always have. My partner and I have multiple successful transportation-related businesses. But we are always looking for great new disruptive investment ideas We especially look for transportation-related, environmentally responsible advancements." He held out his hand in a friendly manner. "I'm Marty Finn. President and managing partner of D&M Motors Limited of Los Angeles. You said your hydrogen rocket can scale up easily and that beating the current land speed record of six hundred and thirty point forty-seven miles per hour should be easy. Right?"

"Yes. That is what I said. But 'easy' is a relative term."

"I understand. Six hundred and thirty is an ambitious goal. But what about seven hundred and sixty-seven miles per hour? Have you thought about seven hundred and sixty-seven?"

"Seven hundred and sixty-seven! You want to break the sound barrier? On land?" I asked, astonished.

"Historic limitations never last. But that's right, son. First you set the stage by beating the Lava Maniac. Next you smash the sound barrier in a hydrogen rocket race car. Do it within an eight-month window, and my associates and I will give you everything you need. You and the Mercury III will be more famous than Neil Armstrong."

"It's the tires. They must be thin and lightweight. But if we make them thin and light, then they can't take the stress at sound-barrier RPMs. At those speeds, tremendous internal forces bear down. It produces a type of rotational kinetic energy, adding weight and stress to the tires. Rubber just explodes. It may be an unsurmountable engineering problem. I don't believe capable tires exist."

"Not to worry. I've already talked with representatives from Goodyear. They're working on a Kevlar composite. The engineers are confident!"

Sara happened to step into the room. "Did you say your name is Marty Finn?" She kept up with the Hollywood gossip magazines. "Your partner is Danni? The famous singer from New Orleans?" she said on impulse.

"Yes. That's right."

Sara was thrilled. "I'm sorry to interrupt, but I would love to meet her."

"I'm sure we can arrange that. In fact, she'll be here in a few minutes," Mr. Finn said as he looked at his watch.

"What is your interest in land speed records?" I wondered.

"Nothing. Absolutely nothing."

"Nothing? I don't understand."

"I'm not interested in speed records at all. However, I am interested in saving the environment, and I am interested in hydrogen as a carbon-free fuel. I drove an experimental Mercedes hydrogen-fuel-cell car a few years back. It changed my way of thinking."

"You're talking about hydrogen fuel cells. Mercury II is a hydrogen rocket. They're very different things. I don't know much about cells."

"Don't you see? Hydrogen needs a watershed moment. When people think of hydrogen, two things come to mind. They think of bomb tests in the Pacific and the Hindenburg.

But breaking the sound barrier in a hydrogen rocket will become that watershed moment. It will change the way people see hydrogen. Think of nuclear power. It can destroy cities or kill cancer cells. People understand this trade-off. Hydrogen deserves the same reasonable consideration. People need help envisioning a future that doesn't exist yet."

"Why only eight months? That's not much time to build a rocket and break the sound barrier!"

"In the nineteen fifties, a fishing boat called *Lucky Dragon 5* was caught in the fallout from a hydrogen thermal nuclear test in the Pacific. Hollywood is filming a big-budget film now that will be released in eight months. It's already an Academy Award favorite. The film is even underwritten by the American Battery Electric Vehicle Association. We need to counter the antihydrogen propaganda the film will generate."

"Why not just continue to refine battery electric cars and support that?" I asked.

"They're interesting, but they're just a short-term bridge technology at best. In the early twentieth century, they competed head-to-head with internal combustions cars. They lost. We don't listen to music on the Victrola anymore. We don't watch Flashmatic TVs anymore, and we don't wash our shirts on a washboard. People are always free to be obsolete if they prefer. But we should not equate that decision with smart environmental stewardship." Mr. Finn paused for a moment and took a sip of his drink. He collected his thoughts and continued.

"I don't want to turn this conversation into a chemistry lecture, but battery electric cars are severely limited in worldwide transportation disruption capability. The batteries are a toxic mess of rare material and minerals found in remote and difficult places. Mining these minerals destroys the environment and introduces great political risk. Mining in politically unstable nations, transportation, scarcity, and war, we would dig ourselves out of the petroleum hole, only to fall into a much deeper quagmire. Twenty percent of the world's cobalt comes from the Congo. Some of the miners are young children. The battery car potential is clearly limited by the unfortunate economic, environmental, and humanitarian reality."

"You said 'young children.' How young?"

"In the Congo mines, it is not uncommon to see children as young as seven. Many are already suffering from chronic lung disease caused by the cobalt dust they breathe. We haven't even discussed poisonous chemicals used in the extraction process or deadly emissions produced in the refining of aluminum, manganese, graphite, nickel, and lithium carbonate. It's an upside-down world when children in Africa work slavishly in hellish conditions so rich people in California can drive battery electric cars and believe they're saving the environment."

"That's terrible. Can't they find cobalt somewhere else?"

"Yes, on the ocean floor. Companies are developing giant unmanned underwater tracked dredge machines that will remotely roam the ocean floor harvesting cobalt. They will destroy everything in their path, and the plumes of silt they churn up will kill everything else."

"I wonder how the environmentalists will feel about their batteries once we start strip-mining the oceans. People need to understand this," I said.

"You think the Middle East has been volatile? Wait till the cobalt wars start!" Marty said after a thoughtful pause. "That's the point we are trying to make. Every nation on earth has

access to hydrogen. When used in a fuel-cell electric automobile, the only thing emitted from the exhaust pipe is pure water! On one side of a watershed, water flows in one direction.
It flows in the opposite direction on the other." Mr. Finn put
his hands together in an upside-down V shape to help make
his point. "Every successful disruption always involves a bril-
liant individual with a great mind and a vision that manages to
break through conventional thinking. When your hydrogen
race car smashes the sound barrier, it will cause the greatest
watershed in environmental carbon-free thinking ever. It will
be a watershed moment, from Hindenburg thinking to em-
bracing the modern hydrogen economy. That will begin a true
sustainable environmental revolution. If you have any remaining doubts, look at the sun. It's basically a ball of hydrogen."

"So. How does D&M Motors make money on all this?"

"First, we want to put the Mercury III on display in our
flagship Los Angeles showroom. Years back, we displayed a
famous gullwing Mercedes Lemans winner. People lined up
around the block to see it. It became our most successful promotion ever. Also, our company has made multiple investments in hydrogen-fuel-cell development companies. Once
hydrogen fuel catches on, we stand to make multiple millions.
The environment wins, you and your team win, and we make
a reasonable return on our risk and investment. This is how
disruption is born. There is always entrepreneur opportunity
hiding in consumer dissatisfaction."

"No one is opposed to a return on investment," I said.

"One more thing. Hydrogen is derived from water. Then
the fuel cell converts it to electricity. The only exhaust generated is fresh and pure water. What if we develop an effective catalyst that could efficiently split that exhaust water to

produce hydrogen again and run it back through the cell, producing more electricity? Have we stumbled upon the energy Holy Grail? A true perpetual energy motion machine?"

"Physics has proven that to be impossible," I said respectfully.

"Maybe. But physicists used to laugh at the Wright brothers and their impossible flying machines too."

"Hello, sweetheart." Danni walked over and introduced herself to Sara first. She turned to me in a businesslike manner. "Can you do what we ask? Can you smash the sound barrier?"

"Yes. I have already done the engineering work, blueprints, plans, and research. With proper funding, and with capable tires, it's not a shoo-in, but yes, I think so. It is just a question of building it."

"Marty tells me it will take one point four million dollars. No problem, but first things first. Our agreement will be predicated on Mercury II beating the Lava Maniac for the national title. Then we go to Bonneville. But no national title means no money, and no money means no Bonneville. It's just business." Danni walked away with her heels clicking on the marble floor. She waved without looking back. A group of adoring fans and a gaggle of paparazzi with their 35mm Nikons waited outside.

"I'll be in touch." Marty shook my hand quickly, hugged Sara, and ran off to catch up. "It's been a pleasure."

# 30

"Sooooo? How do you think that went?" Sara asked me.

"Danni is all business. But after we win at Pomona, it seems we'll have our Bonneville sponsors."

"Is their company involved in racing? I know they sell a lot of Mercedes-Benz cars, but I didn't know they were interested in speed records."

"No. They don't promote any company-sponsored racing activities. But Mr. Finn does think hydrogen will save the environment."

"Save the environment? That's a tall order for rocket fuel," Sara said with the same skeptical expression I had seen when we discovered Henry Ford's desk hiding in a Royal Street antique shop.

"Mr. Finn says hydrogen is a key technology. He believes hydrogen could become a major part of the world's energy mix. He says it could help lower greenhouse gas emissions by twenty-five percent, and he has the money to back his commitments."

"By the way, I think I read somewhere that Danni was involved with that famous Chalmette Aluminum controversy back in the fifties," Sara said.

"Really? How could a glamorous movie star like Danni be

involved in scandal like that? And why would someone interested in carbon-free energy innovations support a plant that
devastated Louisiana's environment and poisoned workers?"

"Money? Maybe? Perhaps we should be a little cautious,"
Sara said.

"I guess I'll ask Mr. Porteous to review everything."

Johnny easily won all the early qualifying races at Pomona,
as did the Lava Maniac. It was late afternoon when Mercury II
pulled up to the prestage beam. The Lava Maniac's huge jet
engine thrilled the crowd with sound and fury, as Shakespeare
said, indicating nothing. Think of a blast furnace with the
door open—impressive heat and sound, but that's about it. A
six-foot-tall wooden fence behind the start line was blown over
by the jet exhaust as it pulled up to the burnout area. Johnny
was not there yet, but I wasn't worried. He was probably saying
last-minute goodbyes to a new girlfriend.

"That beast weighs more than a locomotive. It takes
a long time for it to spool up!" I said. The Reliable guys
agreed. A huge jet-air intake was directly above the driver.
It was not an air-streamed design. Our rocket car carried
the necessary oxygen in a tank without the need for drag-
inducing air scoops.

Johnny was only gone for a few minutes. "I think I could
beat that fat, ugly beast in Grandpa's mobility scooter." He
laughed at his own humor with his usual big cheesy grin. I
reminded him to be safe and pointed out the kill switch again
if anything went wrong. This would be the first time we ran
flat-out full power. We checked and double-checked all safety
procedures, making sure we hadn't missed anything. "This is
it, Johnny. It all comes down to this race." I turned the dome
dial to 100 percent.

"I love you like a brother. I won't let you down. Now let's go destroy this ugly Lava fucker." Johnny shut his visor and settled in.

The huge Lava Maniac pulled up alongside our tiny rocket. I know how David must have felt when he faced Goliath. The track's PA system began playing "She's So Heavy" from the Beatles' *Abbey Road* album. With an unlit cigar dangling from the corner of his mouth and three more in his shirt pocket, the Lava team owner gave me a cocky, angry sideways glance and nodded his head as if he expected to win easily. "Who instructed the track to play that song? That Johnny Rocket is a punk. Turn that damn 'Heavy' song off!"

Johnny was not with a new girlfriend. He had been in the announcer's booth arranging to torment the Lava Maniac one last time before the race. Fans were laughing. Heavy became the Maniac's new nickname, and it stuck.

The Lava team had no way to know that all their calculations were based on our throttled-back 60 percent power races. Now, with our little hydrogen rocket pushing 100 percent power, the Lava team was about to get an unpleasant surprise.

The Mercury II was at full thrust in less than three milliseconds. When Johnny crossed the finish, Lava Maniac was easily thirty yards behind and still not completely spooled up. The power delay was a jet car weakness we had planned to exploit from the beginning. Race fans ran onto the track and carried Johnny on their shoulders back to the pit area. He was treated like a college quarterback who had just won the Sugar Bowl.

"Thank you, everyone!" Johnny attempted to be heard over the adoring crowd. "I want to thank the Mercury II team and especially..." He gave up trying to speak and lifted the huge silver cup trophy high over his head. A reporter for *Motor Trend* magazine tried to push his way to the front like a kid at a Mardi Gras parade.

"Ladies and gentlemen, may I present our new national champion! The world's fastest dragster!" Rock music blasted from the track's PA system, cameras flashed, and dignitaries in suits shook hands with each other.

"That is impossible. Impossible!" the Lava Team owner repeated over and over as he paced back and forth in the pit area. His mechanics quietly packed away tools and equipment.

They loaded the defeated Lava Maniac unceremoniously onto a trailer. They pulled it too far forward, and the over-extended front wheels fell off the trailer. "What else can go wrong today?"

A reporter asked him for comment. "This race was more crooked than a snake with scoliosis!" he said as he spit cigar juice. "I trust the integrity of Chicago elections more than this!"

The angry team owner filed multiple lawsuits challenging his humiliating defeat. They were all thrown out in short order. Of course, the sore loser's legal shenanigans generated great nationwide interest. Sara capitalized with press interviews and appearances.

I received a telegram. "The weight of this moment is not lost on history. Steam replaced wind, diesel replaced steam, and jets replaced pistons. The time has come. Let us welcome in the hydrogen revolution. Congratulations on your convincing victory!" It was signed "Danni and Marty."

Celebrating his victory, Johnny spent a week living it up in Monaco while succumbing to his narcissistic conceits. As a guest of Gulf Racing, he was "officially" there for the grand prix. Now a wealthy celebrity, Johnny bought a dilapidated house across the street from our old high school. "I'm going to tear it down and build a massive mansion right here." The old neighborhood was in a constant state of irreversible decline.

Johnny was making a lot of money, and I expected him to buy a home on the lakefront with all the other "new rich." "Is the old neighborhood the best area for your investment? Have you looked at Lake Vista?" I asked.

"I want to build right here on this spot. That school counselor still works here, driving the same old car, wearing the same cheap Timex watch, and married to the same old woman. He parks in the same spot every day. In the morning I want him to see my mansion. In the evening, I want him to see my mansion. I want him to start and finish his day thinking of Johnny Rocket! I want that bastard to eat his words!"

I was eager to check on the Mercury II and begin working on design drawings for the Mercury III. Eight months was not a lot of time. "Dat gift was delivered a few days ago for you." All the guys at Reliable were happy to see me and seemed eager and excited about something. "I have never seen a delivery crew like dat. They wore white cotton gloves and green jackets. Even da truck's cargo area was air-conditioned. A supervisor showed up after and checked for even da smallest scratches. He polished it like it was a priceless Duesenberg."

"What are you talking about?" I asked.

"You don't know?"

We walked back to the Nutria Works, pushed the sliding doors open, and turned on the lights. The Mercury II was covered with a white cotton cloth and sat in the middle of the build area, where it should be. The tools and equipment were exactly where they should be. My plans and prints were filed away in an old file cabinet. But my green metal US government surplus desk and matching ugly vinyl chair were gone. In their place sat an enormous mahogany desk. I recognized it immediately and approached it slowly while struggling to maintain my composure. I took a deep breath. "Mr. Henry Ford!"

On top of Ford's desk was a sealed envelope with my name handwritten in blue ink. The envelope was made of expensive white linen paper and conveyed an image of prestigious identity.

"Thought you would love to have this. The provenance is beyond question." The note was unsigned.

"Is dis really Henry Ford's desk?" Most of the Reliable guys were in a complete state of awe. "Henry Ford?"

"Yes, this is Henry Ford's desk! Do you know who sent it?" I asked.

"No, we don't. But a woman stopped by to make sure da delivery was satisfactory. She didn't give her name. Thought dat was odd."

"What was she driving?" I asked.

"It looked like a very fancy green Land Rover. Is she family?"

"No, I have never met her. But I often wonder. Do you believe in angels?" Seeing Henry Ford's desk was icing on the cake for my friends at Reliable Reconditioning. Good things had been happening. They loved displaying our national championship trophy in the front office. I thought the shop was the perfect place for it. Engineers from NASA had visited the shop three times in the last few weeks. "They said they were having problems machining certain parts with compound angles for dat new space shuttle rocket motor. Ain't no problem for us. We made dem with no trouble." After testing the Reliable parts, NASA returned with a sole-source contract offer. Sole-source agreements are generally noncompetitive and can be very lucrative.

"Did you negotiate a profitable agreement?" I asked.

"We certainly did, but we didn't negotiate much over money, if dat's what you mean. Everything seemed acceptable in dat regard. But it is rewarding for us nevertheless."

"If it's rewarding, what did you hold out for?"

"We insisted on finally getting dat official visit to da Lockheed Martin Skunk Works. You know, da one we were promised when pistons and propellers were still considered important. They are flying us out dare on a government C-130 Hercules!"

"You held out for a trip? What else did you get?" I was puzzled.

"Respect! Reliable Reconditioning is respected again! Dat's worth more than anything."

# 31

" **P**lease sit down, Sebastian." Mr. Porteous had reviewed the contract offer made by D&M Motors Limited and invited me into his conference room. I took a seat and watched as he read over it one more time. He leaned forward with his glasses resting on the tip of his nose. "It is a very generous document," he said. "Your successful performance is not required to fulfill the terms, only your best efforts. The contract is worth one point four million dollars, paid in monthly installments as Mercury III development continues. The sound barrier must be broken in eight months or less. Otherwise, the contract is void."

"Will I owe D&M any money back if we fail?"

"No. They view this as an investment. They understand and assume the financial risk. Your obligation is to report every month on progress done. If the car is a failure, then you owe nothing, and the agreement is over with no further obligation or commitments by either party. If you are successful in the eight-month window, then you will own the car, but D&M Motors owns exclusive trademark rights, advertising rights, and promotional rights for a seven-year time period. If you break the sound barrier but fail to do so in eight months, then they take procession of the Mercury III and own all marketing rights indefinitely."

"Should I sign?"

"Yes. The agreement is clear and straightforward with no legal doublespeak. Just remember, that eight-month requirement is airtight. You have eight months from the day you sign and not a day more." Mr. Porteous handed me his Montblanc. "The clock starts ticking today."

Major challenges lay ahead—designing the propulsion systems, assembling the propulsion components, installing everything, working out the final design of the Mercury III's aerodynamic structure, and aluminum fabrication. Additionally, the Bonneville record attempts would require various support vehicles, including a trailer designed specifically for the Mercury III, a hydrogen refueling truck, and the air compressor trailer. These had to be designed and custom built.

We moved the Mercury II to Larry's new restaurant, where it was put on display in the entrance. I figured this was much better than keeping it hidden away under a cover in a corner of the Nutria Works where no one would ever see it. Larry offered to cover the cost of the support vehicles.

Everything for the Mercury III was engineered around a twenty-eight-inch-diameter Firestone tire like those used by previous land speed record holders. The tire size was an important factor in designing the cross-section area of the fuselage, drag coefficient calculations, rocket power requirements, and fuel capacity. It was calculated into the design and engineering work already completed.

Mr. Finn called early on a Tuesday morning. "We have great news. I just received a call from Goodyear! The Kevlar sound-barrier tire is ready! They tell me it's capable of one thousand miles per hour! Their tests confirm that Kevlar holds together under incredible pressure, and the larger diameter reduces the centrifugal forces that have destroyed other tires. Goodyear test results are conclusive."

"Sounds great, but what did you say about tire size?"

"Sure, the Goodyear engineers went from the standard twenty-eight-inch tire to a thirty-five-inch diameter design. They said it's the only way to make the sound barrier run safe. They see no other options."

"We can't just change tire size like that. This isn't a Dodge or Chevy sedan."

Mr. Finn promised to have the Goodyear engineers send four tires to Reliable for our design testing and adaptations. "If you need anything else please call."

The 25 percent increase in tire and rim size grew the car design geometrically in all directions. Everything changed, including my cost calculations. First, adjustments to the steering had to be calculated. It only had a degree steering, enough to keep it going straight. Moreover, the original design had faired rear wheels mounted outboard on streamlined beams resembling airplane wings. All that was discarded in favor of open struts without the fairings. Every change affects something else. It is a series of trade-offs and compromises. Without the streamlined wings, lift became a problem, although the rear fin was retained to help keep the car straight with the limited steering. At these speeds it was always a major concern that the car would lift off and crash back down. The wider stance required a redesigned nose to reduce drag, and the new ogival shape helped alleviate pressure buildup if shock waves bounced off the ground at supersonic speed.

The changes added to the car's length. With the new nose design, tail fin, motor, larger fuel tanks, and the driver's seat,

the car became an ogive-shaped thirty-five-foot-long cylinder.
Everything had to change, and that involved lots of new aluminum welds. Aluminum welding requires an extremely sophisticated skill set, but the Reliable guys had that covered.
More time, more money, and additional engineering work
was involved.

Sometimes engineering trade-offs offer advantages.
Mercury III's longer body and redesigned nose now allowed
for a new front-wheel concept I had been thinking about.
Bonneville official rules defined all cars as having four wheels.
Anything less and the racer is classified as a motorcycle, with
totally different rules and design requirements. The rule book
said nothing about the position of the car's front wheels. I
redesigned them together, tucked under the nose, completely
out of the wind. Think of a giant tricycle. The aerodynamics
changed completely as the Mercury III went through the wind
faster than a sailor on shore leave spending his pay.

"A small weekly publication from the Mississippi Gulf Coast
asked for an interview. They want a few quotes and photos.
The whole thing should take thirty minutes tops," Sara said.

"Sure, no problem." I was happy to agree to the unusual request. Usually it was Johnny doing the interviews. This worked
like a football team. The quarterback gets all the attention.
He does the aftershave, car, and credit-card commercials. The
quarterback gets photographed at swanky high-society events
with fashion models from *Vogue* on his arm. No one cares
much about the offensive weak-side tackle. In this case, I was
treated like the unknown lineman. I also knew quarterbacks
couldn't win games by themselves.

"Tell us how a hydrogen rocket motor works. How fast will
this car go? How long is it? Is hydrogen safe?"

"You drive around town every day with sixteen gallons of highly explosive gasoline. Hydrogen is actually safer."

I took my time and answered all their questions completely in concise layman's terms. The reporter took careful notes on a yellow legal pad, and the photographer took a few photos. The interview went well, and I got back to work. The article appeared in print two weeks later. In the cover photo, I was leaning against the chassis frame with a clipboard and cup of coffee. I loved it. Except they got one thing wrong. The caption identified me as Johnny Rocket!

# 32

Regretfully, I intended to inform UNO of my plans to drop out for a year and return to finish my degree later. It was not possible to handle everything currently on my plate. I did not have many classes left to take, but it was just an unreasonable allocation of limited time to continue at this point.

The dean was not surprised. "We've been expecting this conversation. In fact, the chancellor and I discussed your situation recently. You nearly have enough credits to graduate now. Those you are lacking can be covered under the category of 'life experience.' With your list of remarkable accomplishments, no one can argue against it. You will have to finish the current classes you're enrolled in. We can handle the rest. How does that sound?"

"I can do that. No problem."

"There's one more thing I would like to ask," he said.

"What is it?"

"The chancellor and I would consider it an honor if you would agree to deliver the school's commencement address. The faculty and staff are also in agreement. After your address, the chancellor will present you with an honorary doctor of engineering degree."

"I'm honored. I don't know what to say. But I'm not much

of a public speaker. I get very nervous. I want you to understand that. Don't expect great oratory."

"We don't want a fancy speaker. We want you just exactly as you are. The student body will relate to your story."

The dean asked how many seats they should reserve at the graduation for my family and friends.

"Three to five, perhaps?"

"Three to five rows?" he asked.

"No. Just three seats or so. Sara, Johnny, and Larry, and maybe a couple of guys from Reliable. That's about it."

The UNO engineering building was always clean with perfectly polished floors. The reflection off the florescent lights was like mirrors, making the walk between classrooms seem longer than a football field. Final grades were posted outside the dean's office and listed by student number. I still remember my old number, 1667548. Walking slowly toward the postings, I supported my weight by leaning against the doorjamb with my left arm. I scrolled down the list with the index finger of my unsteady right hand. The grades were listed in no specific order, and the ink was smeared from other students doing the exact same thing I was doing.

Finding my number on the left side of the sheet, I moved my finger across to the next column on the right and closed my eyes.

I had done it! I was really going to be a college graduate! The feeling was overwhelming. I double-checked to make sure I had read my grades correctly. I leaned back against the wall and slid down to the floor. Resting my head on my knees, I stayed still for a long time. The honorary doctorate degree was a wonderful honor, and now, with the engineering degree, I had reached a successful climax to a struggle for academic achievement that had plagued my family for generations. My thoughts turned to Dad hiding under blankets late at night with a flashlight reading his hidden books and filling out college admissions applications in secret that he never intended to submit.

I asked the dean for one favor. "Can we play Pachelbel's canon in D major at the commencement? That was my dad's favorite music. He always loved hearing it." I think Dad's death at such a young age gave me a sense of urgency regarding the things I wanted to accomplish. It motivated me but also drove home the realization of the unpredictable, temporary nature of everything.

The UNO photographer was there to record the ceremony. I treasure the black-and-white photos with the university chancellor and the dean. Mostly, I was nervous about the speech and worried about my cap's tassel. Should it hang on the right or left side? All the academic dignitaries wore it on the left; others I saw wore it hanging on the right. I could not establish any rhyme or reason and decided to keep it on the left since faculty and staff had it that way. *They should know,* I reasoned.

I did not realize that if someone already had a degree, the tassel was worn on the left, while undergrads wore their tassel on the right. Once the degrees were conferred, it was then moved to the left. My tassel was in the wrong position. The degree candidates began their procession into the auditorium first. They were excited and happy. I was nervous as hell about the speech. I lined up behind the university chaplain and in front of the chancellor.

I saw Sara, Johnny, and Larry first. Sara was crying. She kissed her hand and touched it to my cheek. She was fighting to hold back more tears. "I'm so happy for you."

Larry moved my tassel to the correct position. "Knucklehead," he said with both hands on my shoulders.

Johnny gave me a giant bear hug. "You done good, college boy. Real good!"

Once the graduates were seated, the faculty, staff, chaplain, chancellor, and I entered. The school quartet began playing Pachelbel's canon. We walked down the center aisle and then turned to the left toward the four steps that led onto the stage. That placed us directly in front of the reserved seating area. Seated behind Larry, Sara, and Johnny were the guys from Reliable. They had brought their wives, children, and grandchildren. All were dressed in their best clothes. It must have been nearly forty people in all. I felt like a celebrity on the red carpet. They clapped and cheered. The wives were crying. Some of the men were crying. They even made a small, tasteful banner: "RESPECT—Thank you."

The chaplain finished his invocation and stepped away from the podium. The chancellor introduced me as the youngest person to ever receive an honorary degree from the university. I took a deep breath and closed my eyes for a moment. At least I wasn't trembling now. I began talking slowly by discussing challenges, hardships, disappointments, the importance of taking calculated risks, and overcoming fear. The lights were hot and distracting. "It is very tempting to take the easy road. Don't do it. My greatest fear is to become a bitter old man sitting in a rocking chair and wondering about the countless things I should have done differently. Bitterness and regret will eat you alive! I don't want to be like Prince Charles, spending life waiting for something that may never happen."

My eyes began to adjust to the harsh lights, and my nerves settled down somewhat. I told the story of the man who gets to the gates of heaven and asks Saint Peter who was the greatest general of all time. Saint Peter points to a quiet individual off in the distance. "That man? I know him from my village. He was not a general at all. In fact, he was only a cobbler with a small shop!" Saint Peter then says, "Yes, that is true. He was a cobbler. But he would have been history's greatest general, if he had been a general."

I talked more about taking risks. "Jackie Cochran was born into poverty, but she became the first woman pilot to break the sound barrier. She was told that women don't do things like that. 'Stay in the kitchen, honey!' She was told that the F-86 Sabrejet was not capable. Excuses, excuses. The air force commanders forbid it. 'Suicidal,' they told her. On May 18, 1953, Jackie flew to thirty-five thousand feet and then, disobeying orders, pointed the F-85 nose directly at the ground and jammed the throttle forward. At seven hundred and sixty-nine miles per hour, she entered the history books."

I changed subjects. "Have any of you ever been crabbing off the seawall?" I asked. "When blue crabs are placed in a bushel basket, they all fight and climb up trying to escape. But if one is about to make it to freedom, the others gang up and pull him back in. Blue crabs keep themselves trapped. Life can be full of people like blue crabs. Stay away from them," I suggested.

In conclusion I talked about something I had learned from the guys at Reliable. "Make sure you know what is most important. Chasing meaningless empty ambition leads nowhere. Dollars are important. But the respect of family and community is earned, never bought.

"Don't worry about reasonable risks, blue-crab people, or failure," I said. "Worry about opportunity you miss if you don't even try. Do those things others only dream of!"

# 33

Johnny was often invited to ride in pace cars as the guest of honor at many NASCAR events. He drove the Indy 500 pace car on the opening lap and announced "Gentlemen, start your engines" at a Formula 1 race in Belgium. I know he was frustrated driving the Indy pace car, since it only went about half the speed of the actual race cars, but Johnny did say running the famous track was a cherished experience. "I love the smells and sounds of this place. The exit out of turn three is crazy scary! All you see in front of you is the opposite wall! Most of all, I loved driving over the yard of original bricks at the finish."

Johnny was also doing personal appearances at state fairs and car shows, where he signed autographs and posed for photos. Promotors loved him because of the large crowds he could draw, and Sara sometimes traveled with him to make sure the PR was handled correctly. A dragway in Illinois sponsored a huge jet dragster exhibition. It was the first time four jet-engine dragsters had raced at the same time, side by side. Johnny waved the flag to start the race. The crowd went wild when the announcer said, "Starting our race today is our new world champion, hydrogen innovator, master of speed—Johnnnnny Roooooooocket!"

The Pollution Punisher was never intended to win real races. It was the only jet dragster ever designed with two seats. The engine sat in the middle, with the seats just below the massive air intake. It was the Cyclops on steroids. Built for promotional purposes, the passenger seat was reserved for politicians, VIPs, or thrill seekers willing to pay $1,100 for a five-second ride. Not a true dragster, it was more like professional wrestling—exciting to watch but staged.

Ten thousand fans showed up for an antique and historic racing event in Tampa. Held at an abandoned airfield, the historic races sponsored by the Sportscar Racing Vintage Organization (SRVO) went on all day. Triumph, MG, Maserati, Lotus, and Ferrari were all well represented. The vintage racing events were considered an amateur sport where the thrill of seeing vintage racers on the track outweighed the desire to win. The day's vintage events concluded with the Pollution Punisher and Johnny Rocket doing an exhibition run. Johnny waved to the crowd, strapped his helmet tight, and climbed into the passenger seat that was situated inches above the front wheels. "I'm excited to see what this dinosaur can do," Johnny said to the driver on the other side, a young man he had never met. Johnny expressed no concern.

"You are in for quite a treat, Mr. Rocket. Hold tight."

The Christmas tree counted down. Johnny waved and smiled. The jet engine ignited with an orange exhaust flame and thunderous roar.

As I said before, I never like getting unexpected calls at unusual times. They don't bring good news. This one was from Sara.

"He's dead! He's dead! Johnny's dead!" She was crying uncontrollably.

Midway into the quarter-mile run, the Pollution Punisher's right front tire suffered a blowout. The aluminum rim disintegrated, spraying jagged broken pieces like shrapnel through the thin fiberglass body. The suspension collapsed, causing the car to swerve right and then hard left and back again. It tumbled end over end five times before pencil rolling another two hundred yards, finally coming to rest in a field at the end of the old runway. Then the fire started. Johnny was probably dead long before that.

He had a closed-casket funeral.

When the blowout occurred, the young driver was paralyzed by fear. Investigators said Johnny reached across the out-of-control car and pulled the steering wheel hard right. This might have caused it to tumble out of control. It also caused it to avoid the crowded viewing stands, saving many lives.

Johnny's old high school counselor authored a touching tribute. It was printed in the *Times-Picayune*.

Johnny was one of the few people able to live life on their own terms. He chased dreams with a passion seldom seen, especially so with his youthful, abandoned sense of urgency. The mansion he built near the old school inspires hope in a dying neighborhood. Every day, I park in the same spot, as I have done for decades, but Johnny's success has become a beacon of new hope and inspiration. I love seeing his mansion every morning and every evening. Sometimes I stay in my tired old car a few extra minutes and admire Johnny's success. It means that life does not need to be stagnant, that difficult odds and challenging circumstances can be overcome. I don't know why he decided to build his home here, but I am happy he did. When freshmen students see it, they say, "That's Johnny Rocket's house. He lives in our neighborhood." That is a powerful message.

I was tough on Johnny because I knew no other way to reach him. Johnny was never meant for a college classroom, and I said so. He hated me for it, and perhaps I should have been more diplomatic. But I like to think Johnny's passion was partly a result of his determination to prove me wrong. Johnny is a role model for kids growing up in poor neighbors and tired old high school guidance counselors still hoping to change lives. Although he had no formal education, Johnny taught us all. Rest in peace, Johnny Rocket.

Easygoing and carefree, Johnny had no fear of death and thought he could avoid it forever. He believed that acknowledging risk would end his racing career. No one was surprised to see Johnny had done nothing to prepare his financial affairs. He had no will or financial adviser. In fact, he still had not filed his tax returns from last year. Johnny's bookkeeper tried to reach him fourteen times before giving up. The estate was tied up in legal knots for years. However, Johnny did leave money to support industrial arts classes at the old high school, and he owned a single premium term life policy paid in full. Sara was named primary beneficiary.

"I loved Johnny." Sara placed her hands on my shoulders and looked apologetic. "I know. We all loved him," I said. "No need for apologies."

"I want time to think. Everything has happened too fast. I'm going out west for a while. Utah, Colorado, or

Wyoming...I'm not sure exactly where. I'll come back soon."
She told me that I was a great guy.

"You don't have to leave. You know, I want to work this out."

"I don't know what I want. The friendship you and I have is special, but no one can ever love me the way Johnny did. I need to sort things out. It's something I must do on my own. But I will come back. I promise," Sara said.

"I'll be here." I believed the lies because I wanted to, not because I had to. But the realization still cut deep. I wasn't surprised that Sara loved Johnny. I already suspected that. I was deeply saddened by the fact that she never loved me.

She left with only her car, clothes, and the money from Johnny's life insurance. I found Karen's pottery on my kitchen table with a short note. "Promise to remember our wonderful French Quarter weekend. If you never forget it, you won't struggle to understand why I must leave. Sara."

Sara said she would keep in touch, but I knew that was just a lie. I know how these things go. Why does everyone looking to find something go west? No one ever tries to find themselves by heading east to Hoboken, New Jersey, or something. I hate the west!

# 34

"Mr. Ainsworth, I need someone experienced at Bonneville to drive the Mercury III. Can we talk?"

"Of course. Sorry to hear about Johnny. He was a gifted driver. But I'm available anytime. In fact, I planned on taking a week off to visit the Glenn Miller festival in Clarinda. Why don't you come up and join me? I'll show you around up here."

Clarinda, Iowa, is famous as Glenn Miller's hometown. There is a Glenn Miller museum and annual festival. It is also the birthplace of 4-H, and Johnny Carson grew up just down the road. Clarinda's historic Carnegie Library building is now an important modern art museum, and the county courthouse has been restored to its original 1890s magnificence. The tiny house where Glen Miller was born is restored and open to the public.

"You'll love the Midwest. After the festival I'll take you to my shop just up the road. The original Green Monster is stored in a shed on the property. I'll love to give you the tour."

The first available flight from New Orleans put me in Kansas City, Missouri, the next day. It was a two-hour drive from the airport to Clarinda. Plowed fields lined the road on both sides. "I want to take you to one of the best restaurants in the Midwest,"

Art said as we headed to Iowa in his International Scout pickup truck. He still had his unkept salt-and-pepper gray hair. We pulled up to a Casey's gas station, convenience store, hunting supplies, and restaurant. "Aren't you getting out?" he asked.

"Here? Is this where we're eating? Isn't this a gas station?" "Just trust me. I hope you brought your appetite," he said.

Mr. Ainsworth was right. Casey's did have the best chicken and pizza in the entire Midwest. Probably two dozen people came in and out within fifteen minutes after the lunch counter opened. They also served cafeteria buffet-style lunch, and that line extended to the back door. Today's special was bacon-wrapped meat loaf with whole-kernel corn and mashed potatoes with beef gravy. "Take a seat. I'll order for you."

Everyone was dressed in heavy-duty Carhartt work clothes, I'm guessing agricultural. They were friendly and loved talking politics when not discussing crops and land prices. "Corn looks good. Prices are better than last year. Let's hope the feds don't screw it all up." Mr. Ainsworth filled my plate with a taste of everything available. "I know New Orleans is famous for those cute hoity-toity French restaurants. But I promise you this: no one ever leaves Casey's hungry. That's a guarantee."

The chicken was as good as any I ever had down south. The corn was sweet with a mountain of melting butter, and the meat loaf was remarkable. I ate like Henry the Eighth and probably gained ten pounds. I think I felt so comfortable and at home because the people were hardworking, honest hometown folks, just like my blue-collar friends and family in New Orleans. The guys with the Reliable team would love Casey's.

"If you like this, wait until tomorrow. We're having dinner at Bruner's on the town square. The steaks are so big they serve them on twenty-inch platters instead of plates."

We watched the nation's best high school marching bands parade around the courthouse square competing for the Glenn Miller Festival championship trophy. The friendly locals treated me like family, offering me hotdogs, sausage sandwiches, grilled corn on the cobb, and fried pork chops on a stick. Those were made famous at the Iowa State Fair. We drank Iowa wineshine. It was local wine fortified with brandy and the only forty-proof wine I have ever seen.

I was announced as a visiting guest to the area and friend of Mr. Ainsworth. We shared a picnic table with a proud sixth-generation Iowa farming family. "They grow the best corn around, and they have hundreds of heads of cattle. Each one of them cows is well taken care of," Art assured me. "They are also developing a new process to turn corn into fuel. They call it ethanol, and they say it could be great for Iowa's economy and the environment."

"That sounds very interesting."

The oldest daughter, Harper, was a grad student at Iowa State studying agriculture science. We talked about everything and felt like we had known each other for years. "You have a wonderful accent. It's so seductive. Where are you from?" she asked again.

"New OR-linz."

"I'd love to read about New Orleans. It seems like a magical city, and I love the way you say it."

The bands played more Glen Miller hits, and the festival's lucky drawing winners were announced between songs. After the music competition ended, the next highlight of the festival was the naming of the Ms. Clarinda Community Award. Harper won, in recognition of her efforts to develop a computer-assisted corn-planting program. I knew very little about computers. My high school had one, but it was only for the smart kids. I had peeked at it occasionally through a small window in a locked door.

I admired Harper's intellect and beauty. She walked off the stage, clicked the heels of her Ariat farm boots, swung around, and reached for my hand. Still not much of a dancer, I did the best I could. We danced again and again. "I know a quiet place where we can go," Harper said, smiling suggestively. Later in the evening, after sundown, we planned to sneak off together, walking along a path toward the city park and recreation center.

The path was lined with birch, elm, and ancient hickory trees. Harper pointed to a beautiful Kentucky coffee tree. Its muscular branches reached skyward, then arched back toward the ground. They formed a crisscross latticework perfect for climbing. "Kids say this is the best tree in the entire county. I agree. I think I climbed it every day during many long Clarinda summers growing up here."

The coffee tree stood strong and determined, inviting and nonjudgmental. Harper stopped and turned to me. Moonlight was beginning to penetrate through the branches as we pulled each other close. Sheltered under the tree's protective embrace, we talked liked old friends, watched the hours drift away, and loved each other. Harper offered weak defense.

"When will you get back to Iowa? Soon?"

This concept of true love is a superstitious myth. Think of an inflatable mattress. It seems comfortable, but there is nothing there. In the end, I know these things turn out the same. Someone always leaves. So why bother when the result will remain the same? My parents were married for years, but in other ways, they were already apart. Sara and I were never really together. I thought we were, but I was wrong.

"Sebastian, please promise to remember me and remember this night forever," Harper said as she wrote her number on a Casey's napkin. I do treasure those memories with her, and when things turn difficult, they provide comfort from life's storms. Those memories take my mind to a better place. Then I smile.

It occurred to me that I would essentially head east, then south to get back home. Not east all the way to Hoboken, New Jersey, but east nonetheless. I wonder if Harper will keep her promise and remember me. I think that's all anyone can ever ask for.

"Are you ready to see my baby?" Mr. Ainsworth asked early the next morning.

That was what I had been waiting for. But I was surprised to see the original Green Monster up close. Much of it seemed hand fabricated and pieced together in a homebuilt haphazard fashion. The frame was a massively overbuilt steel box and not the well-sorted chrome-moly tubes I had expected. "I salvaged that from an abandoned farm combine left in a field. I paid the scrap dealer twenty dollars for the whole thing and stripped it down. That John Deere frame is strong as an ox. I was once a farm equipment repairman. I don't know much about torque, stress, twisting, or rotational forces. But I do know how John Deere builds combines. That J-79 jet engine was salvage too. A repairman left a bolt that was ingested into the engine. I bought it for scrap value and just cut out the damaged blades and their counterparts to maintain balance. It worked fine," Art said. The Green Monster's body seemed to be held together with sheet metal screws, and the fuel tank was lifted from an old Mack truck. This famous Green Monster world record holder had started life as a John Deere farm combine. Who knew? I was even more impressed now. Mr. Ainsworth had broken multiple land speed records and hit 576 mph in this!

I was fascinated by this haphazard homebuilt champion jet car. Especially interesting was the unique suspension design compensating for the immense weight of the jet engine. When I turned back around, Mr. Ainsworth was hanging by his fingertips from the door sill. His knees were bent, and he was swinging gently back and forth. "Mountain climbers do this all the time. I hang by my fingers two hours every day. It builds up strength, agility, and reflex speed in my arms all the way to my fingertips. Great training technique for race car drivers," he said.

I did think it was odd to see Art hanging from the ceiling like a bat, but anyone willing to drive a John Deere farm combine at six hundred miles per hour is going to be a little odd. Art hopped down from the door frame and leaned against the dusty Green Monster. "So, you're looking for a Mercury III driver to break the old six hundred and thirty mile-per-hour record in your hydrogen rocket. Is that right? And what about this short timeline?" he asked.

"The eight-month timeline is not a problem. I had the plans, drawings, and engineering work all completed months ago. The Reliable guys don't need me babysitting them. They're more efficient than a Formula 1 pit crew and are already way ahead of schedule. As for breaking the old six hundred and thirty mile-per-hour record, that is not the goal."

"I don't understand, then. What is the goal?"

"The target is not just some run-of-the-mill race-car speed record. I want a driver willing to go seven hundred and sixty-seven miles per hour. The goal is not just a new trophy on the shelf. The goal is to make history!"

"You want to break the sound barrier? That is crazy insane and maybe impossible! Your hydrogen rocket is unproven at this level. Your technology is new. You completely redesigned everything to accommodate larger tires, and you want me to climb in and break the sound barrier? Just like that?"

"Yes. Just like that! Are you interested?" I asked him.

"Damn right I'm interested. Count me in!"

"Great! How long will you need to train?"

"Train? It's just about keeping the vehicle steady and under control. At about four hundred miles per hour, it'll start to skate like a car on a frozen road." Art used his hand to illustrate how a car slides out of control on ice. "All you need to do is stay in control. That's it. How much training does a caterpillar need to turn into a beautiful butterfly? None. Right! It just comes natural."

# 35

Realizing the urgency of meeting deadlines, the Reliable team worked nonstop. Their enthusiasm was contagious, with everyone happily working the long hours. Someone once said aerodynamics are for people who can't build powerful motors. To break the sound barrier, we needed both an aero body and a badass rocket motor. The Mercury III's central body was designed and built with ring and stringers divided by bulkheads for additional strength, like airplane monocoque construction. The aluminum body panels were riveted to the frame, forming a strong, durable aerodynamic skin that also acted in a load-carrying capacity, allowing us to reduce chassis weight. I borrowed that idea from Lotus. They designed the first Indy racers that used the car's engine block as part of the frame. That was a groundbreaking engineering concept.

The Reliable team devised a way to eliminate body buckling and flutter at extreme speeds by changing the size of the individual aluminum body panels. "We solved a similar problem with the P-38 Lightning. This will work." I trusted them to fill in and improve some of my engineering suggestions.

"We also made adjustments to the nose-cone design."

They created an aluminum monocoque shell with a fiberglass-and-Kevlar sandwich lining supported internally by a welded steel frame attached to the first bulkhead. The high-pressure air tanks used for pumping the hydrogen fuel were mounted in this area. The Reliable guys also discovered a problem with the rear frame section supporting the engine, wheel struts, tail fin, and braking parachutes. The aluminum monocoque construction used in other areas was not suitable here because of the extreme high loads. So the team came up with a stronger welded nickel-steel tube layout and employed it without problems.

We had these multiple design issues to overcome if we were safely going to go supersonic. Think of a soft-drink bottle rolling around on the deck of a boat in high seas. It's impossible to calculate the bottle's movements because there are just too many unpredictable variables at play. I decided to trust the knowledge of the Reliable guys over my own limited engineering skills, understanding the value of the experience I just didn't have.

Aerodynamics dictated the final layout of the front suspension and steering system. The idea was to go perfectly straight at speed, so the steering ratio was ninety to one. We designed the front with a coil spring setup, but we didn't use suspension at all in the rear. The back tires provided adequate shock insulation. I was still concerned about the tires, but they were spin tested up to 850 mph and performed fine. Our top speed expectation of 775 max should not be a problem. We were ready to get Mercury III prepped for painting and applied multiple coats of primer and hours upon hours of wet sanding while we debated a color scheme.

"Hello, young man. How are you?"

"I'm doing fine, Mr. Finn. Everything is going great."

"I see you're ready for paint and ahead of schedule. Danni would like to suggest a color scheme, if that's OK."

"Sure, but we were thinking of something patriotic. The Reliable guys suggested that," I said.

"Danni wants the Mercury painted green and blue. She says that will represent the environmental advantages of hydrogen, and it will be great for our advertising and marketing efforts. I agree with her on that. I'll send color samples."

"Wonderful suggestion, Mr. Finn. Thank you."

"How long will the painting take?" he asked.

"Not long. A week, perhaps."

"One more thing. We're opening a new Mercedes dealership in Dallas. It's our first venture in Texas. The expansion is important to the long-term success of the company. Danni wants the Mercury III at the Dallas showroom for the three-day grand opening party."

I politely reminded Mr. Finn about the tight Bonneville schedule, but saying no to a financial backer is never a good move. "There is also time involved with planning, transportation, loading, and unloading, and the ever-present risk that something could go wrong."

But his mind was already made up. "You said you're ahead of schedule. Right?" "Yes, sir. We are."

"Then perfect. See you in Dallas!"

I admit, the green-and-blue paint combination looked awesome. We also painted the custom trailer to match the Mercury and strapped it down tight on the trailer bed. Once loaded up and ready for transport, it looked like some type of secret NASA space project and was sure to draw a lot of attention on the road. Two Reliable guys had their CDLs with the necessary endorsements to haul such a long tractor trailer. I also hired a highway escort service to help keep traffic safe, for good measure. We would follow up in a Ford crew-cab pickup. Our convoy pulled on to I-10 at the Gentilly on-ramp and settled in for an uneventful drive to Texas. With a twelve-hour cushion including fuel stops and lunch built into our schedule, there was no need to push the 55 mph speed limit. The weather was perfect, with only a few isolated clouds rolling across a cobalt-blue morning sky.

Near Bator Rouge we picked up LA 1. The old two-lane state highway ran from Grand Isle to Shreveport and was still the quickest way to cross Louisiana from north to south. Otherwise, we would have to backtrack to Mississippi and I-55 or go all the way to Houston and head north on I-45. We stopped for lunch near Alexandria in Rapides Parish at a run-down Pizza Hut.

"Mister, is this a UFO?" Four young boys on bicycles were circling the parking lot arguing over the strange craft they had discovered.

"I think it's a secret Russian missile or something like that. Not a spaceship," the other boy said with authority.

I gave them each a framed publicity photo taken at the nationals. "It's a rocket race car!" The escort car pulled out first, followed by the other vehicles. Everything was fine until Natchitoches. That was where the careless driver of a Chevy Vega decided he wanted a closer look and drifted behind the escort car and directly into the path of our oncoming tractor trailer. The well-trained Reliable driver swerved to avoid crushing the small Chevy, probably saving the driver's life. I saw white smoke from the truck's wheels as its air brakes locked up, leaving black stripes zigzagging across the road. The driver swerved back right, but the soft banked shoulder couldn't support the truck's momentum and weight, causing it to tumble over and slide sideways into a muddy drainage ditch.

"Oh my god!" The Mercury was lying on its side in the shallow ditch with sunlight reflecting off its new paint. I expected the worst. Thankfully, our drivers were climbing out of the sideways cab uninjured. The reckless Vega driver took off. I didn't see any apparent damage to the Mercury. It seemed the Reliable guys had done a great job strapping it down, saving the car from possible ruin as the trailer took most of the impact.

Police arrived, as did a reporter and photographer from a local paper and TV station.

"What exactly happened here?" Many embarrassing photos were taken.

"I'll be right back!" I took off running as fast as I could back to the Pizza Hut. It was a long run on a hot day, but I had no choice. I was sweating, and my heart was racing. Clearly, we were going to have a challenge reaching Dallas on time, and I knew the Pizza Hut had a pay phone.

"Mr. Finn, we have a problem."

"Every major media outlet in Texas is here expecting your arrival. Figure it out," he said after I explained the situation.

We would need a large six-axle recovery tow truck to right our tractor trailer. There was one in the area, but it was still two hours away, in Shreveport. The police accident report took time to complete, and the tractor trailer had to be checked out before getting back on the road. The local volunteer fire department used its hoses to clean off the red mud and gunk that was caked on everything. The Louisiana State Police provided a trooper escort with flashing blue lights and sirens all the way to the Texas border. With all that, we arrived in Dallas only fifteen minutes late.

Mr. Finn was right. Turning the corner in front of the new dealership, I was amazed at the incredible turnout. There must have been seventy-five large cameras on tripods, photographers with handheld cameras, flashbulbs everywhere, and thousands of people lining the block on each side. Even a helicopter hovered above. It seemed as if we were celebrities arriving to walk down the red carpet on awards night.

"This is bigger than the Cowboys' Super Bowl celebration!" our escort driver said on his CB radio.

I was thinking that it would take one hell of an advance job to organize this. But then again, D&M Motors was a large company with an entire public relations department. This time the news coverage went national and way beyond the racing community. Every national network morning news show ran a Mercury III story. They covered the hydrogen angle, the rocket motor, and the supersonic aspects of our quest. They interviewed "expert" talking heads pontificating about the difficult odds of a successful outcome. They even used the Natchitoches accident to add a human-interest angel to the reporting. "After an unfortunate accident, the world's first supersonic hydrogen race car arrives in Dallas."

Danni did many of the national TV interviews in person. "Well, sweetheart, hydrogen fuel is the future, and the Mercury III is going to remove all doubt about that. This is not just an attempt to break the sound barrier on land. It is an event destined to change the way the world thinks about energy." Now I understood why companies hire celebrity spokespeople. Danni was remarkable in front of the camera. Her affiliation with the Mercury project added legitimacy and credibility we would have struggled to achieve otherwise.

"The Natchitoches accident report says there was no evidence of any Chevy Vega in the area," Danni said later, after the successful Dallas event.

"But I saw the whole thing happen. He fled the scene before police arrived." "Maybe so. Did you get his license plate number?"

"No. I didn't think about that. I was worried about the Mercury and the drivers."

"Look, sweetheart. If you can't prove it, it didn't happen. It seems like driver error to me.

Fire him!" Danni insisted.

"Fire him? Why? He did nothing wrong. He has a wife and three children in private schools."

"If he did nothing wrong, then who did? Someone is always responsible. This time we can place the blame for the screwup on a truck driver. But if you don't fire him and he screws up again, then your judgment is questioned, and you are fired for poor management. One more thing, sweetheart. You planned the route? Right? It was your decision to take Louisiana 1, right? That is an old, unsafe two-lane highway clearly not suitable for such a big tractor trailer. Somebody will get thrown under the bus. You understand what I'm saying? Don't you?"

"Yes. I think so."

"Fine. Remember, business is business. I expect you to protect our investment. Put all the blame on the reckless truck driver and fire him now! My PR team will clean it all up with a press release in the morning."

"OK, Danni."

# 36

I started receiving mail from across the country. Most of it was like fan mail, asking questions about the Mercury. A few letters were from people seeking jobs or money, and some were just plain weird. A fella claimed to have researched every automobile manufactured in the US. He had production numbers, brands, costs when new, engine-block identification numbers, and even paint-color availability going back to 1895. "It's my life's work. This detailed information has tremendous value," he said in a cover letter stained with some type of greasy fingerprints. Fried chicken? "I want to offer it to you first, before the Smithsonian gets their greedy hands on it." I politely declined.

Asking for financial help, a lady in Alabama said she was living in a trailer without electricity or running water. "I tape newspaper to these thin walls and windows for insulation. My floor is covered with cardboard to keep the cold out. I get the cardboard boxes from behind the Winn-Dixie store. I ran a hosepipe from the next trailer to flush my toilet. I can't even afford a litter box for my five cats. It's been twelve years since my husband blew himself up cooking crack in the garage. All I need is a little temporary financial help until I get back on my feet."

Another guy had purchased a stainless-steel DeLorean. It's difficult to paint stainless steel; that's why the cars were all just polished metal. "I had it painted red three different times at great expense. After a few days, the paint always peels off in long sheets. I think my jealous neighbor is pouring acid on my car. Luckily, the body shop is happy to continue repainting it."

Another guy I never met asked me to be godfather to his newborn son. I sent back generic letters thanking them all for their interest in the Supersonic Mercury III and a signed publicity photo.

"You can't solve all the world's problems," Danni said when I asked how she handled this aspect of celebrity, especially with strangers asking for money. "I never send a rejection letter under my own signature. You don't want to provoke anybody. I created a fictitious associate vice president for administration instead. 'Danni has received and read your recent letter and request for assistance. However, she is currently traveling and has asked me to respond. Unfortunately, currently we are unable...Signed, Mr. Howie W. Simsno.' I never say no to anyone, but my fictious vice president always does. He is a real heartless curmudgeon." Danni laughed.

I had never heard of the National Association for Climate Concern until their senior vice president called. "We have a powerful climate initiative underway. It presents a great plan designed to reduce carbon fuel use on a worldwide palette of new concepts." That sounded interesting enough. I took the bait and accepted the dinner invitation.

We enjoyed shrimp and seafood-stuffed eggplant at Mandina's on Canal Street. The dining room was lined with Jazz Fest posters. Especially interesting was the original first-year 1969 poster with the Olympia Brass Band. It is extremely rare, and Mandina's is the only place you will ever see one. When I asked about the National Association's purpose and mission, my host was vague and tried to redirect my line of questioning. I smelled a rat!

"We work to make sure developing nations can meet their long-term carbon reduction goals as set forth in multiple UN climate studies."

"How do you do that?"

He tried another deflection.

"Here's the problem. Wealthy nations can afford to implement alternative clean-energy programs because they have become rich using fossil fuels since the dawn of the industrial revolution. But most of the carbon dioxide generated today comes from underdeveloped nations because they cannot afford anything else. That's why they destroy rain forests, pollute rivers and lakes, dump trash in the oceans, burn wood to stay warm, and have so many children."

"I see your point," I said.

"So the best way to meet future carbon reduction goals is to help developing nations build strong economies. The choice should not be between fighting poverty and saving the environment. Do you follow me?"

"Yes."

We spent a few moments discussing the dessert menu with our waiter. He recommended the pecan pie.

"These countries need affordable energy today so we can have clean air tomorrow. Once they become wealthy, they will implement all the expensive new clean technologies we are developing in America. Today, poor nations are denied cheap sources of energy they need to build economic development, or they expect American taxpayers to pay the cost. They need coal!"

"Excuse me! Did you say they need coal?"

"Yes. Coal is cheap, accessible, and easy to transport. Developing nations can't afford windmills, liquified natural gas, cobalt batteries, or hydrogen fuel cells. If environmentalists want to minimize carbon dioxide in the future, they should call for burning more coal in China and India today. Coal is the energy source we should be using now to save the climate tomorrow."

"That is certainly an interesting twist on mainstream environmental thinking. What do you want from me?" I asked, just to be polite. This guy was a real knucklehead.

"We just want you to postpone a hydrogen watershed moment for a few years, and we want you to set a new land speed record as well. You have worked very hard. You deserve that success. Just don't go supersonic. A short hiatus in your sound-barrier ambitions could be extremely lucrative for you and us."

"Are you asking me to sell out everyone who has supported me, funded the Mercury project, and believed in it? Is that what you're asking?" Annoyed, I excused myself to the restroom.

Standing in front of the urinal, I was shocked when a hand reached around my waist from behind and tugged on my pants.

"Excuse me!" I turned around quickly.

I didn't know that shady deals are usually consummated in the restrooms of expensive restaurants. In restrooms it's easy to see if anyone is around, and there is not likely to be video or audio surveillance there. My dinner host was trying to stuff a thick envelope filled with cash into my pocket. When I excused myself from the table, he took that as an indication of offer acceptance.

"This is only a down payment," he said.

"I'm curious. Are you trying to delay all new energy advancements?"

"No. Only hydrogen. Lithium and cobalt batteries are no threat because those elements are too scarce to result in any sustainable legacy disruptions. Hydrogen, on the other hand, is a coming revolutionary change. Think of all the jobs supported by the coal industry."

"Jobs? Drug cartels and the mafia can use the same logic. Thanks for dinner, and you can keep your money." I picked up my coat and left. The night was damp with a thick fog. I decided to refuse the cab ride and enjoyed quiet solitude walking home.

Thinking about this coal industry bribe offer, I began to realize that perhaps Mr. Finn's belief in the coming hydrogen economy was closer than expected.

"I would like you to stop by the office tomorrow morning. How does ten work?" Mr.

Porteous said he wanted to discuss patent applications for our multiple hydrogen innovations.

"Perfect. See you tomorrow," I said. Patents were something that had never occurred to me before.

I noticed a green Land Rover parked nearby but thought nothing of it. After all, there were lots of Rovers around New Orleans, and it was not unusual to see one.

"Mr. Porteous will see you now."

I was led into the conference room.

"Would you like some coffee?"

"Yes, of course."

Mr. Porteous was sitting at the long table looking over open files. An attractive middle-aged woman wearing a beautiful string of white pearls and a snug-fitting black dress extended her hand in a pleasant way. "I would like to introduce you to Sabrina," he said. I recognized her from Dad's funeral. She had been standing alone under an overhang as the rain came down.

"You look so much like your father. He was about your age when we first met." I noticed tears in the corners of her blue eyes. She was overcome with emotion. "I think about him every day and miss him so. He will always be the love of my life."

"I have a few things to look over. I'll let you two get acquainted." Mr. Porteous closed his files and left the room.

Sabrina sat at the end of the table, and I sat in the next chair. Clasping my hands in hers, she wondered where to begin.

"Like you, your father was smart. He just never had a fair chance. He was proud and didn't want help, even when the bank was taking his house. He was stubborn, but, Sebastian, he loved you more than anything else. After the cancer diagnosis, I promised him I would look after you. His greatest dream was to see you receive a university degree. I was at UNO for your commencement address. I know your father was there. I could feel his presence."

I asked about their relationship.

"I made a regrettable decision. I traded love for money and married an egotistical corporate lawyer. He eventually became a full partner. He's a good provider, keeps me safe and warm. But I don't love him. Not the way I loved your father, anyway. I would have never ended it. Your father ended it. Broke my heart into a thousand small pieces."

"What happened?" I asked.

"A junior partner at my husband's firm tried to gain a professional advantage by blackmailing my husband. A private detective took photos of me and your father together. When my preoccupied husband expressed indifference, the outraged partner sent the photos to your mother. She was stunned in a devastated way. Your father decided to try to save his marriage. I cried for weeks but respected his decision."

"That explains so much, especially why he never confronted her about the male friends always showing up. I thought he lacked a backbone, but perhaps he felt responsible for it all." Those family memories came back like ghosts from a painful past. "I tried to forget most of that," I said, feeling familiar knots in my stomach again.

"I'm sorry to have caused so much trouble. Your mother was never able to overcome her feeling of betrayal, and your father was overwhelmed with guilt. I caused so much havoc, which I regret. But I loved your father more than anything. I still do. I will never regret that."

"You were willing to give up everything to be with my dad? Would you have left your husband?"

"Yes. Beyond question. In a second! Even now, I would sacrifice everything just to see him again, even for only a minute. He is always my true love."

"You know, he never stopped loving you," I said.

"How could you possibly know that?"

"I know because he saved your letters. Every single one of them. All those years, he saved your letters."

Sabrina clinched her pearls and cried. "I miss him so."

The door opened slowly, and Mr. Porteous sat back down at the conference table. "Let's get down to business for a few minutes." He explained how the patent-approval process worked. "The approval is just the first step. The US Patent Office does not defend anything. Lawyers do that," he said.

"Sounds expensive. Can I afford this?"

"It's all covered. The applications and legal defense of your patents. It's all covered." I looked at Sabrina. "Thank you. I feel like I have an angel looking after me."

"Please give me a list of the unique components you've developed and designed for the hydrogen rocket. Let's start with that," Mr. Porteous said.

"Sure. First, there's the closed-loop exhaust system. You've already seen that. I also developed a shock-absorbing system inside the motor to reduce resonance vibration. The amplification of the oscillating force threatened to rip the motor apart. We solved that problem with a shock system like the shock absorbers on your car. The chamber pressure control device I built limits and controls fuel, allowing the rocket motor to be throttled. The other engineering problem addressed combustion instability. Simple baffles solved that issue. Finally, the hydrogen fuel tanks had to be insulated. We developed a honeycomb-type mesh that worked perfectly. That may cover the propulsion systems. Do you want to discuss the aero body, suspension system, and nose-cone construction?"

"I'll get things going. This is a long application process, so I had better get started." Mr. Porteous left the conference room, walked over to a group of six interns in a nearby cubicle area, and began barking orders like General George Patton.

I sat at my small kitchen table thinking about Sabrina and Dad's story. My coffee cooled as the evening passed. Perhaps my cynical attitude was wrong about everything, especially love. Maybe I gave up too easily. I seemed to think about Harper a lot. She was always on my mind.

Maybe finding love was worth the risk of another disappointment. I pulled out my wallet and unfolded the Casey's napkin I had carefully placed there. The number was written in green ink with a small sketch of a tree and the words "remember me." Staring at the phone, I started to dial the number a few times but hung up before completing the call. The kitchen lights were dim, and I played Pachelbel's cannon on the cassette player. This time I dialed the entire number.

"Hello, Harper. How are you?"

# 37

The weather in Western Utah is unpredictable, and winter comes in fast. The Bonneville speed trials are over for the year with the first snowfall or heavy late-autumn rain. With a comfortable three-week window remaining to meet the eight-month contractual deadline, I was confident. We picked up I-80 east of Saint Louis, heading through Iowa and on to Salt Lake City. Art would be waiting for us in Clarinda.

It turned out that Harper's work with computers to improve the efficiency of corn farming also applied to our speed trials. "We can track the changes between each practice run, thrust changes, wind effects, temperature effects—all of it. Then we can make real-time adjustments capitalizing on all this new data the computers will generate." Harper said it was the first time technology would be used this way. She had a trailer full of monitors, hard drives, sensors, and cables. It was all property of Iowa State University, on loan to Harper for her thesis work. "I can't wait to see you again," she said, hoping we could find some time to be alone together.

"Will it be too much of a distraction if we share a room?" she asked. "Of course not. I can't wait to see you. I always got you on my mind."

There is not much going on between Salt Lake City heading west to Nevada on I-80, except for a few abandoned silver mines, rotting old wagons here and there, remnants of the original Intercontinental Railroad, and the Bonneville Salt Flats. We set up in the small town of Wendover, which is about thirty miles from the flats, and planned to stay three weeks. Wendover is famous for one thing. The crew of the Enola Gay trained at the Wendover Air Base.

West Wendover is a thriving city on the Nevada side of the state line, with legalized gambling, alcohol sales, and prostitution. To avoid distractions, we rented rooms in a quiet Holiday Inn roadside motel in Wendover, Utah, and settled in to break the sound barrier. We set up tents for the equipment, a tarpaulin to protect Harper's computers, and adjusted the Mercury's cockpit area to Art's specific suggestions. We moved the pedals back three inches and the steering wheel forward. This was the first time Art had sat in the Mercury. He asked for additional seat padding for his lower back and more grip tape on the steering wheel. "My office now feels just about right," he said. We planned a short engine test on day two, measuring rocket thrust acceleration output and Art's familiarity with the dash and control layout. Additional test firings were also important for Harper to establish data baselines.

Speed was timed for a flying mile, but it took some distance to get up to full speed and a few miles to come to a safe stop. We lined up across the width of the course at arm's length and walked the entire thirteen-mile distance. Any debris, loose stones, or even shallow pools of rainwater could spell disaster at supersonic speeds. Aircraft carrier crews do this before flight operations, where even a small loose bolt sucked into a jet engine could lead to engine failure and loss of the aircraft. Sailors call it defodding the flight deck. We were concerned with tire stability and directional control at supersonic speeds and were determined to leave nothing to chance.

I directed the small group of dedicated reporters to stay back near the press tent. At this early stage of testing, I had not expected to see any media, but I was wrong. Harper stood behind her wall of computer screens, hard drives, and cables. She gave an enthusiastic thumbs-up signal when everything was set. "I'm good! I'm good!" The crew loaded a very small amount of hydrogen, uncoupled the fueling lines, and backed the hydrogen fuel truck away. Art was strapped in, his breathing system checked, and the canopy locked into place. The parachutes were packed and rechecked.

A taxi appeared in the distance, throwing up a large trailing cloud of salt dust. Mr. Finn had arrived in time. "I wouldn't miss this for anything."

"This is just a five-second acceleration test from a dead stop. The real excitement will start when we go for the sound barrier. That's in a few days. Glad to see you," I said while asking him to stand back at a safe distance near Harper.

"This computer technology is amazing," Mr. Finn said after Harper gave him a very quick rundown. "I've always been captivated with interesting innovation," he said.

"Four, three, two, one, ignition!"

The Mercury accelerated under its own power with the planned short burst of thrust for the first time and sped down the course. Our other tests were all static up to this point.

"Shut it down!" Harper was first to see a problem.

A loud bang and a ball of flame indicated a rocket motor malfunction a moment later. This is the type of early setback that cannot be foreseen, but it is best to uncover it during testing and address the issue beforehand. That is what testing is designed for. I was not overly concerned.

"We never reached more the sixty percent power. Looks like an internal engine failure involving the hydrogen fuel intakes," Harper said while focused on her data readouts.

"Just before the explosion, everything began shaking violently. It felt like I was in a clothes dryer. I reached for the shutdown lever, but there was no time," Art said.

"Is this serious?" Mr. Finn asked.

"Can't expect to break the land sound barrier without any setbacks. This is to be expected," I reassured him.

It seemed the explosion was caused by a failure in the hydrogen heat exchange section of the fuel injection system. That caused a deformation, further restricting exhaust flow and increased back pressure. A hairline fracture had gone unnoticed. It might have been caused by the Louisiana 1 mishap or during our cross-country transportation trip to Utah or by poor design. Nevertheless, it was necessary to redesign the injector system and catalyst pack. I was also concerned about the silver catalyst screens. The pure silver mesh had a melting point just above normal operating temperature. If they were damaged or melted, hydrogen flow would be further restricted.

I expected them to be destroyed. The melting point of silver is 1,763 degrees Fahrenheit. "The downstream combustion chamber temperature at the time of the explosion reached twenty-five hundred degrees," Harper said while poring over her data sheets. "Looks like we were blowing raw hydrogen out of the nozzle just before the failure," she added.

We pulled the engine, confirming the worst fears. The entire first-stage heat exchange injectors would need to be discarded and the second-stage injector system moved forward to the combustion chamber. It was an hour back to the Salt Lake City airport, and I made a connecting flight in Cincinnati to get back to New Orleans. This was my only option to get home that day. The long flight gave me time to work out the engineering issues, and the guys back at Reliable were waiting to fabricate the new designs. I called ahead to line up all the materials necessary to build a new catalyst pack. Harper had enough data to begin analyzing handling characteristics, thrust output, and speed changes. Meanwhile, the Bonneville team went over everything with a fine-tooth comb looking for any additional cracks, especially in the inner walls of the rocket chamber.

Unable to find pure silver wire mesh, I was told it would be at least a two-month wait.

That was unacceptable.

The Reliable guys had a workable suggestion using materials readily available. "A silver-plated nickel catalyst should work as good as da pure silver."

"How will the thin plating hold up under the heat-generating catalytic cycle?" I asked.

The Reliable team suggested applying a porous hard coating over the silver plating.

Something like ceramics. "Da hard ceramics should prevent any damage to da plating." At this point we had no other options. "Let's give it a try," I said.

Finding someone capable of producing the necessary specialized ceramic coating remained a challenge. A steel fabricating company in Chicago had industrial heat-treating ovens but a six-month backlog. "Every job is important. There is no way to bump you, or anyone else, up the list." I could think of only one other person with ceramic knowledge and expertise. It was a long shot but worth the effort. I called Karen in LaGrange, Georgia, and explained our situation.

"I hand build coffee cups, trays, and decorative art. I'm not a materials engineer, I'm an artist," Karen said.

"I've seen your remarkable work. I don't think what I'm asking is such a great leap." I explained our situation in detail and the specifications.

"Well, that shouldn't be a problem. If your coating needs a maximum heat tolerance of twenty-five hundred degrees, we're good. My L&L kiln will fire above cone ten."

"What is cone ten?" I asked.

"Cone ten is the highest temperature any potter would ever use. We can fire above that. Perhaps three thousand degrees! You can go all the way to Chicago, but you will never find anything better than Georgia red clay and an L&L kiln."

The Reliable guys began building the screens and headed to LaGrange, where Karen was developing the ceramic coatings. I finished building the new injectors. Within three days I had the finished screens in my luggage and the injectors complete. I was ready to fly back to Salt Lake City that morning.

Harper was waiting for me at the airport. "I have some bad news," she said.

"Did we find additional cracks in the motor?"

"No, the rocket is fine. It all checked out. But just as I was leaving to pick you up this morning, two OSHA inspectors showed up."

"OSHA! What the hell do they want?"

"They received an anonymous complaint about safety conditions."

"Anonymous! I bet that is those idiots from the coal lobby. Who's talking with the inspectors now?"

"Mr. Finn said not to worry. He would handle it." "Thank God he's here."

"I also have some good news to share. I extrapolated the few seconds of data we gathered before the malfunction. If we carry the statistics out to a full thirteen-mile speed-trial run, it seems we would have not just reached the sound barrier, we would have smashed it!"

We worked nonstop to repair the damage and reconfigure the engine hydrogen injection system. Karen's ceramic work was perfect. I was also able to eliminate the old problematic heat exchanger. When it was all done, I calculated the maximum thrust at fifteen thousand pounds. In less than two days, we were ready to do another short four-second power burst to test these changes.

"Fire! Fire!" Harper was first to see black smoke seeping from a seam between the body and the nose cone. The cone was attached with fasteners spaced apart every three inches. Courageous crew members grabbed wrenches and frantically worked to remove dozens of screws and bolts. Water and chemical-extinguisher powder were pumped in through every available opening, dousing the blaze. Injuries included blisters and minor burns but, thankfully, nothing too serious. The hydrogen tanks were depressurized, and the car was pushed off the course. The nose cone was off, the front body panels removed, and everything was covered with black soot and white powder. Reporters were eager to get embarrassing photos of the beautiful Mercury III in this undignified situation. We covered the damaged area with a brown tarp.

Apparently, the explosion and extreme vibrations damaged a coupling near the fuel tank, causing the fire. A faulty line connected to a regulator that pressurized the hydrogen tank was to blame. Because of the quick thinking and brave action, damage was minimal, but it would be another two days before we were ready to test again. On the bright side, the OSHA inspectors had left a few hours before the fire happened.

All the fire and heat damaged lines were replaced, and the entire system was pressure tested twice. A new regulator valve and line was moved outside the body as an additional safety measure to prevent a fire recurrence. The nose cone was replaced, the body panels reinstalled, and the Mercury was polished from front to back and ready to race again.

The crew decided to blow off steam and enjoy an evening in West Wendover. Dinner reservations were made at a steak restaurant in a popular casino, and a fabulous Las Vegas–type dance show started at seven o'clock. It had great reviews in the local paper. The casino's nightclub never closed.

"The casino outing sounds great. But I have a better idea. Why don't you and I stay in for the evening?" Harper suggested.

"I was thinking the exact same thing!"

Harper opened a bottle of the forty-proof Iowa wineshine she had squirreled away in her luggage and locked our motel room door. "This is the stress relief I have in mind." She unbuckled my belt and unzipped my pants with one hand. They fell around my ankles. With the other hand she playfully pushed me onto the bed. "Lie back and enjoy!"

After two hours we were exhausted and left the TV on for background noise before falling asleep. It was the first time

I had seen the movie trailers for the new film about the aboveg-round thermonuclear hydrogen bomb tests in the 1950s. *Lucky Dragon 5* showing soon. My self-confidence melted away like ice cream in the summertime.

"This must be the film Mr. Finn was worried about. The one funded by the Cobalt battery companies. Looks like a big-budget blockbuster. The clock is ticking down, and we haven't even matched the old land speed record, much less gone su-personic. Maybe we're wasting everyone's time and money. I'm sure Marty and Danni are disappointed by now."

"Did you expect this to be easy? The setbacks are just a part of the field-testing process.

You know that. You have to keep trying," Harper said.

A reporter with *National Hotrod Trends* magazine, published in Milwaukee, said he had a deadline and needed more inter-views to complete his article. He asked to join the crew on the casino outing. The reporter seemed more interested in the Nevada culture of gambling, prostitution, and alcohol than our supersonic rocket. When the article appeared, it was all about the crew's evening in West Windover. He wrote chiefly about Nevada gambling and legalized betting on sporting events including auto racing, abundant prostitution opportu-nities available inside the casinos, and drinking. The article was titled "Hydrogen Bad Boys." It deliberately left the false impression that we were a ragtag bunch of nonserious jokers and clowns. What else could go wrong? I asked Mr. Finn how to fight this type of unfair press coverage slander.

"You want to shut your critics up! Stop feeling sorry for yourself. Get back to work, and smash that fucking sound barrier!"

# 38

It was a cloudy and windy morning. Winter was approaching fast, with an early cold front heading out of Canada. According to weather reports, we could expect a three-hour window of clear weather in the afternoon. I started the day by reading a note of encouragement Sabrina had sent. "I have read the recent articles and understand things at Bonneville have been challenging. I am reminded of an old French expression your dad said from time to time, 'Marche ou Creve.' It is the motto of the French Foreign Legion—March or Die. Never quit. Keep marching forward regardless of the obstacles ahead," she wrote. I had forgotten, but I now remembered Dad said that when the '47 Mercury was towed away after that surprise flood.

Art was hanging by his fingertips in the hotel room door jamb. "Are we racing today?" "Go suit up."

The cool morning was spent double-checking everything. All four tires were fine, the hydrogen tank pressurized, and the parachute packed and tested. The tires showed almost no wear because of our lightweight design and precise steering control. The Mercury tracked perfectly straight. Art was strapped into his "office," and the canopy was closed and locked into position. The Mercury was pushed down to the rolling start line. Art had previously mentioned that he had had some trouble seeing the track mile markers. We purchased four-by-eight sheets of plywood, painted them green, and set them up every quarter mile, indicating distance. The wind died down in the afternoon exactly as predicted, and the sky cleared to a deep autumn blue.

Four, three, two, one, ignition. At eighty miles per hour, the push car backed away as Art ignited the rocket motor. Somehow, he managed to disconnect his air supply line, so he spent the entire run with his right hand holding an air valve open so he could breathe. The run was uneventful and nearly perfect but deeply disappointing. At full throttle in perfect conditions, the top speed on the timed mile reached 614.60 mph. It was fast enough to set a new land speed record, but not supersonic. The wind was picking up, and we were unable run a second confirmation, so we didn't even have a new official land speed record. We could set an official record later, but that seemed anticlimactic.

I knew almost immediately that the run was really slow. The injector changes had a meaningful negative impact on maximum thrust output, and there was no time for additional major changes. Our eight-month contract was up in just two days, and the first snowfall could happen anytime. I thanked everyone for their remarkable efforts and planned to deliver the disappointing news to Mr. Finn.

"We were so close," Harper said as she looked over the data collected from the latest run while packing up her equipment. "Everything was functioning as expected. Those new ceramic coatings are the biggest surprise. They were barely warm. I think they could function well at thirty-five hundred degrees, from the looks of this data profile."

It hit me like a sledgehammer. "Thirty-five hundred degrees! Harper, that's it! You're a genius. I love you! Art, don't go anywhere. You're about to smash the sound barrier," I said excitedly while running to the Mercury III. Harper's computers were right. The ceramic coatings were in near-perfect condition, and the silver showed no signs of melting.

"How long will it take to get a shipment of ninety-eight percent pure peroxide out here?" I asked the crew.

"One day. We have a supplier in Nevada. But pure hydrogen peroxide is dangerous stuff."

"I know that. It is also one hell of a propellant! Get the damn hydrogen out here now!" I demanded.

"I don't understand. What am I missing?" Harper asked.

"Don't you see? We held maximum thrust back intentionally because the melting point of silver was too low, and if the silver catalysts melted during a run, the rocket would have exploded! That's why we've been running diluted peroxide and lower fuel pressure all this time!"

Mr. Finn arranged a police escort for the fuel truck, Art hung by his fingers, Harper spent hours reviewing her data, and I paced back and forth. My nerves got the best of me, and at 2:00 a.m., I threw up.

The orange fuel truck arrived at 5:00 a.m. It was plastered with hazardous cargo signs and escorted by three state troopers and a fire truck. The sky was cloudy, but the wind was calm. The Mercury was fueled and prepped. Art climbed into his office and strapped in. The parachutes were checked again. With a black marker, I wrote three words on the tail fin: "Marche ou Creve."

"What difference will this fuel make?" Mr. Finn asked.

"It's going to be like strapping afterburners on and jamming the throttle down. You're about to see what hydrogen can really do!"

Art held up a finger, spun his hand around in circles, and pointed forward. "Let's go!" At eighty miles per hour, the push vehicle backed away, and Art fired the rocket engine.

It was at full thrust instantly.

Still miles away from the measured mile markers, a huge rooster tail of salt dust clouded the horizon. The sound grew deafening, it was a thunderous rumble more felt than heard. The ground shook like earthquake tremors beneath its power.

"That's a sonic boom! That's a sonic boom!"

Art entered the measured mile at 778 mph! His official mile speed was timed at 786 mph. There was nothing to celebrate yet. The Mercury would be quarantined overnight and watched over by land speed officials. No additional changes or adjustments were allowed. The average of two runs on consecutive days would determine our official speed. We were at the mercy of the weather. Word spread quickly: "Sound Barrier Shattered by Hydrogen Rocket Car" was the headline of every newspaper in the Western world. Somehow our small group of dedicated reporters swelled to thousands the next morning. They assembled along the measured mile with movie cameras and recorders.

We were delayed until late afternoon as the Canadian cold front approached quickly. With little daylight left, we had a small acceptable window; Art was strapped in and the canopy locked in place. This was it—do or die. At 80 mph the push car backed away. Art hit the measured mile at 810 mph. Most reporters had never experienced a sonic boom up close. They covered their heads with their hands and bent down in fear. It looked like a duck-and-cover atomic film from the 1950s.

Art's official measured mile time on the second day was recorded at 823 mph. He was officially the world's fastest man. We towed the historic Mercury III back to the staging area and parked it in a tent. We planned a celebration at the Nevada casino. Art started the celebrations early with two bottles of Iowa wineshine he passed around.

"You did it!" Harper gave me a passionate kiss. "We'll celebrate in style later," she promised.

"Well done, young man. Nice work." Mr. Finn put his arm around my shoulder. "Incredible!" He opened a case of Dom Perignon, pulled the cork on one of the bottles, and sprayed everyone. Marty gave a short speech about the great future for hydrogen as a green fuel. "I'm heading back to LA now to celebrate with Danni," he said.

The first snow flurries began to fall.

Harper and I planned a short private celebration in our hotel room before heading off to the casino party. The telephone was ringing off the hook.

"Should you answer that? They keep calling!" Harper said.

"No. Probably just another reporter. It can wait." Eventually, I got out of bed and picked up the phone.

"Thank God you answered!" The call was from one of the mechanics who had stayed behind to pack up some equipment and tools. "There are two goons here in suits with a huge tractor trailer truck to pick up the Mercury! They have legal documents and some type of court order!"

"Is there a name on side of the truck?"

"Yes. D&M Motors," he said.

"Oh no! What is today's date?" I asked Harper as my heart sank into my stomach. I dropped the phone and sat on the edge of the bed.

We had broken the sound barrier in eight months and one day. With so much going on, I had lost track of the calendar. Danni and Marty now legally owned the Mercury. I arrived back at Bonneville in time to see the truck's taillights heading out to LA. I didn't bother to call Danni. I already knew what she would say. "It's business, sweetheart. Just business. Nothing personal."

# 39

Was I tricked into losing the Mercury III? Maybe, but no one forced me to go to Dallas. I could have said no. Was the increased tire size change a setup? Who knows? Nevertheless, everything worked out. Danni and Marty displayed the Mercury at the Mercedes dealerships first. The crowds were remarkable. Then it went on tour around the country and even spent time in Germany and England. *Time* magazine said the Mercury III was more famous than the Lunar Rover, Chitty Chitty Bang Bang, and Herbie the Love Bug. We succeeded in setting a land speed record that would last for decades, and we succeeded in creating the hydrogen watershed movement.

Japan and Germany invested heavily into hydrogen-fuel-cell development and research. In the US, President George W. Bush declared, "The hydrogen economy has arrived," and he dedicated valuable time in State of the Union addresses to speak about the importance of America's leading technology in green, non-carbon-based hydrogen energy. With government support the US led the world in hydrogen fuel development. Hydrogen companies experienced skyrocketing stock prices and massive support from important environmental groups.

Politics! President Obama was not going to allow the
Republican Party to declare an environmental victory as important as this. He instructed his secretary of environmental
quality and the Energy Department to defund most hydrogen
development grants awarded under the previous administration and redirect everything, dismissing hydrogen power as
"fool cells." Taxpayer-funded subsidies were offered to rich
people buying expensive battery electric cars. Will environmental groups support the coming strip-mining the oceans
and children dying in Congo mines for cobalt? We'll see.
Inefficient and expensive windmills were built by the many
hundreds of thousands, destroying the usefulness of valuable
agriculture land and killing endangered birds. Carnival bark-
ers and charlatans capitalized on this environmental misdi-
rection and became ridiculously wealthy modern-day robber
barons at taxpayer expense. It was a costly eight-year hiatus
from serious environmental progress in America. There are
now huge financial incentives to continue along this mis-
guided path, throwing good money after bad. Meanwhile, the
climate crisis grows more and more threatening.

Is time running out? Yes. Have we wasted too many years
already? Yes. Is it too late?

No.

Things are changing. The American hydrogen industry
has survived years in the wilderness and emerged stronger.
They perfected the technology, starting on a small scale with
forklifts. Now the entire materials-handling industry is facing
disruption. BMW, Coca-Cola, FedEx, Home Depot, Honda,
Lowe's, Walmart, and many others use hydrogen. Fuel cells
are being deployed at airports, in over-the-road trucking, and
at stationary power backup applications like hospitals and cell

towers. Fuel cells are also being used for carbon capture, with renewable biogas for fuel flexibility.

Asia and Europe never lost hydrogen faith. Japan is using decades of hydrogen R&D to develop a "Woven City" using hydrogen as the core power source. Applications for fuel-cell long-haul trucks and city buses are spreading across Europe and Asia. The Netherlands Operates hydrogen train. Daimler is ramping up production of fuel-cell trucks. Toyota is currently testing hydrogen trucks at the Port of Los Angeles, and a South Korean Company has developed lightweight hydrogen-fuel-cell systems for long-endurance commercial drones. European natural-gas pipelines are adding hydrogen to the natural gas to reduce methane pollution. The 2020 Summer Olympics in Japan will showcase the country's technology lead in hydrogen energy advances. These Olympics will be known as the Hydrogen Games.

My hydrogen patents generate monthly cash flow from licensing agreements handled by Mr. Porteous. If you did the math, then you must be wondering what happened to the $150,000 cost I overestimated and charged to D&M for the development of the Mercury III. I invested nearly every penny in the ethanol plants operated by Harper's family in Iowa. If Danni were to ask about the $150K, I would say, "It's just business, sweetheart. Nothing personal."

"Marche ou Creve"

## THE END

# EPILOGUE

It is true that one of the world's largest aluminum plants was built in the early 1950s south of New Orleans. It was shut down by 1983. How the plant ended up here is still a puzzling mystery wrapped in political intrigue. We may never know the truth. This fictionalized account of the political skullduggery involved is as plausible as any other explanation offered by real historians. Americans love the expression "no taxation without representation." But we don't talk much about the statement's inverse, "no representation without taxation." Tax revenues from heavy industry along the Mississippi River and the oil and gas industry paid the bills in Louisiana. If people are not taxed, then it's not their money on the line, and they tend to stay disengaged. Furthermore, if politicians don't have to ask voters for tax increases, they are more likely to be reelected, and the cycle continues.

# ACKNOWLEDGMENTS

I have had the pleasure of getting to know Richard Keller. He is the engineer behind the successful Blue Flame land speed record holder. It was a natural-gas-powered rocket car that set a land speed record of 630.478 mph on October 28, 1970, at the Bonneville Salt Flats. His record lasted for thirteen years. Richard is still a competitive cyclist. Meeting by chance at a cycling event in Alabama, I happened to mention how fast 45 mph downhill feels on a bicycle.

"Fast? Yes. But it's nothing like setting a land speed record!"

Now he had my attention. Multiple conversations over dinner followed. This fictional account of a hydrogen rocket land speed record car would not have been possible without studying the significance of Richard's remarkable achievements.

Made in the USA
Columbia, SC
08 October 2022

69091704R10174